PRAISE FOR
__TED ALLBEURY__

"That old pro, Ted Allbeury,
does it again in *Deep Purple*...
Mr. Allbeury is a very deft operative."
—*New York Times Book Review*

⋈

"A classic writer of espionage fiction."
—**Len Deighton**

⋈

"A master of the genre."
—*Los Angeles Times*

⋈

"Mr Allbeury is a writer of espionage novels
that often soar above the genre."
—*The New Yorker*

⋈

"Does the name Ted Allbeury ring a bell? No?
You've led a deprived life."
—*Chicago Sun-Times*

⋈

"No one picks through the intelligence maze with
more authority or humanity than Allbeury."
—**Sunday *Times*, London**

⋈

"Ted Allbeury is perhaps the best,
most authentic and skilled spy novelist
in a very crowded business."
—*Toronto Sun*

⋈

"Allbeury is arguably the best teller of
spy tales to come out of that growing group
of authors who were spies themselves,
and I include John le Carré in that judgment."
—*Washington Post*

Also by Ted Allbeury

A TIME WITHOUT SHADOWS
ALL OUR TOMORROWS
THE LANTERN NETWORK
THE STALKING ANGEL
THE JUDAS FACTOR
THE SEEDS OF TREASON

Published by
THE MYSTERIOUS PRESS

TED ALLBEURY

DEEP PURPLE

THE MYSTERIOUS PRESS
New York · Tokyo · Sweden · Milan
Published by Warner Books

MYSTERIOUS PRESS EDITION

Copyright © 1989 by Ted Allbeury
All rights reserved.

Cover illustration by Sonja and Nenad Jakesvic

The Mysterious Press name and logo are trademarks of
Warner Books, Inc.
Mysterious Press books are published by
Warner Books, Inc.
666 Fifth Avenue
New York, New York 10103

A Time Warner Company

Printed in the United States of America

Originally published in hardcover by The Mysterious Press.
First Mysterious Press Paperback Printing: January, 1991

10 9 8 7 6 5 4 3 2 1

Peace dies when the framework is ripped apart. When there is no longer a place that is yours in the world. When you know no longer where your friend is to be found.

—Saint-Exupéry, *Flight to Arras*

CHAPTER ONE

As Hoggart stood waiting for the double stream of traffic to clear he looked across the street at Century House. It was a glorious summer day but not even the bright sunshine could make the tall building look anything but grim. Perhaps it was appropriate that the headquarters of MI6 should look implacable and forbidding in its public face. But it gave a false impression all the same. The people inside, like the staffs of any large government organisation, were just people. There were flowers in vases in the typing pool, there were disputes about holiday schedules, rivalries, and even long-historied feuds. The most modern pieces of high technology still had to give way sometimes to no more than the hunch of an experienced man. There was loyalty and ambition, and sharp academic minds that probed the accumulated field-wisdom of experienced agents. There were love affairs and mild sexual harassment, prejudices and deviousness, and evidence of most of the frailties that human beings are prone to. There were strict

1

upholders of the law of the land and others who deemed justice more important, and recognised that they were not synonymous. There were several scores of people who knew more about what was going on in the world than most heads of government knew; and there was a handful of people who knew enough to bring to an ignominious end the careers of at least fifty public figures. Strangely enough, the knowledge led to a tolerance of behaviour in others that would have been unacceptable by their own scales of values. But none ever confused tolerance with trust. Newcomers learned early on that trust was not valued in the ranks of the Secret Intelligence Service. Trust was like belief, and implied an absence of fact. And in SIS even facts were subject to double and quadruple checks. Both elements, the law and justice, required it.

It was almost five minutes before Hoggart was able to thread his way through the temporarily halted streams of cars and lorries to the other side of the street.

He showed his ID card at Security and waited as they logged his arrival before taking the lift to the ninth floor, and the office he shared with David Fletcher.

• • •

It was mid-afternoon when Hoggart came in, exchanging brief greetings with Fletcher before settling down at his desk.

Hoggart was reading a file, turning the pages slowly, once or twice turning back to read the text again. He had a heavy-weight boxer's build so that although he always wore snappy clothes his bulging muscles seemed to make his jackets look a couple of sizes too small, even when they were new. He had a big, haphazard sort of face but it was his hair that you always noticed. Jet black and brushed straight back from his forehead, it always seemed lank, as if it needed a shampoo, and it never lay flat, so that it looked like the raised hackles of an angry dog.

Then Hoggart looked up and saw Fletcher watching him. He pointed at the file. "Have you read this?"

"What is it?"

"The surveillance report on the suspect KGB guy at the Soviet Trade Mission." He looked at the file cover. "Barakov. Igor Barakov."

"Yes. I've read it."

"D'you remember the physical description?"

"More or less."

"So what the hell does etiolated mean?"

Fletcher laughed. "That's a bit of original Anthony Renshaw. He edited the report. It means—pale—wan—kind of washed-out."

"Jesus wept. Has he ever done any actual fieldwork himself?"

"I don't think so. He had the usual training courses way back. But he's always been an administrator. Looking after the likes of you and me."

"How the hell do you get a job like that?"

Fletcher grinned. "You have an old man who's head of a merchant bank. Then Eton, Balliol, a stint in the Foreign Office, Washington and Bonn. You speak fluent Russian. You are naturally charming. You mix with the top people who are old family friends—and you work very hard." He paused. "He's very good at his job. And he's at arm's length. He doesn't get emotionally involved like we do." Fletcher paused. "Somebody has to, you know."

"He's like something out of P. G. Wodehouse or a Noël Coward play. He even looks like one of those creeps in a fashion ad in the Sunday magazines."

"What does it matter what he looks like? We do our jobs and he does his. That's all that our lords and masters expect of us. We put our fingers in the holes in the dyke but he has to have a wider view than we do." He paused and smiled. "If it was left to the likes of you and me every Russian in London would be in the Scrubs." He stood up, pushing back his chair. "Are you taking over the Barakov surveillance?"

"No. I'm working for Renshaw doing my share of decrypting the last material from 'Needle.' He says you're doing the second batch."

"Is that the . . . ?" Fletcher waved his hand because his sense of security even inside Century House was too ingrained to let him go further.

Hoggart nodded. "Yeah. That's the one."

Fletcher stood up. "I'm going for a coffee. D'you want one?"

"Thanks. Same as usual. Half and half with two sugars."

• • •

The street of grim Victorian houses was at the back of Euston Station. Once the houses of artisans, they had been crudely converted into flats of various sizes. On the top floor of one of them a small boy sat reading a tattered comic. He was pale, with thick black hair and a bruise on the side of his face. He heard the voices and footsteps on the bare, wooden stairway outside and then the sharp, peremptory knock on the door. The boy ignored the knock, standing up to look out of the window. There was more knocking and then the jangle of keys and the door opened. A large woman and a police constable were standing there.

The woman smiled, and said, "Hello, Eddie. I'm Mrs. Hopkins—d'you remember me?"

The small boy stayed silent, and the smiling, stout woman edged into the room. "Where's your Ma, Eddie?" The boy pointed to a closed door and the woman walked over slowly and opened the door to the only bedroom. A woman lay on the filthy bed, smoking a cigarette, tapping the ash into a cup of cold tea. The stout woman said quietly, "I've come for Eddie, Mrs. H. The court order, you know." She paused. "Can you hear me, Mrs. H? We've got to take him away."

Mrs. Hopkins waited and the woman on the bed slowly turned her head to look at her. For long moments she looked without speaking; then she said harshly, "What you waiting for, you stupid cow?"

"We're taking young Eddie into care, Mrs. Hoggart."

"Tek the little bugger, he's no bloody use to me."

For a moment, Mrs. Hopkins hesitated, non-plussed. She was used to mothers who fought like wildcats to keep their children. Screaming abuse, calling on the saints, cursing her and those she might love, praying that she might die slowly and painfully. Cancer was their favourite choice. And then she gathered her wits and turned to the boy.

"Collect all your clothes and your toys, boy. Everything you've got."

Ten minutes later the pitiful possessions were wrapped in a couple of pages of The Sporting Life. *Two vests, two shirts, a pair of socks, two tattered boys' comics, and a Christmas card.*

* * *

The estate agent's details had described it as a "maisonette on three floors." Anthony Renshaw referred to it as his "pad" but it was a bit more than that. With three bedrooms and in King's Road, Chelsea, it had been a good move when he had taken the last twenty years before the lease ran out at a price that amounted to £1,000 a year all in. And these days he could probably sublet it for that much a week if he threw in the carpets, curtains, and a bit of furniture. Most of the furniture had come from the second floor of Austin's of Peckham Rye. That wonderful emporium, known only by word of mouth, where the shrewder members of the upper classes and the Diplomatic Corps furnished their houses. Renshaw's flat was essentially a male domain but not aggressively so. The photographs on the wall of the music room were mainly of jazz musicians and members of London orchestras past and present. The maleness came from the obvious comfort of the place. The leather of the settee and armchairs was soft and yielding rather than the stiff, buttoned leather of club furniture. There was one original nude by Annigoni in sanguine but the rest were mainly signed limited editions of modern prints, traditional rather than experimental.

The most obviously lived-in room had polished floorboards and plain white walls. The Bechstein grand was piled with music. Mostly standard classics with a preponderance of Chopin and

Brahms but a leavening of jazz, some of it in manuscript, and ranging from Fats Waller arrangements to Scott Joplin originals with handwritten annotations that softened the master's precision.

A woman came in daily to clean and tidy and they left each other notes. Hers written in careful capitals and his with Greek "e"s and precise punctuation.

Tall and lean with an actor's studied movements, he both dressed like and resembled a young man from the era of flappers and tea-dances. But in fact he was approaching his forty-sixth birthday. His voice was not quite a drawl but the mixture of languid delivery and precise choice of words had not endeared him in his earlier years to some of his rather earthy superiors in SIS. But the talent was too obvious to be permanently ignored and several new brooms had raised dust to his advantage. He was now in charge of all operations involving penetration of the KGB and the GRU.

When he had first moved in to the flat he had been able to park his Austin-Healey 3000 in King's Road itself but these days, even for loading his gear for the weekend on the boat, he had to park at the far end of Royal Avenue.

He stood for a few moments looking slowly round the sitting room and then picked up the canvas hold-all and the cellular phone.

It was a Friday night but the traffic out of London and down to the coast was comparatively light, and he was on the outskirts of Chichester just under two hours later. A few miles down the A286 he turned off at the cottage that marked the lane to Birdham and a few minutes later he was at Birdham Pool. He drove cautiously, trying to avoid the permanent potholes on the jetty, and parked directly behind his boat, which was moored stern-on with an alongside pontoon on its starboard side.

Aquila was a fifty-foot twin diesel cruiser on a Halmatic hull built to Lloyd's 100 A1 specification with fuel capacity that could take her down to the Med. But Renshaw used her mainly for day trips to the Isle of Wight and weekend trips across to France and Belgium. He was a regular and considered a competent skipper by the locals.

There was another two hours tide he could use and he ran up the engines as soon as he was on board. As he checked the warps to the for'ard piles he stood looking across the pool toward the lock that led to Chichester channel. There were lights on a lot of boats and a faint sound of music from the Birdham clubhouse and its Friday night hop. And just enough wind to set halyards and sheets clinking and clanging against metal masts. Twenty minutes later he eased her into the lock and threw one warp to the keeper and then the second, holding the tail of both when they were looped round the bollards and turned back to him, as the water level went slowly down.

"Where you off to tonight, Mr. R?"

"Only across to the island, Mac. I'll be back on the midday tide tomorrow."

"You notified the coastguard?"

"I'll go through Channel 16 as soon as I'm over the bar. Have you had any Admiralty chart changes this week?"

"No, Mr. R, but the Harbour Board said the bar had shifted and they've put a temporary can to mark the new entrance."

Renshaw laughed. "A bit late, if you ask me. See you tomorrow, Mac."

"Good trip, sir."

"Thanks."

As Renshaw slowly eased forward the throttles he put on the searchlight to observe the portside piles marking the narrow channel that led to Itchenor Reach. There were a few boats even at that late hour making their way up towards Bosham but by the time he was level with the East Head beacon he was on his own and heading for the Nab Tower.

• • •

The small studio flat was in one of the old buildings in a street just off Arbat Square, which marked off the old part of Kalinin Prospekt from the new. But she knew that she was very lucky to have it, and even luckier to have a Moscow residence permit. The residence permit was her own work. A reward for gaining a one-year scholarship to the Bolshoi from her home town of Tula, 180 kilometres south of Moscow. Tula has few claims to fame but is recognised as the home of the best sweet biscuits in the Soviet Union, *Tulskie Pryaniki*. It is also respected for its iron foundries. Her father was a leading official in the foundry workers union and that might conceivably have helped a little in the award of the scholarship. She had never been certain whether the afternoons she spent with the director of the Youth Theatre had made any difference or not. But in his untidy room at the back of the theatre on Kominterna Street there had been half-promises of influence that might be used, in the intervals of their love-making. It was certainly her beautiful face and her lithe young body that had got her Yuri Lensky, and through him the studio flat.

Lydia Malikova was twenty years old and her beauty and a comparatively small talent would have ensured her a reasonable standard of living even in Tula, so Moscow had turned out to be something of a disappointment. Small talents seemed even smaller in the rarefied atmosphere of the Bolshoi, and the female dragons of the ballet school saw beauty as no more than a distraction from total dedication.

She had met Yuri Lensky at a Kremlin reception for the musicians of the Czech National Orchestra. He was one of a group who were discussing Smetana and Dvořák and he had suggested that it was time somebody choreographed a ballet for the *furiant* from *The Bartered Bride*. The others in the group had said it wouldn't work. It was too fevered to sustain. But she

8

had contradicted them vehemently and as the only dancer in the group they had given way to her gracefully.

He had taken her for a meal at the Rossiya after the reception and a few meetings later she had spent the night with him at a dacha at Kolomenskoye. Right from the start he had made clear that he was not only married but happily married with a daughter whom he very dearly loved. Had he been some other man, she would have found the relationship abhorrent but he was not only a very attractive man, he also had a charm that was in no way contrived. She had no idea what he did but he was obviously a man with considerable power and influence.

She was wearing the dress he had bought for her at a recent stop-over in Tokyo. It was his favourite. White silk, with a faint pattern of pink roses on the skirt.

They were seldom able to go out together because he was determined not to risk disturbing his relationship with his wife. He never talked about her but always answered questions about her with what sometimes seemed undue honesty. But he didn't treat her like most of the Kremlin's oafs treated the young girls they slept with: making it brutally clear that it was nothing more than sex. And sex that was no more than a few minutes of crude animal lust. But Yuri was quite happy to spend a few hours with her, talking and listening to music on the hi-fi. He actually listened to what she had to say as if it mattered, and although he sometimes disagreed or laughed at her views on life and destiny, it was gently done.

He never said that he was a journalist, he just talked as if he were. But she knew that he wasn't. Not even an editor would have his freedom and self-assurance. She guessed that he was probably KGB although he didn't fit the usual stereotype of a KGB officer. But she knew that they weren't all thugs. Like many of his generation, the war babies, he knew almost nothing of his parents and could remember very little of his childhood but he seemed to take it all in his stride. Not like some of them who wore their misery like medals for all to see.

She hurried to the door at the first ring of the bell, and there he was, his face impassive but his grey eyes smiling as he kissed her cheek and gave her the small posy of flowers.

• • •

As they sat drinking tea and eating sweet pastries Lensky said, "What was all the excitement about across the corridor?"

She grinned. "The people next door have got a new car. They can't stop talking about it."

"What is it?"

"It's only a Zhiguli."

"What are you doing at the theatre now?"

"I'm giving talks to the juniors about dedication and all that crap."

"You don't go along with dedication?"

"Not if it really means being eternally grateful for the Party kindly allowing you to use your only talent."

Lensky smiled. "So be dedicated and forget about the Party. Just get on with your work—and your talent."

For long moments she looked at his face, and then she said softly, "Because I don't have a talent, Yuri. Not by Bolshoi standards."

"Is there anything else you'd rather do?"

She shook her head and then said, "Tell me you love me, Yuri. Say something nice."

Lensky put his arms around her, holding her close and as she rested her head on his shoulder he gently stroked the long black hair. "Lydia Alexandra Malikova. You're very young and very beautiful. And I love you very dearly. Moscow isn't very far from Tula on the map but it's very far from Tula in its thinking. This is a tough city, my love, and the first thing you have to learn is not to inhale. Just relax and enjoy being here. Be an observer for a bit, not a participator. You're very intelligent and in some ways very naive. You'll succeed some way if you're patient." He kissed her mouth gently and then drew back to look at her face. "Are you worried about you and me?"

She sighed. "Yes, a bit."

"What bit?"

She looked at his face and said softly, "I think you know which bit."

He nodded slowly as he looked back at her and then said, "Is it Halenka and Katya that worries you?"

"In a way it is, and yet it isn't them."

"So what is it?"

"It's you. I can't understand you."

He half-smiled. "What can't you understand?"

"How can you love Halenka and me at the same time? It isn't possible to love two people at the same time."

"There are different kinds of love and different kinds of obligations of love."

"Tell me."

"Do you think your parents love you?"

"Yes, I'm sure they do."

"Do you love them?"

She thought for a moment before she said, "Yes, but not as much as they love me. They think about me all the time and I go for weeks without thinking about them."

"You remember telling me about a dog you had—a shepherd dog called Khan who was killed by a car?"

"Yes. It was the first time I really felt sad."

"Why were you sad?"

"Because I should have taken better care of him. He was mine and I missed him terribly. We went for walks every day together. He used to come and meet me out of school."

"Did your mother love your father?"

"Yes. She adored him from when she was sixteen."

"But she loved you too."

"Yes. But not in the same way."

"So you think that there's more than one kind of love? More than one kind of loving?"

"Yes. Of course."

"Except for me. You don't think I should have different kinds of love?"

"You tricked me, Yuri." But she smiled.

"No. I just explained something as best I could. I love Halenka, I love Katya, and I love you."

"In that order?"

"That's the chronological order. You're last because you came last into my life. But I've got enough love for all of you."

"I can understand Katya, she's your daughter. But not Halenka and me at the same time."

"I love Halenka because she is my wife. We've been married a long time and she has always been a good wife. If I were not married already I would certainly ask you to marry me. I think you would be a good wife too. But I am married and I would no more want to hurt Halenka than I would want to hurt you. I have responsibility to you both. Different responsibilities."

"Have you had a mistress before?"

"No, never. I've had sex with women other than Halenka. But that's all it was."

"You're a strange man, Yuri. I don't properly understand. But I love you very much." She smiled. "Let's go to bed."

• • •

Lensky had only been twice to KGB headquarters at Dzerdzhinski Square since the days when he had been a captain. And that was nearly five years ago. Neither did he ever wear his uniform. His special ID had a different name and a serial number that precluded anyone from questioning what he wanted or what he was doing, whether they were KGB, GRU, police, or militia.

Apart from the family apartment in the modern block facing the Moskva River he had four other places that were set aside for his use. A room at the Moskva Hotel was permanently available for him, and on the opposite side of Marx Prospekt he had a room in an old house in a small street, Georgyevsky Pereulok. Yet another place was in a block in Red Square near the GUM building, and the dacha at Kolomenskoye was also his to use.

There were at least a dozen senior officers who worked for Directorate S of the First Chief Directorate who had similar responsibilities. Directorate S was responsible for the control and operation of all "illegals" and Lensky was concerned with both the First and Second Departments covering the USA and Britain. Officers like Lensky were known only to a handful of KGB officers whose rank was at least full colonel, and they all had several identities, names, and documents. These men were administered by a small and tightly secure staff from offices in a concrete basement complex under the Nikolsky Tower in the Kremlin.

• • •

The meeting with Ulianov had been planned to last the weekend but there were still things to discuss by the Monday afternoon. Lensky was glad that they had arranged the meeting at the dacha. It meant that they could walk in the woods between sessions and get some fresh air. Although they were both colonels, Ulianov was the senior. He was in his early sixties and had been a colonel for at least ten years. They got on well together despite the differences in age and attitudes. Ulianov went by the book: for him it was bureaucracy that preserved the security of illegals' operations, but he seemed to accept that in Lensky's operations bureaucracy sometimes had to turn a blind eye. Men in hostile environments thousands of miles from Moscow's support could not always see the wisdom of restrictions that seemed to hamper their operations. There were lessons to be learned from both

13

sides and Ulianov accepted that what looked efficient from an office in Dzerdzhinski Square didn't always work on the ground.

When they decided that they would have to carry on over to the Tuesday they had taken a break and walked to the lake. It was a perfect summer evening and they sat on the trunk of a fallen tree watching the rings on the water from fish rising. But even in that setting Ulianov's mind was on work. He had reached down and picked a wild orchid and as he looked at it he said, "What did you think of the report on the Walker case in America?"

"I think our people let it get out of hand."

"In what way?"

"First of all, Old Man Walker was doing it solely for money, and with that kind of informant you've got to watch his life-style. They aren't savers, they're spenders, and sooner or later somebody's going to notice."

"Go on."

"That relationship had gone on for years and it's easy for both sides to get complacent. They get away with it for so long that it seems like it will go on for ever. They keep to the routines of dead-drops and contacts but it's all become a ritual. They don't expect anything to go wrong."

"But it was the wife who gave him away."

"Like I said, they should have watched his life-style. He was a wife-beater on one hand and going with young girls on the other. And he was a boaster. There were at least ten people who knew what he was doing. Sooner or later somebody was going to talk. Our people kept to the rules on procedures but they should have watched his private life."

"Maybe we should accept that there's a limit to the useful life of any informant. A couple of years and then we cut off?"

"No. That's a waste. It takes a long time to establish a top-grade informer." He shrugged. "It depends on the person. Old Man Walker got about three hundred thousand dollars out of us but we got information on their submarine operations that was so valuable that you couldn't put a price on it. It's a matter of temperament. Walker was cunning but he wasn't intelligent. He was a moron and we should have recognised that. He was greedy so he was controllable. We didn't control him."

"Is it possible to do that continuously?"

Lensky shrugged. "I do it with my people in London. It's in their interest. It's insurance. And it keeps both sides up to the mark."

"At all levels?"

"Yes. No exceptions."

"Including the top man?"

"Yes. But he's no problem. He's in the business and he knows what it's all about."

"What's he like?"

Lensky threw a pebble into the lake as he thought about what to say without giving offence. Ulianov hadn't used the codeword that preceded any exchange of information about the man. He turned to look at the older man, smiling as he said, "I keep my own rules too, Colonel."

Ulianov smiled and stood up. "We'd better get back."

CHAPTER TWO

Despite the sunshine the gusty breeze had made the girls and young men wear jackets and sweaters around their shoulders as they sat eating their brown-bag lunches in Farragut Square. And the gusts of wind gave the sound of the US Marine Band playing a selection from *Oklahoma* a strangely distant uncertainty.

The man in the light mackintosh sat watching the young office workers eating, talking and laughing. The girls in bright colours, the men more soberly dressed until the evening. They were strange people the Americans. Tough and ruthless but strangely naive, with childish enthusiasms. So ignorant of the rest of the world unless there was some current news story that made them realise that Europe and the Middle East could affect their own lives and prosperity. Capable of great generosity and warmth for the underdogs but strangely antagonistic if an underdog eventually became capable of looking after itself. What they lacked was not energy or determination but a sense of destiny. They were all going in different directions. But that was what democracy was all about. Every man was his own political party. And Moscow was going to bury them, just as Khrushchev had once told them openly. They were going to learn that innocence can be another name for ignorance. The British understood the realities of life. They'd been at it for years. They were getting bloody noses from the KGB all the time but they would recognise the truth when they heard it.

He looked at his watch and stood up. Tomorrow was the day. He walked up to Massachusetts Avenue, past the British Embassy and its huge statue of Winston Churchill, and then back to his room at Hotel 1440 on Rhode Island Avenue.

• • •

Sir Roland was standing talking to the Polish ambassador as he watched the dancers. He had decreed that there would be none of this modern pop stuff. It was going to be good music: Kern, Irving Berlin, Rodgers and Hammerstein, and that sort of thing. Thanksgiving seemed to be a mixture of harvest festival without the hymns and the sort of dos the Queen gave for the staff at Christmas at Windsor and Buckingham Palace. Until he became Her Majesty's Ambassador in Washington he had never been too clear about what Thanksgiving was all about. But he'd checked on it and thought it was rather a nice idea. Typical of the Americans to make it always a Thursday. That meant at least five days' disruption, if you counted a day of preparation when most of the embassy and at least half of its staff were away from their duties. There would inevitably be more trouble from Angela about the meanness of the Foreign Office.

Poor Krelski was in one of those periods when the American Poles were ostracising him. Some trial of a dissident in Warsaw or an insult to the Pope. They were always feuding about something or other. As they chatted away he wondered how it was that naval attachés always got hold of the prettiest girls. They were always so young, the girls, so cuddly and yet so sexy.

And then he saw Patton, the First Secretary, pointing towards the alcove. He excused himself and made his way to where Patton was waiting for him. When he had closed the door Patton turned and said, "We've got a walk-in."

"A what?"

"A walk-in, sir. A Russian defector."

"Oh for Christ's sake. Why couldn't the stupid bugger wait until we open tomorrow?"

"He's KGB, sir. Or claims that he is."

"Where is he?"

"We've put him in the annexe with Mason."

"What's the chap want?"

"Wants to see a senior intelligence officer."

"Well Mason's not one of them, is he now?"

"No, Your Excellency, but Pritchard wouldn't see him. Says it's not policy for these chaps to meet an intelligence officer until their bona fides have been established."

"Why not, for heaven's sake?"

"The walk-in could just be checking on the identities of our intelligence people."

"That's more than I can do with the Foreign Office in cahoots with them half the time." He paused. "What does Pritchard want us to do?"

"He suggests that the Russian has a preliminary de-briefing with Miss Pollard."

Patton saw the first glimmer of hope on Sir Roland's face. "That should teach the bugger a lesson." He shrugged. "If that's what Pritchard wants then I approve. But they don't do it here, they take him to one of their places. Make that very clear."

"I'll do that, sir."

• • •

The house in Cleveland Park had been built in 1905 and it still had an air of rural peace despite the fact that it was only a short walk from the metro station. But inside it had been gutted to suit its current owners, a company based in the Channel Islands called Mivi Investments. A title devised by a *Times* crossword fanatic in one of the more mundane departments of SIS.

The room used for de-briefings looked much as it had originally looked in 1905. Apart, that is, from two wide-angled video cameras secreted in twin sconces of wrought-iron, painted white and shaped like full-blown roses, in different corners of the room. And an array of microphones at several levels in the cornices, walls, and wainscoting of the room. The adjoining room was like a recording studio with video recorders and players, Revox tape recorders, and a control panel set in a custom-built desk.

Pritchard had arrived half an hour before the Russian was brought in and he had checked the equipment and set up the control panel ready for recording. He lit a cigarette and made himself comfortable as he heard them coming upstairs to the next room.

Vera Pollard was in her early fifties, Deputy Cultural Attaché at the embassy for the last five years. A handsome woman whose gentle face was deceptive. A double-first at Oxford, she had played hockey for her college and for England, and had one of those calm, analytical minds that the Foreign Office so rightly treasures.

The Russian looked as though he was also in his early or middle fifties. Tall and thin with a dark complexion and thin black hair, he looked as if he was likely to be originally Armenian or perhaps Khazakhstani. He was wearing a grey woollen shirt and a brown jacket with baggy trousers that gave him an old-fashioned appearance. He had a worn leather briefcase which he held on to as Vera Pollard pointed to one of the armchairs. When he was seated she sat down facing him.

"It's Mr. Yakunin, isn't it?"

The Russian nodded. "Yakunin, Igor."

"Would you like something to eat, Mr. Yakunin? Or a drink maybe?"

"No thank you. Maybe later."

"How can I help you?"

"You are an intelligence officer?"

"No. But I am an embassy official. We felt I should talk to you first. Just to make sure that we are in a position to help you."

"It's me who helps you people, not you helping me."

"Tell me," Vera Pollard said softly as she smiled at him.

"I am a major in the KGB. I work for one year here in the United States and I wish to defect to the British."

"Where have you been working, Mr. Yakunin?"

"In Los Angeles and in New York."

"And what were you doing?"

"I have Canadian documents and I have run two networks of agents in the United States."

"Why didn't you talk to the CIA? Why us?"

"They're too clumsy. And the most important information I have concerns the British not the Americans."

"What kind of information is that?"

Yakunin shook his head. "That's only when I'm sure of your people. I risk my life but they risk nothing."

Pritchard pressed the button and he saw Vera Pollard glance briefly over the Russian's head to where the red light blinked silently to tell her to end the interview.

• • •

Vera Pollard had taken Yakunin to one of the security bedroom suites, shown him the various facilities, and a Royal Marine from the embassy had reported to Pritchard to act as guard for the night.

When Vera went in the control room to see Pritchard he was listening again to the tape of the brief interview. As she sat down he switched off the recorder.

"Thanks, Vera. What did you think of him?"

"He's tense but I guess anybody would be tense doing what he's just done."

"He could be a 'plant.'"

She smiled. "I'd still be tense if I were a 'plant.' I'd wonder if I were going to be exposed and what would happen to me if I were." She paused. "What would happen to him?"

"Depends on how long it took us to rumble him."

"He's going to be a difficult client."

"What makes you think that?"

"I'd say he's an arrogant man. A bit full of his own importance. Quite sure that he's bringing over the Crown Jewels and expects a lot more than three cheers for handing them over."

Pritchard smiled. "There's a car to take you back to the embassy. You must be tired."

She nodded and stood up, walking to the door when she turned to look at him.

"What are you going to do with him?"

"London are checking on him. If he's positively identified I'll fly over with him tomorrow. They'll take him over."

"Will you have to stay?"

"No. I'm not a Russian speaker and I'm not an interrogator either. And a de-briefing can take months."

"See you when you get back and I'd love to know how it all works out."

Pritchard smiled. "I refer you to Section 2 of the Official Secrets Acts, my dear. My lot are very fussy about it."

She raised her eyebrows. "Saving it for their memoirs no doubt." She closed the door behind her before he could reply.

• • •

Hawkins met him off the plane at Heathrow. They didn't go through immigration or customs. They didn't even enter the terminal building. There was a silver grey Rover 2600 drawn up on the tarmac. They went straight to the safe-house in Kent.

CHAPTER THREE

The outside of the old Victorian house just off the Fulham Road looked as unprepossessing as the day it was built. It stood four-square to the road with its small front garden and jutting bay window, defying the march of time. But inside the battle had been lost in the early eighties when its ample interior had been converted into four studio flats, the current euphemism for one largish room with a small bathroom and kitchen. To say that the conversions had been lovingly done would be an exaggeration, but they had been done with a touch of affection here and there. The flat that was occupied by David Fletcher and Rachel Meyer had a well-polished pine floor and white walls, and old-fashioned second-hand furniture that was assembled in a single area of the room, near the window. At the other end was an upright piano and plain shelves stacked with the scores of almost every concerto, sonata, and trio that had ever been written with a cello as its principal instrument.

They had eaten their evening meal and Rachel was annotating the fingering changes required by the new permanent conductor of Capital Symphony for his version of Britten's Cello Symphony. David Fletcher was lying with his feet up on the chintz-covered sofa that his parents had given them when they decided to live together. It had been impossible to explain to them why they hadn't yet decided to marry but were both perfectly happy to live together. His mother often said that they both looked more married than a lot of married couples she knew.

He watched as she bent over the music on the wooden stand, so beautiful and so intent on her work. Swishing the long, silky black hair impatiently aside when it touched the music. Leaning back automatically from time to time to ease the discomfort in the muscles of her back that plagues all cellists.

When she walked over and sat on the sofa pushing his legs aside, he said, "Does it really make a difference what finger plays the note?"

She smiled. "Not always. But there are some places where if you use the wrong fingering the bowing gets in a mess. It's like getting out of breath."

"Play me that thing I like. I've forgotten what its called. 'Variations,' or something like that."

She smiled, stood up and walked over to her music area, taking her cello from where it leaned against the piano and the bow from where it lay across a pile of music. For a moment she closed her eyes as she sat down, and then she played the opening bars of Rachmaninov's "Variations on a Rococo Theme." She played until the variation changed and then she walked back to him sitting beside him. "Why do you like that so much, David?"

He smiled. "I don't know. I think because it makes me think of you." He paused, smiling as he looked at her face. "It's very beautiful."

She kissed him gently and then said, "Don't forget we're going to see your parents. You need a shave." She laughed softly. "Your mother would be more shocked at you not being shaved on a Sunday than the fact we're living in sin."

"Have you thought of anything for the old man's birthday next week?"

"Well—not slippers, pyjamas, or ties anyway." She paused, smiling. "I have thought of something that I'm sure he'd like."

"Tell me."

"How about we buy him a season ticket for Middlesex Cricket Club and he can snooze away in the nice sunshine."

"That's great. He'd love that." He hugged her with enthusiasm and then sat up. "I've just remembered. I got something for you."

He reached under the sofa and gave her a square, flat envelope. As she tore it open he said, "I'm sure you'll hate it and say it's just schmaltz."

She looked at the sleeve of the disc. It was the Cliff Richard and Sarah Brightman duet, "All I ask of you," from the *Phantom* musical.

She took his hand and walked across the room and put the disc on the record-player. She stood with his arms around her and her head on his shoulder until the song ended and then looked up at his face. There were tears in her eyes as she said, "It's very you. Very us. Thanks."

As they drove across to Hackney where his parents lived she watched his face as he drove. He was not handsome but he was attractive. Brown eyes, strong jaw, and his mouth permanently ready to smile. She was aware that she didn't understand him, something she had always thought was essential to loving a man. But somehow it didn't seem to matter any more. She knew she loved him, and that was all that mattered. What she didn't understand was not some darkness or reticence in his mind, just that there was more there than she knew. She knew vaguely of his work and found it equally incongruous. She could understand how they used that quick, sharp mind, but what on earth did they do with that big warm, loving heart?

• • •

Tony Renshaw put aside the new issue of *Motorboat and Yachting* and answered the telephone. It was Mackintosh's secretary. The Director General would like to see him at seven at the Reform Club. He would be waiting by the tape machine and a private room had been booked already. He could expect to be away by no later than ten o'clock.

• • •

In fact Tony Renshaw was better known to the club servants than Mackintosh was. His father and an uncle had put him up for membership when he was eighteen and with due deference to its democratic tradition he had been kept waiting until he was twenty before he became a member. But that was in the old days when all London clubs were vying with one another for new members, when aristocratic property owners were quadrupling rentals at every break clause in the lease.

He preferred the Savile and that was what appeared in his *Who's Who* entry, along with Ronnie Scott's in Frith Street. The entry for Ronnie Scott's was no more than cocking a snook at the Establishment. He had only been once to the jazz club, and had disliked it intensely. He had disliked both its loucheness and the fawning adoration of the audience who so obviously knew nothing of music or technique. His taste was more for Bad Tuesday's on Third Avenue, which he always visited on trips to New York.

As Renshaw walked into the club the porter pointed to the far corner of the entrance hall. "Sir Graham is over there, sir, talking to Lord Harper. He said for you to join him."

Mackintosh had his back to him as Renshaw approached but his companion's face lit up, beaming as he turned away from

Mackintosh. "Tony, my boy. How nice to see you. How is your father? It's months since we met but I've been overseas." Then apologetically he said, "I say, let me introduce you to Sir Graham." He laughed, "Great panjandrum of one of our private armies."

"We have met, Archie," Renshaw said, smiling. "We know each other quite well."

"Good, good. Well I must be getting on my way." He grinned. "Only popped in really to get the last race results on the tele-thing." He turned to Mackintosh. "Good to see you, old chap. Keep up the good work."

As Mackintosh and Renshaw walked slowly up the broad stairs together the atmosphere was distinctly frosty. Sir Graham Mackintosh didn't like influential men knowing his juniors better than they knew him. And neither did he like being described as a "great panjandrum" as if they were all in some Gilbert and Sullivan opera.

The meal had been very nearly a silent feast but when the waiter had cleared away and poured them coffee Sir Graham said, "Tell me about your friend in Moscow."

"You saw the report on the two members of the TUC General Council?"

"Yes. When are you going to deal with them?"

"I want to make sure that when we pull them in there's no chance of anyone connecting the action to information from 'Needle.' He's more valuable to us than a couple of subversives in the trades unions."

"I was amazed at what he said the French were up to. They really are the limit. Do you think the Americans know?"

Renshaw smiled. "Not unless we tell them."

"What do you think?"

"I think that's for you to decide, sir. Maybe after consultation with the PM. But I suggest we keep the report on the relationship between Gorbachev and the KGB inside the department."

"Did you go along with his analysis?"

"It's all we've got, sir. Everything else is conjecture. The media have given up trying to decide what's going on inside the Kremlin because of all the contradictions. What 'Needle' is telling us is facts. He's there. Right where it's all happening." He paused. "He's given us the names of the senior people on both sides of the struggle."

Mackintosh's washed-out blue eyes looked at Renshaw's face. "Do you believe it?"

"I believe that this is how he sees it. I suppose he could be wrong. Or things could change."

"D'you know what worries me about all this?"

"No."

"It seems too good to be true."

"You mean the situation in the Kremlin?"

"No. I mean the flow of information."

"You think he's making it up?"

"I just don't know. Everything you've ever been able to check on proves that he's on target. No . . ." he shrugged and smiled wryly. "We've never had anything like it before. Not just in my time but for decades. Do you trust Charlton?"

"As much as I trust anyone. Anyway, he's no more than a go-between. He doesn't know what he's passing on. He's just a messenger. He doesn't have time to look at anything. The schedule is very tight. Our chaps at the embassy will have picked it up from the drop within an hour of Charlton getting it. He's never even met 'Needle,' he doesn't know who he is. And the contacts and dead-letter drops are fixed by London."

"How many people know about 'Needle'?"

"You mean people in SIS?"

"Just people."

"Just you, me, and Fletcher and Hoggart who do the decoding, and it's passed straight to me. They get a condensed brief from me. Even when they have decoded they would have no idea who the code-names refer to."

"Does Charlton's editor know that he's helping us?"

"No. Nobody knows anything about him and 'Needle' except you and me. And anybody you've told." Renshaw waited as if he expected an answer but Mackintosh didn't respond.

Mackintosh picked up the cup of cold coffee and sipped it slowly.

"Who's seen the section you deciphered yourself? The long piece on the arms control meetings?"

"Nobody. Just you. I've done a précis that you can distribute if you so wish, but I felt that the subject was so important and so controversial that you ought to have a literal and full version of his actual assessment. Maybe for the Foreign Minister or perhaps direct to the PM."

"What did you think about it?"

"Well it's obvious that Gorbachev really does mean to do a deal on intermediate-range missiles and 'Needle's' evaluation is that if they're forced to then they'll link it to an agreement on short-range missiles."

"And open inspection of destruction on both sides? He really thinks they'll go with that?"

"That's what he predicts. And zero-zero missiles is what the West has always said it wanted."

Mackintosh shook his head slowly. "That's what they say in public. But there isn't a government in NATO that isn't scared stiff at the thought." He paused and looked at Renshaw's face. "The Soviets would have achieved everything they wanted if such an agreement was signed."

"Why, sir?"

Mackintosh smiled. "You know why as well as I do. Three good reasons. First it would mean nothing left on either side in Europe except conventional ground forces. The Warsaw Pact outnumber NATO forces by five or six to one. Secondly, it would have 'uncoupled' the US from Europe. The only real defence we have of Europe is the Atlantic Alliance. Nobody admits it in public but we all know it. The Americans are not going to launch inter-continental ballistic missiles to protect Europe, even if they're attacked themselves. And thirdly the public will believe that without nuclear weapons in Europe then we have peace in our time. And they'll thank the Soviets for it." He paused. "They'll be wrong on both counts."

"Is all that the current Cabinet's view?"

"Who knows? Not me."

Then he said, "Now let's talk about you, Tony." He paused. "You're a head of section and you're too good to move to something that would give you promotion. Do you mind?"

"No, sir. My seniority isn't affected and I've no ambitions in other areas."

Mackintosh nodded, his lips pursed, and then he said in routine social tones, "And how's the boat?"

Renshaw laughed. "She's fine. I'll be down there as usual at the weekend."

Mackintosh stood up unsteadily and recovered himself before he said, "You don't mind if we call it a day now?"

"Of course not, sir."

• • •

There were lights on all over the house as the taxi dropped him in Eaton Square. Some of the windows were open and as he paid the driver he could hear the babel of voices and bursts of laughter. The Honourable Mary de Freitas was celebrating her twenty-fourth birthday. She was one of a large group of acquaintances of many years standing who would have been friends to any other man. But Tony Renshaw was not a man for friends. He enjoyed their company, their wildness and indifference to the rest of the world, and their determination to be happy. Few of them actually were happy but an outsider would not have recognised that.

They saw themselves as the "new-wave" but in fact they belonged in the twenties along with red Alfa Romeos, the Charleston, and tea-dances. The offspring of wealthy or just titled families. A lot of Mitford girls and Bertie Woosters with a leavening of artists, musicians, and not very successful writers who were taken up in some burst of enthusiasm and dropped with equal suddenness when they became so used to the crowd that they had the effrontery to behave as if they really were one of them.

Tony Renshaw had once tried to work out the common denominator of the crowd. It wasn't money. Some were stinking rich but some were virtually penniless. It wasn't good looks. There were real beauties but there were many who would have been flattered to be described as *jolie laide*. And the men ranged from rowing hearties to closet gays. With a flippancy that the crowd would have approved of he came to the conclusion that probably the only thing that they all had in common was that their mothers or grandmothers had all once danced with the Prince of Wales. And in a few cases perhaps a little more than just dancing. Those partners in mixed doubles at Fort Belvedere who ended up playing different games.

An hour later he was sitting at the piano with a crowd around him, joining in as he sang and played the old Noël Coward songs. They liked even the sad ones. When he had played Scott Joplin's "The Entertainer" three times and had done a take-off of Errol Garner doing "Misty," he closed the piano lid firmly and stood up. But his hostess had clamoured for just one more. He laughed and asked her to choose.

"The one you always play last. About deep purple."

He sat down, opened the lid and sang and played and there was silence as they listened—"When the deep purple falls over dreamy garden walls . . ."

• • •

When it became obvious to Department S that Yakunin had defected it was assumed that he had defected to the Americans, and the Soviet Ambassador in Washington had made the usual heated protests to the State Department, including a demand to be allowed to interview him, and the standard allegations that he had been drugged or kidnapped or both.

The State Department's indignant denials of any knowledge of Yakunin or any defector had been genuine. But the Russians were used to such denials and saw them as no more than the usual diplomatic rigamarole that was normal to any government including themselves.

It was almost two weeks before it dawned on both the Americans and the Russians that Yakunin might have defected to the British. The same ritual dance was conducted with the British Ambassador and the lapse of time allowed the First Secretary who dealt with the complaint to feel quite genuinely affronted by the Soviet accusations. Yakunin had virtually never existed so far as the embassy was concerned. Just another of those shadowy figures that their devious colleagues of MI6 spent their time with.

In Moscow there had been several meetings with Ulianov and some diplomatic criticism of lack of supervision, but fortunately he had recorded his own critical messages to Yakunin's director on the ground because of reports that Yakunin was acting too independently. There were reports back from the director of illegals who covered networks based on Washington, protesting that Yakunin was providing results that only his methods could have produced. He pointed out that he himself had obeyed his orders from Moscow and only a month earlier had talked severely to Yakunin about his behaviour. He went on to suggest that it was possibly those talks that had led to the man defecting. Yakunin had been angry and indignant at the attempt to restrict him and the director referred to a number of reports that had been made in the past about Yakunin's idiosyncratic character. He was a very difficult man to control. But Moscow would surely agree that the information obtained from the Walker circuit had been worth appeasing a difficult agent.

The usual damage control operation had been established and it was only then that the full extent of what Yakunin could reveal was established. Yakunin was one of the old KGB hands who had been involved in illegals' affairs for many years. His regular visits to Moscow meant that he could talk not only about his own operations but about many others, too. Ulianov was ordered to suggest some way of counteracting Yakunin's defection. And it was to have top priority in timing, budget, and facilities. For the first time in his career Ulianov was under real pressure from his superiors.

• • •

David Fletcher had bought a copy of the *Standard* on his way home but hadn't read it until later. He had only skipped through it and was ready to pass it over to Rachel when he saw the paragraph in the Stop Press column after the late race results. It was printed in extra-bold type but was only eight lines. An agency report. It said that a usually reliable source had claimed that a top Russian official and a British journalist named Charlton had been arrested and charged with being spies for a foreign government. The source suggested that a full-scale public trial was likely.

CHAPTER FOUR

*T*he management committee had dealt with next year's budget and had heard the secretary's report on planned expenditure. There was a minor tussle about the allocation of funds for a second-hand billiard table because a governor who was an accountant wanted to be seen as a liberal, and a governor who was a kindly parson was anxious to show that soft hearts were not synonymous with soft touches. When tea had been taken the committee settled down to the last item—grammar school scholarships. St. Joseph's Orphanage was proud of its alumni who had gone on to success in the outside world, and the facts showed quite plainly that almost all of them had had grammar school scholarships.

There were four names on the list and two had been approved with little discussion. But there had been lobbying beforehand and small deals done without a word spoken. A vote in exchange for an implied promise to support a request for a part-time football coach.

The secretary read out the remaining two names together.

"And now, ladies and gentlemen, we come to Edward Montgomery Hoggart and James Walker." He paused. "We can only choose one of them, as you know. You've seen the reports on the two boys." He looked at the older of the two women. "Miss Cately—could you give us a lead?"

Miss Cately was in her middle forties. Still pretty, with a well-boned face and smile wrinkles by her eyes. But they were rather sad eyes and she sighed as she looked at the others around the table. She spoke quietly so that they had to listen attentively.

"Edward Hoggart has been at St. Joseph's since he was eight years old. He's very bright. Does well in class. Two teachers have given him adverse reports despite his work. They found him both aggressive and violent." She looked at her notes. "He has run away twice and has been brought back by the police. On both occasions he had been found hanging around with undesirables. The last episode was just over a year ago.

"In the case of James Walker there is little I can add to the reports you have been given. He had done well in class and in his exams and Mr. Sproat who takes him for art says that he has a very definite natural talent. No adverse reports and a very cooperative boy all round. Well liked by all the staff."

There was a long silence and then old Major Payne said, "Who do the staff favour?"

"James Walker, Major," Miss Cately said quietly.

"Then I'd go for the other chap—whatisname—Parker."

Before Miss Cately could correct the name, Mr. Stroud, who was the staff representative on the committee, bristled and said sharply, "The staff would very much resent your implication, Major Payne. I'm shocked. In fact I must lodge a formal protest."

The secretary, who saw his role as rushing in where angels fear to tread, said with an aggravating smile, "Perhaps we should hear the major's reasons before we rush to conclusions, Stroud." He turned to the elderly man who was being so awkward. "Please take us into your confidence, Major."

"No question of me confidence, old chap. Just simple logic. You've got one lad who's good at art who everybody likes. He's going to make it anyway. On the other hand you've got a bright lad with certain blemishes—handicaps—whatever you care to call them. He'd get the most benefit from a grammar school education." He turned to look at the staff member. "Can't see any need to get all wound up about it, Stroud."

The Reverend as peacemaker said, smiling apologetically, "Perhaps we've got the parable of the prodigal son in real life here."

Padstow, a wealthy builder, said gruffly, "What's their backgrounds?"

Miss Cately said, "Edward Hoggart came to us from the courts, as a child in need of care. His mother was an alcoholic, his father was seldom around. He was a petty criminal. A very unsuccessful one. James Walker's parents were killed in a car accident. There were no relatives willing to take him."

The secretary allowed a few moments of silence and then said, "Perhaps we'd better vote on it."

After some discussion they voted and the secretary read out the result.

"It's—six votes for James Walker and two for Hoggart." He smiled at the major, "Sorry, Major."

The major shrugged. "How much do we have to pay the grammar school?"

"We get special terms—two hundred a year."

"How about we compromise. We put them both up and I'll pay meself for the Hoggart boy. How's that suit you?" He looked around at his colleagues and there were embarrassed murmurs of approval and thanks.

• • •

There were times when Major Payne suspected that his sister Amelia would have made a better army officer than he had been. A sharp, *crisp mind and a forthright attitude to life and living. It was, perhaps, typical of her character that out of a lavish endowment of four Christian names she chose to be known by the one he found the least endearing.*

She was arranging chrysanthemums in a cut-glass vase as they talked, briskly tearing off surplus leaves and jabbing the thick stems into a piece of foam rubber at the bottom of the vase.

"You're wasting your time with that boy, George."

George Payne took a sip of his whisky and loosened his leather belt before he replied.

"What makes you think that, dear?"

"I don't think it, George. It's a question of fact."

"Go on, my dear. Get it off your chest."

She sighed. "How I detest this tendency to sloppy speech. Get it off my chest indeed." *She paused.* "Tell me why you got involved with him in the first place."

"He's just one of the orphanage lads. Needed a helping hand, that's all."

"You're going to get no thanks from the likes of him. Takes it all for granted. All take and no give."

"He doesn't have anything to give, does he now."

He spoke quietly and she turned from her flower arranging to look at him, aware of the sadness in his voice.

"He could show a bit of gratitude, surely."

"You don't indulge in gratitude if you come from his kind of background. Kids like that are like wild animals. Always on the run. Waiting for the next blow to fall. He gets a bit of peace with me at the weekends. He'll be all right. Just takes time."

"Let's hope you're right, George," *she said appeasingly as she stood back to examine her vase of chrysanthemums.* "You know, George, if truth be told, I don't know why people go on so much about chrysanths. They're very sameish and frightful colours. Belong in cemeteries not country cottages."

He laughed. "Never thought about 'em, my dear. But I'm sure you're right." He smiled. "You generally are."

• • •

Eddie Hoggart was always embarrassed when he could be seen walking with the old man when he was wearing his riding breeches and leather boots. He had real affection for the old man who had shown him such kindness but he wasn't mature enough not to be embarrassed by some of his idiosyncrasies. They stood that day at the bottom of the slope that led up to the cottage. It wasn't really a cottage, it was four farm workers' cottages made into one.

The old man waved his walking stick towards the long building. "I'm going to get them to put a bathroom in next to your room, boy. Be ready when you come next time." He turned and looked at the boy. "How old are you now, Eddie, remind me?"

"I'm eighteen in October, Major."

"And then what?"

"Depends on my Matriculation results."

"What do you think you'll get?"

"French, geography, and maybe physics."

"Not English?"

"No. Definitely not."

"And what if you get the two?"

"I don't know, sir. I'll have to think about it."

The old man pointed with his stick at the wooden bench. "Sit down, lad."

When they were both seated the old man said, "Why not go in the army, boy? Good games player, boxing, decent exam results: you'd stand a good chance of getting a commission. And the life would suit you."

"They wouldn't have me."

"Why not?"

"I've got a police record."

"*Oh for God's sake, that was just a boyish prank. Six months' probation. That's no problem. I can see to that.*"

"*I wouldn't want to let you down, sir.*"

"*You won't, lad. I'll see you don't.*" He paused, "*The main thing is, would you be interested?*"

"*Yes. I would. If they'd have me.*"

"*I'll get you an interview as soon as you get your exam results.*" He stood up. "*We'd better be going in or we'll get bawled out by Mrs. Taylor for letting our food get cold.*"

Eddie Hoggart had become a surrogate son for the old man who had had no children and whose wife had died not long after the end of the war. He had had plenty of opportunities to marry again but he had seen it as bordering on impertinence that any woman should think she could replace his Alice. He had been better than most fathers would be, guiding and observing but never interfering. Eddie Hoggart came as near to loving someone as he would ever come.

The army had taken Eddie Hoggart, accepting the minor blot on his record with much the same attitude as the major did. He had done his three months' basic infantry training and had been posted to a Royal Corps of Signals training unit where he had trained as a radio operator. It was during his course that a notice was posted on the unit's notice-board calling for applications from French or German speakers.

The old services' motto of "Never volunteer for anything" made him ask the old man, when he was on a forty-eight-hour weekend pass, for his opinion. The old man had advised him to check out what was on offer. Six months later Eddie Hoggart was a lieutenant in the Intelligence Corps. Five weeks' SAS-type training in survival and self-defence was followed by a weapons course. A year's routine duties penetrating suspected subversives in the armed forces was followed by an intensive Russian course and then a further year of advanced Russian.

At that point Hoggart was approached to join M16 on a grade higher than his army rank. He hadn't rushed into a decision but after ten days' thought he accepted. From then on he wore civilian clothes and worked from Century House.

The major died a few months later and left Eddie Hoggart his medals and £500. The rest of his estate went to Cancer Research. It took Eddie Hoggart quite a time before he got used to not having a home to go to and the wise old man to discuss his problems with.

CHAPTER FIVE

Hoggart found that the records on Yakunin were sparse. He was born in 1936 in Smolensk. No record of his parents after or before the war. He had been in the siege of Leningrad and, with a group of "lost" children, had been evacuated to an orphanage just outside Alma-Ata. There were several blank years and no further information until 1959 when his name appeared as a trainee militia-man. A year later he had been transferred to the Frontier Police. Then came two years at Moscow University but no details of what he studied. But his student serial number indicated that it was probably some science subject. The first indication of his transfer to the KGB came in 1964 when he was noticed as a regular visitor to the KGB offices in Kiev. The man he was frequently seen with was a KGB captain in First Directorate administration, and shortly after he had been seen at a Czech Embassy party given to a US trade delegation visiting Moscow. There was no record of a marriage or a family and from 1968 there were no further entries apart from a record of his promotion to KGB captain in 1969. The only visual material was a grainy photograph of Yakunin sitting at a pavement café in bright sunshine with an unidentified man. There was no indication of where they were but a photo analyst had suggested that it could be somewhere in California because of the style of the woodwork used in the shop front and the style of the furniture.

Eddie Hoggart had been ordered to take over the de-briefing of the Russian and having read the sparse information on file he knew that he would have to go slowly. His first objective must be to establish that Yakunin was the man on their file and then fill in some of the gaps and get him to define what his recent operations had been. He made arrangements to move into the safe-house where Yakunin was being held.

• • •

As Hoggart drove south down the A21 all the traffic was coming the other way, from the coast. The day-trippers to the seaside towns. The dinghy sailors and windsurfing fanatics with their kit lashed onto roof-racks. It had been a real summer Sunday, and they had left it to the last minute before they headed back to the London suburbs.

Just after the sign for Lamberhurst he took the right fork off the coast road, up through the picturesque village and up to the Down where he turned right, past The Swan and on past the small row of houses that faced the vineyard until he came to the farmhouse where he turned slowly down the rough track that led downhill.

Hoggart drove his car into the old barn. There were two white Land-Rovers already there and instinctively he put his hand on their radiators one after the other. They were both cold. The farmhouse itself lay well back from the road down a dusty dirt track that skirted the main yard. He stood looking across the valley to the hills. The long rows of the vines ran from north to south, and some kind of machine was spraying the rows, the liquid fanning out, catching the sun and a spectrum of rainbow colours.

As he turned he saw a man watching him from the shadow of a beech tree. He was one of the security guards in charge of the safe-house. He walked over to him carrying his canvas hold-all and without speaking held up his ID card for the man to check. He was obviously an old hand and he reached out for the card and checked it carefully, routinely holding it slantwise against the light to see if there was any sign of obvious alterations. When he handed it back he said quietly, "Can I help you?"

Hoggart smiled and said, "Where is he?"

"He's inside. In his room."

"How's he been?"

"Totally non-cooperative. Bloody-minded and constantly complaining."

"About what?"

"That he's not being treated with proper respect."

Hoggart smiled. "Sounds ready for me. Which is my room?"

"Number four, sir. The last on the left at the top of the stairs."

As he walked up the stairs Hoggart was conscious of the warm, musty smell of the house. Most safe-houses smelt odd, no matter how clean and tidy they were kept. Cabins rented out for holidays were the same, as if they were ailing from being nobody's home. Places that had once been homes that were now unloved, just places that housed one transient after another.

He unpacked then washed his face and hands, looking out across the valley as he dried his hands. There was an evening mist beginning to hide the trees along the edge of the vineyard. He opened the old-fashioned sash-window and took a few deep breaths before he walked out of the room and along to the far end of the landing. For a moment he hesitated at the closed door, then knocked and walked in.

The Russian was sitting in an armchair, smoking, the ashtray on the floor beside him piled high with butts. He looked older than Hoggart had expected, and he looked back at Hoggart as if he were a prisoner rather than a defector. Maybe that was just what he was.

"Mr. Yakunin?"

The Russian just nodded, his eyes intent on Hoggart's face.

"Would you prefer to speak in Russian or English, Mr. Yakunin?"

Yakunin shrugged. "Is OK with me either way."

"Let's start in English and we can change over if it doesn't work out."

Hoggart pulled up the other armchair and made himself comfortable.

"How about food and drink, Mr. Yakunin, are you getting what you want?"

The Russian shrugged. "Those things aren't what I came for. They don't matter."

Hoggart smiled. "They count if they're not provided. But let's get talking." He paused. "I'm an intelligence officer, Mr. Yakunin, and I'll be staying here at the house with you so that we can talk."

"And after the talk?"

"I don't understand."

"After the talk will you and your people act on what I tell you?"

Hoggart smiled. "That's for others to decide. It depends on what you tell me."

"You've got big problems in your organisation."

Hoggart laughed. "There's problems in the KGB too."

"Problems of traitors?"

Hoggart had been at it too long to fall for that one. A "plant" on a fishing expedition? He shrugged. "Who knows? How about we get down to basics?"

"You're not interested in traitors?"

"Let's just do it bit by bit. We'll come to the traitors when we've established the groundwork. Tell me about yourself, and what you've been doing."

"My name is Yakunin. Igor. I am a major in KGB. First Directorate. Department S. I have been for several years an illegal in United States."

"Any family, Mr. Yakunin?"

"No. No family. No living relatives."

"When were you recruited into the KGB?"

"Why do you ask me—you're sure to have some sort of file on me?"

Hoggart took a deep breath to control his irritation. "It's a standard procedure, Yakunin."

"I'm not interested in procedures. I have things to tell you and that's all that matters."

"Do you regret going to our embassy in Washington?"

"Why do you ask that?"

"Because we can make arrangements for you to be sent anywhere you want. You came to us voluntarily but if you've changed your mind about having done that—now's the time to say so. But . . ." and Hoggart waved a monitory finger towards the Russian, ". . . if you want to stay—you do it our way. Is that understood?"

The Russian stood up slowly and walked to the barred window, the setting sun lighting up his face. Hoggart watched him as he stood looking out across the valley. It was a face from a medieval painting. Gaunt, with hollow cheeks, a prominent nose, and a full sensual mouth. Heavy-lidded eyes that even in profile looked tired of the world and its ways. When the Russian turned to look at him Hoggart looked back implacably. If the Russian wanted to play games he wasn't going to join in. When Yakunin walked back slowly and sat in the chair he said, "I joined KGB in 1963."

Hoggart nodded. "Tell me what you studied at the university."

"English and electronics."

Hoggart smiled. "You speak very good English. Were you as good at electronics?"

"Just enough to talk about it and understand the answers to my questions."

"Was it electronics you were covering in the United States?"

"That was the prime target area."

"What was your cover?"

"German technical journalist."

"What particular area of electronics did you cover?"

"Weapons control, guidance systems, and computers."

"Who was your contact in the States?"

"Nobody. Just dead-drops arranged by radio from Moscow."

"Where's the radio now?"

"I left it in the States."

"In Washington?"

The Russian shook his head. "No. A long way from Washington."

"If my people want to locate it I assume you'd cooperate."

"Let's see how we go."

Hoggart sighed. "Is something worrying you, comrade?"

"Yes."

"What is it?"

"It's you people. You're wide open to the KGB and you don't realise it. I don't want to end up face-down in the Thames."

Hoggart stood up, walking to the door before he turned to look at Yakunin. "Mr. Yakunin, I've de-briefed a number of Warsaw Pact defectors and I've never come up against somebody with your attitude." He paused. "Maybe you'd better think over your position overnight and make sure you wouldn't rather talk to the Americans or somebody else. Goodnight."

He closed the door before Yakunin could reply.

CHAPTER SIX

*T*he stone facade of Great Marlborough Street Magistrates Court has a cheerful, welcoming face that belies its Dickensian interior. The probation officers and elderly police officers are all helpful and amiable to their visitors but very concerned that the dignity of the courts should be upheld.

The waiting area for Court Number One seems to have been designed by an architect who had been influenced by the design of the bathhouses in ancient Rome. A large and well-proportioned room, its walls lined with wooden benches that were crowded on most mornings with the left-overs of minor offences and criminal acts. Real criminals were inevitably moved on to a Crown Court.

The solicitors and their clerks were barely distinguishable from their clients. Sombre and seedy dress and a permanent air of suspense and irritation with clients who, even with their own advisers, maintained an instinct for evasive answers to straight questions. The solicitors relieved their tension by pacing the open area, looking and sometimes nodding at their colleagues, and sometimes pushing head and *shoulders into the door marked* COUNSEL AND OFFICIALS. *The court was closed to the public while it was dealing with half a dozen cases where prisoners had been in custody overnight. There were sixty-four names on the court-list in the glass frame. All due to be heard that day.*

It was almost eleven o'clock before the door was opened for the public to enter the court. There was a single bench that held about twelve people and room for a few more standing behind the bench.

It was an hour before one of the elderly constables signaled to the five chattering girls that their time had come. In court they went one by one to the stand as they were called by the usher. The police prosecutor read out the same formal charge for each of them—"that on the 28th of June you were loitering in Curzon Street with intent to solicit for prostitution." The magistrate was used to the ritual. The plea of guilty in the barely audible little-girl voice, the slightly bowed and contrite head as seen in TV courtroom dramas, the fine of £25, and then the next name was called.

The only exception to the conveyor-belt justice was the last girl. Young and very pretty, her face and body an odd contrast of innocence and flaunting sensuality. Like the others she was charged and pleaded guilty, but the magistrate looked across the court at her and asked, "How old are you?"

"Eighteen."

The magistrate looked to his right where the woman probation officer sat alone at her small desk. She answered his unspoken question with a small lift of her shoulders and a shake of her head. For a moment he was silent and then he looked at the girl.

"I'm going to remand you for fourteen days. You will not be in custody but you must cooperate with the probation officer and appear in fourteen days' time . . ." He looked at the usher who said, "Fourteenth of July, sir."

The magistrate noted the date, nodded at the girl in the dock and the probation officer took her through the door marked FINES.

• • •

After half a dozen interviews with Jacqui Lovegrove, the court probation officer felt that she needed to discuss the case with a senior probation officer and the meeting was held at the Community Team's offices in Rathbone Place.

Maggie Castle, the senior, folded her arms and leaned on the table.

"I've read all the reports, Helen. Tell me what you think?"

"The only facts I've got are that she lied in court about her age. She's not eighteen. I couldn't get out of her her real age but she's definitely under-age. And a clear case of incest by the father."

"Has he been interviewed by the police?"

"No. She swears she won't testify against him."

"How old was she when he first had intercourse with her?"

"As near as I can get she must have been about twelve when it started and maybe a year later before there was full intercourse."

"And you think the mother knows but doesn't care?"

"I'm sure she knows. I couldn't pursue it with her. It had to be just a chat. She's scared of her husband. A lot of hospital treatments for assaults but no prosecutions. She's not only scared of him, she's entirely dependent on him. I'd say she's jealous of the girl."

"I think I'd better talk to the girl. Can you bring her here tomorrow?"

"Yes, of course."

* * *

There were three chintz-covered armchairs and Maggie Castle was impressed by the girl's obvious self-confidence. After the routine preliminaries she said, "Tell me about your relationship with your father."

"I ain't going to shop him in court so don't think I am."

"I just want to understand, Jacqui. What you and I talk about is confidential. We'd just like to help if we can."

"So what d'you wanna know?"

"Tell me how it started?"

"They'd had a flaming row, him and my Mom, and she went off to stay with one of her pals. He got into my bed that night and started touching me up. And a few weeks later he started doing it all the way."

"Did you object when he got in your bed?"

She shrugged and half-smiled. "No. What's the good. When men want it they're gonna have it."

"Were you scared that he might knock you about if you refused?"

"No. He only beats her because she taunts him. He's easy if you treat him right."

They had gone on talking for over an hour before the girl left. Maggie Castle had phoned her junior and fixed a meeting for the following afternoon.

• • •

Maggie Castle shook her head. "There's no point in bringing all this out in court. First of all she'd deny everything and secondly she's got it all worked out. She's quite shameless. And like most of them she tells so many lies that the stories end up being contradictory."

"We could suggest she's put on six months' probation. She is in moral danger after all."

"She's not, you know. She's got it all worked out. Or she thinks she has. And right now it works. It was incest all right, but it wasn't a rape. She was a willing partner. And now she's got him exactly where she wants him. And he's not the only one. She knows more about men than you and I do. She's very pretty and she's got that cute innocent face. But believe me she knows she's got what men want. And she's going to use it."

"If she was on six months' probation at least I'd be able to keep an eye on her. Sooner or later she'll get into trouble."

Maggie Castle smiled. "OK. Suggest that. The court must have suspected she was under-age or very near it."

• • •

The big Jaguar stopped at the south side of Soho Square and the driver looked at his watch as he locked the car. As he turned towards Fifth Street the girl stopped him.

"Are you Nickie Bodoni?"

The man's dark eyes went from her face to her sweater and then back to her face.

"Who are you, kid?"

"I'm Jacqui. Somebody told me you were looking for a hostess at your club."

"Who's somebody?"

"He told me his name's Caruana. Lew Caruana."

"Where did you meet him?"

"At the pub in Old Compton Street."

"How old are you?"

"Seventeen and two months."

He smiled at the juvenile precision. "You've got nice tits for seventeen, honey."

She smiled up at him. "D'you wanna see them?"

"Have you worked as a hostess before?"

She shrugged and smiled. "Kind of."

He looked at his watch. "Ask for me at the door about eleven. I'll tell 'em you're coming. What's your name?"

"Jacqui."

"OK, Jacqui. Be seein' you." As he moved away he stopped. "They'll nick you for sure if you hang around the square. Better go down by the bottom of Wardour Street."

• • •

The big bruiser on the door asked her her name and when she told him he led her down the dimly lit wooden steps and along a narrow passage. He opened a door and pointed inside.

"Wait there, kid. I'll get the boss."

The room was like a room in a film. Leather furniture, deep wall-to-wall carpet, chrome and glass, and pine strip ceilings and walls. A hi-fi was playing a Beatles tape as she looked at herself in a pink mirror.

They both knew the rules of the hostess and club owner game, and an hour later they were both in bed. He left at six in the morning and told her she was hired and could stay in the flat if she wanted to.

He was back by seven in the evening and not in a good mood. He sat looking at her as she put on her make-up.

"Where d'you get those rags you're wearing?"

"Top Shop."

He took an elastic band off a thick roll of notes and gave her two fifties.

"Get something classier, kid, and chuck that stuff way. The guys who come in here are men with dough. They ain't interested in punk girls."

She turned to look at him. "You wanna bet?"

He smiled. "You're a cheeky little bitch, aren't you?"

She laughed. "No. But I know more about what men want than you do, buddy."

For a moment he was tempted to slap her face but as he looked at her his lust took over and he pulled her down onto the couch.

• • •

Jacqui Lovegrove had stayed with Bodoni for three months, and she had enjoyed it. Teasing the suckers with her young body but seldom delivering. Aware of the power that her body gave her over men. All kinds of men from the well-off louts in Bodoni's club to the smooth sophisticated clientele at the clubs where Bodoni took her himself. He showed her off like a boy with a new toy and then became jealous if other men talked to her.

Bodoni had a wife and a large house in Hampstead but every day he stayed with the girl until the early hours of the morning. Even on Sundays he told his wife that he had to go and make up the books.

It was at Charlie's Place in Frith Street that she met Harry Gardner. He had written his name and telephone number on the flap of a packet of Stuyvesants and there were five twenty-pound notes folded up inside. She had phoned him two days later when Bodoni was at the local Customs and Excise Office going through his VAT returns. She had gone to Gardner's flat in Hertford Street by the Hilton. He had been smiling and amiable but there had been no pretence about what he wanted. Three hundred a week or five hundred if she'd satisfy a few special business friends as well. And, as he said, a damn good time into the bargain.

His lust for her was quite obvious in his eyes and she decided to test her attraction for him by refusing his offer. And she'd judged him correctly: he'd upped both parts of the deal by another hundred. When she was getting dressed afterwards he'd told her that she should stay with Bodoni until he contacted her. He didn't want to offend or annoy Bodoni for various reasons. Things would work out all right.

And they did. Bodoni had an unofficial visit from a man who worked for the local authority's club licensing department. A lugubrious looking man who asked him if he knew that one of his hostesses was under-age. A Miss Jacqueline Lovegrove. A hundred pounds and an evening on the house had cheered up the perceptive official no end.

Bodoni had been puzzled when he told the girl that she'd have to leave. She didn't look upset. Not even surprised. He had had one last night with her and he'd given her a small slab of gold that he swore was worth at least £200. She was surprised that she got £230 for it when she sold it a week later.

* * *

She found that her life with Harry Gardner suited her well. He was a big, self-confident man. Good-looking in an old-fashioned way. Thick black hair, military style moustache, and a rather florid complexion. He dressed extremely well and seemed to spend money as if he didn't need to count it. He always referred to his friends as businessmen but it was obvious that they were criminals. Gang-leaders, top men in organised crime who were as at home in New York, Amsterdam, and Ankara as they were in London. Sometimes she was excluded when business was being discussed and when she joined them she found them amiable and friendly despite their hard eyes. When he went out to clubs and expensive restaurants in the evenings he took her with him and made sure that she was treated with respect. There was a lot of sex but it was normal and routine, and from time to time he "lent" her to one of his associates after a meeting at the flat or sent her by taxi to an influential man staying at one of the top London hotels. The money he paid her was always in cash and she had accounts at several banks that added up to just over ten thousand pounds. On her birthday he gave her a party at an exclusive night-club and a silver fox cape.

He made monthly trips abroad that seldom lasted more than two or three days. And when he was away there was a minder left in case she needed anything. It was when he was on a trip to New York that the minder was a Sicilian named Gianni. Gianni was in his thirties. Handsome and macho, with a reputation as a stud, with a string of women clamouring for his attention. His supercilious grin as he looked her over and his apparent indifference to her had annoyed her enough to make her test him out. She hadn't met the old traditional Palermo ploy before and she was on the bed by the second afternoon. She was unfortunately also on the bed the third day when Gardner walked in.

He had stood there without speaking, his face impassive as he watched them both dress and when Gianni had left Gardner started unpacking his two leather cases.

"I'm sorry about this, Harry. I was a fool."

He looked up at her, smiling. "Happens in the best families, honey." He paused. "I'll be out for the evening. That gives you time to pack and leave."

"Is there anything I can do to make up for it?"

"Yes. Keep out of my way for the next few weeks."

"I'm terribly sorry, Harry."

"Of course you are. We're all sorry when we get caught." He smiled amiably. "Your little friend couldn't scrape together fifty quid so don't look to him for support."

• • •

The next year had been a bad year for Jacqui Lovegrove. Harry Gardner had obviously put the word out that she was no longer welcome at the clubs where she could make good money. It slowly came down to casual pick-ups in bars and drinking clubs. But she was determined not to go on the streets despite a lot of smooth talking from the pimps who worked the Soho area. Her young body still had its usual effect on men but now they were no more than paying customers.

Almost as if she had finished serving a prison sentence things began to improve. Twice she'd been taken to one of the better clubs by men who were regulars there and slowly she was back inside the magic circle again. But she no longer had her influential sugar-daddy and despite the improvement she was lonely. The men who had her wanted her body, not her company. They had homes and families to go back to and she was just one more pretty club girl who did it for money. She put on a good front as the wayward daughter of a wealthy family. A big house in the country and a doting father. Sometimes he was a leading heart specialist, sometimes a wealthy landowner. Her mythical father changed roles to suit the listener, a Walter Mitty once removed.

She was at the Monte Cristo Club that particular night. There was a big fight on at Wembley Stadium and the club was virtually empty. Just two men in deep conversation. She recognised both of them. One was a fence and the other was a skilled driver for big robberies. A free-lance who only did six or seven jobs a year.

When she saw the stranger walk in she thought for a moment it was Harry Gardner. The same big build, the same mass of dark hair, and the same rugged face. She heard him ask for a Glenlivet and as he waited for the barman to pour the drink he turned and looked at her. Her face, her breasts, her legs and then back to her face again. It was the kind of look she got from men who fancied her. But he turned back to the bar, holding up the glass to look at the golden liquid before drinking it straight down. He ordered another drink and took it over to one of the tables in the alcove. She saw him look at his watch as if he were expecting somebody.

The two men at the other table left separately a few minutes later, the driver nodding to her as he passed. Then the man with the whisky was looking at her and she walked over and sat in the alcove beside him.

"Hi, I'm Jacqui. You waiting for someone?"

"Have a drink, honey."

"Thanks. Can I have a port and lemon?"

He smiled and signalled to the barman, who seemed to know what the girl would ask for. When he took it across the man asked for an evening paper. When the barman brought back a folded copy of the Evening Standard *the man left it folded on the table.*

"Why did you smile when I wanted a port and lemon?"

"It's kind of old-fashioned."

"And you don't like old-fashioned things?"

"What did you say your name was?"

"Jacqui. And I'm eighteen."

"And you're very pretty, too. But I expect you've heard that before."

She smiled at him. She was on her own home ground now. There were just the ritual steps to come of a not very complex dance.

"Are you a tits or leg man?"

She saw his smile fade, and he shook his head. "Don't waste your talents on me, honey. You'd be wasting your time."

"Why should I be wasting time?"

"I'm not a john, kid."

She shrugged. "So what? You've got nice brown eyes and a nice voice. There's nobody here but us. Costs nothing to be friendly."

The man smiled. "You're right of course. How about another drink?"

"I'll buy you one." She turned and signalled to the barman, who brought the drinks over with a bowl of nuts. As she raised her glass to him she said, "By the way, what's your name?"

For a moment he hesitated and as a compulsive liar she knew he was lying when he said, "Tom. Most people call me Tommy."

She smiled. "Cheers, Tommy."

"Cheers, Jacqui." He paused. "Have you seen a film called Crocodile Dundee?*"*

"No. But I've heard about it. Sounds good. Have you seen it?"

"No. Would you like to see it?"

"You mean tonight?"

"Yes. Why not?"

"I've got to hang on until the club's busy again after the fight."

"It'll only take a couple of hours and you could come back afterwards."

She laughed and looked pleased and very young. "OK. Why not? I'll get my coat."

• • •

They had gone out together a dozen times. To cinemas, to the Zoo, to the Thames at Marlow, to the Natural History Museum, and three times to meals at luxury hotels. But they ate mainly at Lyons Corner House opposite Charing Cross Station. He had never had sex with her, nor even suggested it. Not because he didn't find her sexually attractive. Not even on high principle. It just didn't fit their relationship. And he had other girls he could sleep with anyway. He had seen through the blarney, the doting father stuff, and had wondered what made her so insecure.

They had arranged to meet that evening at the Monte Cristo Club and as he made his way to the bar he looked around but could see no sign of her. As he leaned forward to order his drink the barman said, "How is she making out?"

"Who?"

"Jacqui. Your girlfriend."

"I guess she's OK. I was expecting her to be here before me."

The barman looked at him. "D'you mean you haven't heard?"

"Heard what?"

"She's in hospital. Some jerk beat her up real bad."

"What hospital is she in?"

"I don't remember." He turned and spoke to the waitress. "Which hospital is Jacqui in?"

"Jacqui—oh yes, Jacqui—she's in the Middlesex."

"Don't bother about the drink."

• • •

He took a taxi to Mortimer Street and when reception told him there were no visitors allowed after 8 P.M. he used his ID and was given fifteen minutes and warned not to tax her strength.

Her eyes were closed and there was a plastic tube from a drip taped into her nose and most of the rest of her face was hidden by bandages. One arm was heavily bandaged and strapped across her body. He looked at the charts at the foot of the bed. She'd been there three days already, and that was about all he could understand of the charts. After they had seen his ID they'd told him that she had been sexually assaulted and beaten up. There was still a possibility of some internal injury that they had not been able to detect. What mainly disturbed them was her lack of will to live. She was holding steady but by now she should be showing some improvement, but she was not responding to the treatment.

She was in a private room but there was no sign of anything personal. She had had no visitors and they had had to incinerate her clothes. He stood looking at her. She looked more like a child than a young woman. He sat down gently on the side of the bed and took her free hand in his and said her name quietly, again and again. A few minutes later she opened one eye.

"It's me, Jacqui. It's Tommy. Can you hear me?"

She made no sign but he saw her chest heave as she sighed deeply and her fingers clasped his and then relaxed.

"I'd have come before but I didn't hear about it until I went to meet you at the club tonight. Is there anything I can get you? Anything you want?"

Slowly she disentangled her hand from his and moved it to push aside the bandages across her mouth. He could see the swollen lips as she spoke.

"They tell you what—what happened?"

"Yes. They told me. Don't talk about it now."

Her voice quavered as she spoke. "I'm scared, Tommy. I've never been scared before."

"Don't be scared, honey. Nothing like this is ever going to happen to you again."

"They did it deliberately. To warn me off."

"Who did?"

She shook her head slowly. "I don't know, Tommy. I don't know." *And he knew that she was lying.*

"Doesn't matter, but you can be sure it won't happen again. I'll see that it doesn't."

"You don't understand."

He nodded. "I understand, little girl. I understand."

"The man who did it said you're an undercover cop from the Drugs Squad—are you?"

"No."

"Honest?"

"Honest."

"Would you do something that would help me get better?"

"Of course I would."

"Tell me your name. Your real name."

"Why do you want to know?"

She looked away for several moments and then turned her head to look at him. "It would show that I mattered. That I'm not just a slag."

For a moment he hesitated, then he said softly, "My name's Eddie. Eddie Hoggart."

CHAPTER SEVEN

Hoggart had had three long sessions with Yakunin and the Russian seemed to be more relaxed. There had been very little progress beyond establishing that Yakunin genuinely was KGB and had worked for Department S. The Russian was less defensive now but it was obvious that he had something to say that he felt was highly charged and he wanted assurance that he was safe in revealing whatever it was. Assurance that could only come from some sort of trust in his SIS handler. It had been agreed in the section that it was going to be a long, slow haul but there was a feeling that the pay-off could be worthwhile.

• • •

Hoggart smiled as he sat looking at Yakunin. The Russian had taken a liking to chocolate éclairs and he sat there looking like a small boy at a party, his mouth covered with chocolate and cream. For the first time ever the Russian smiled as he wiped his mouth with a Kleenex.

"They are fantastic, comrade. I could eat them all day."

"Didn't you try them when you were in the States?"

"I never saw such things."

"How did you like it in the States?"

Yakunin shrugged. "They gave me no problems."

"Tell me about your networks."

The Russian stood up and walked to the window, standing there for several minutes looking out. Then he turned and looked at Hoggart.

"There were no networks. Just me alone and sometimes two others."

"But you told them at the embassy in Washington that you ran two networks out of Canada."

"Why should I tell that woman what I do?"

"How about you tell me."

Yakunin walked back and sat in the chair. When he had lit a cigarette he looked at Hoggart.

"I ran John Walker. That was a full-time operation."

"Who was John Walker?"

"John Anthony Walker, late of Norfolk, Virginia, and the United States Navy—arrested by the FBI on May 20, 1985, and serving a life sentence for selling top-secret information to the Soviet Union."

"That was the case where half his family were involved and he informed on the others as part of a plea-bargain deal?"

"That's the one."

"And you were his control?"

"Yes."

"Will you talk to me about it?"

"No."

"Why not?"

"Because you'd pass it to the CIA and they'd bust a gut to get me extradited and put on trial."

"We haven't even told the Americans that you've come over to us and there are no circumstances where we would let you be extradited anywhere."

"If I talk what becomes of me? How do I live?"

"Provided you have really cooperated with us to the very best of your ability you will be given a new identity and a British passport. You will be paid a pension that will allow you to live comfortably. And if what you tell us has an ongoing significance you would be paid as a consultant to the organisation."

"And my safety?"

"You would have a new name and a new identity. Not more than half a dozen people would know anything about it. You'd have a code-name."

"What about physical protection?"

"What makes you feel that would be necessary?"

"I've been in the business a long time, comrade Hoggart. They would want to kill me."

"There's been no sign of any KGB activity directed towards you so far."

Yakunin smiled. "Of course not. They will be doing a damage evaluation exercise and they will look at what they think I can tell you. They will take steps to reduce the damage. Change codes, pull back other people and so on. The same things you must have done when Philby came over to Moscow and later when Blunt confessed."

"So?"

"But what I have to tell you people they don't even know that I know it. So if I tell you and you deal with the problem they will realise who has given you the information. They would spare nothing to get their revenge on me."

Hoggart was silent for several moments. Realising that the

de-briefing was moving into a decisive phase and not wanting to make a wrong move.

"You know Igor, whether a man is CIA, KGB, or SIS, if he is very senior he always feels that his current operation is the most important item in the organisation's programme. We all feel like that. It's part of the job. It justifies some of the maybe unpleasant things we have to do." Hoggart paused. "Are you sure that you're not exaggerating in your own mind what you have to tell us?"

Yakunin sighed. "I'm quite sure." He lit a cigarette and then looked across at Hoggart. "If somebody had come over with *proof* that Philby and the others were traitors—long before you even suspected them—would you have thought that was important?"

"Of course we would."

"Well what I have to tell you is more important than that."

"So tell me," Hoggart said quietly.

Yakunin shook his head slowly. "When I'm ready I'll tell you."

"Tell me about John Walker and how you ran him."

"Tomorrow we talk about it. A little."

• • •

Hoggart had had a video recorder linked up to Yakunin's TV and they had sat watching a cassette of *Moscow on the Hudson*. Yakunin was much amused at the antics of the two Russian circus men trying to defect in New York. Keeping up a running commentary of advice and criticism of their naivety, as if it were really happening rather than a film. But he had been moved by the ending and there were tears in his eyes as he turned to Hoggart . . .

"He'll never survive. They'll eat the poor bastard."

"It's only a film, Igor. It's just entertainment—a comedy."

Yakunin looked at Hoggart for long moments, slowly shaking his head. "You understand now why you people worry me?"

"I don't see the connection."

"You people make films like that because you believe life's like that. Everybody kind and helpful and Russians are country idiots who need a helping hand." Yakunin's face was contorted as he shouted. "They're smarter than you people and smarter than the Yanks. They like you to believe they're innocents abroad. They aren't. They never were. Not even in the days of the Tsars." Then he seemed to deflate like a punctured tyre. "I was crazy to think you people knew what you were doing."

Hoggart spoke very quietly. "Do you want to go back to Moscow, comrade?"

"I can't go back. You know that."

"And you know it too. So just relax." He paused. "Did you ever handle a case where somebody had defected to the KGB?"

"No. It wasn't in my area."

"Well let me tell you that the KGB go through the same procedures that we're going through. I've dealt with a number of Soviet defectors and I'm used to the problems they face."

"What problems?"

"They go from a closed and privileged group like the KGB, where they are important and respected. They come over here and suddenly it's different. They're out of their environment. It's a strange country. They are important but not in the same way. They wonder if they did the right thing. And they miss Moscow. They miss silver birch trees and *piroshkis* and the routine of everyday life. Even *Pravda* and the newsreader on the TV news. If, like you, they're used to living in the West they still have doubts. Before, there was always Moscow to go back to. Their roots were still there. But when a man comes over he's pulled up his roots." Hoggart paused to make the point. "It takes a lot of courage to come over and it takes a different kind of courage to go along with one's new circumstances. It takes time, Igor. And it's best not to rush things."

"How old are you, comrade?"

"I'm forty-four next month."

"You sound older than me. But maybe you're right. We'll see."

• • •

There had been the usual protests from the British Embassy about the arrest of Charlton and when, as always, they had no response there were requests for a visit by a member of the embassy. His editor had flown in to Moscow and contacted senior Soviet diplomats but to no avail. The Foreign Minister had sent a personal note to his Soviet opposite number but had received neither a reply nor an acknowledgment. So there was some surprise in the embassy when they were offered a meeting with Charlton.

The First Secretary had gone himself and had taken the precaution of writing half a dozen questions on cards so that the journalist could nod or shake his head in answer if the interview was unsupervised. It was taken for granted that the meetingplace would be bugged and the conversation monitored. It was when he came back from that interview that he had a meeting with the Ambassador in their top security "bubble" in one of the embassy's smaller rooms.

"Where did they take you, Stephen?"

"Out to the new KGB building on the Ring Road."

"What's it like?"

"Modern architecture. And inside it could be IBM. Bright lights, teak furniture, Swedish style. Big mainframe computers. An air of efficiency. Not that I saw very much."

"Did you see him alone?"

"Yes."

"That makes me suspicious for a start." He paused. "How did it go?"

"He's lost a lot of weight and looks about ten years older. I showed him the first two cards and he just shrugged. He gave me a note for his parents that I've handed over to Security before it goes in the bag." He sighed. "I'd say he's at the end of his tether. Or very near. And resigned to his fate."

"What fate?"

"I'd say that he's talked and they've got all the evidence they need to convict him. Despite the possible monitoring I asked him right out if he'd been involved in any kind of espionage activity and he looked at me strangely for several moments and then just shrugged and looked away without answering."

"What sort of strange look?"

"I may be wrong, but my impression was that he was sure we knew that he'd been used by our people and that I was trying to sell him down the river by asking him. So that the monitors might assume that we weren't involved. A pretty naive view but these people are naive anyway. Or they wouldn't get involved in the first place."

"You never know what tale they've been told by our people. Patriotism and the rest of it." He sighed. "Is there anything more we can do, or that London can do?"

"Just keep up the protests as usual."

• • •

There were to be no members of the foreign media allowed in the court but Novosty would hold a press conference after the court hearing each day. When the Novosty man announced that the trial would start in two days' time he had mentioned off the record that trying to get information from a Soviet citizen would not only be a serious offence, but would also be a waste of the media's valuable time, because there would be no public allowed in court. The case was to be tried in closed court. Only officials and witnesses would be allowed in.

• • •

Four TV teams had waited outside the court hoping to get shots of the accused arriving but the police and militia in plain clothes had bundled them roughly back to their vehicles and ordered them to leave. When crew leaders asked why they were banned the police pretended not to understand English.

The Moscow press corps had been surprised at Novosty's efficiency when they called a press conference at 6 P.M. the first evening of the trial. But the statement was brief and uninformative.

The accused were being tried separately, the Britisher first. The trial judge was a woman. Judge Abromova. The accused had admitted to acting as a go-between between the Russian defendant and the British secret service. Sentence would be passed when the main trial was completed.

The Novosty spokesman had asked if there were questions but had refused to describe the judge's dress or career, the words of the actual charges, the statute number under which the accused were charged or any details of the defence lawyers. He said they were irrelevant questions. When asked the name and position of the accused Soviet he hesitated and then said that the man concerned was a senior civil servant who worked in one of the defence departments of the Ministry. When that unleashed a torrent of further questions he shook his head and left the podium.

There was no press conference called on the second day but on the third day a conference was called for 4 P.M.

Both accused had been found guilty of espionage on behalf of a foreign power. The British journalist had been given a sentence of seven years' forced labour, and it was pointed out that the law would have allowed a sentence of up to twenty-five years. The Soviet accused had been given a life sentence.

The spokesman had surprised the media people by giving the name of the Soviet prisoner in answer to a question from the Press Association reporter. The Russian's name was Denikin. And no further information would be forthcoming.

In the following day's papers in most European countries the name Denikin had been linked to the KGB and the linkage was attributed to "usually reliable sources." Two days later it was widely reported that there were strong rumours in Moscow that in fact Denikin had been executed during the night after the trial was over.

The embassy sent copies of the relevant Soviet media reports of the trial to London. All SIS records of Operation Needle were put on two microfiches and the originals destroyed. Discreet hints from Soviet contacts over the following weeks suggested that Denikin's wife and child had vacated their apartment and that their Moscow residence permits had been withdrawn. They had not actually been seen by neighbours or acquaintances since the day that Denikin had been charged and jailed.

CHAPTER EIGHT

*E*ddie Hoggart had found her a room in Paddington and had driven her there when she was discharged from the hospital. And he'd taken her that evening for a meal at Bertorelli's in Queensway.

Her room was a fair size. Clean and reasonably furnished, with a telephone and security locks that he had fitted himself. When he showed her how the locks worked he'd asked her if she was still scared.

She shrugged her shoulders. "A bit."

"Why?"

"Like I told you, they think you're an undercover cop from the Drugs Squad."

"If anyone says that to you ask them to check me out at West Central nick."

"They wouldn't believe what the cops said."

"The drug pushers know people they can check with. Anyway, that's what you should say. Did you know the man who beat you up?"

"No. But I know who paid him to do it. The bastard gave him a message to give me."

"Who was it paid him?"

"A man named Sid. Sidney Cash."

"Where's he hang out?"

"He's got a pad off the Euston Road and he supplies drugs to pushers in Soho—and he's got two minders."

"Good for him." He paused. "How are you off for cash?"

"I've got enough to get by on."

"How long for?"

"Six weeks. Eight if I'm careful." He was a nice guy but he didn't need to know everything.

"There's some booze in the kitchen cupboard. How about you pour us both a drink?"

She laughed. "OK. What you want—whisky isn't it?"

"That'll do fine, honey."

When he was leaving she stood by the door with him. She looked up at his face.

"Can I ask you something personal?"

"Yes. But I might not answer it. What is it?"

"Are you a queer?"

She knew by his laugh the answer. "What makes you think I might be?"

"You've taken me places, given me meals. You bothered about me in hospital. You found me this place. But you've never made a pass at me. I don't understand."

"What don't you understand?"

"Why you bother with me if you don't want to go to bed with me?"

For a few moments he stood without speaking and then he said softly, "Sit down and we'll talk about it."

She sat beside him on the small couch, watching as he poured himself another drink. Then he turned to look at her.

"D'you remember the barman in the Monte Cristo—James or Jake—whatever his name is?"

"Yes. Of course I remember him," she said softly.

"He talked to me one evening about you." He paused and looked intently at her face and then looked away. "Seemed to know a lot about you."

"Like what?" And her voice was almost a whisper.

"Told me about your old man and what he did to you. And how things turned out for you."

"When did he tell you this?"

"Before I met you actually. Maybe a couple of days before. It was just gossip. But I recognised you from the description when I saw you."

"And what was the description—long legs and big tits?"

"Doesn't matter what the description was. It was the background that mattered."

"Oh yes. Screwed by her dear old dad who pimped for her on the side. Great."

He smiled at her. "Why don't you just calm down and shut up. And let me finish."

"I don't want to hear about my background, understand?"

"I just wanted to say that I didn't make a pass at you because I thought that somebody who was friendly without wanting to sleep with you might make a change."

"And you're the Fairy Prince. Is that it?"

"No," he said quietly. "But I had a background like yours and the only person I've ever cared about was kind to me without wanting anything in return. All the others treated me like shit. Like people treated you. I didn't want to join the others. That's all."

"You're a strange man, Eddie."

"Why?"

"I don't know anything about you. And I never believe anything that men tell me. But I believe you. What you just said."

Hoggart smiled and stood up. "I'll pop in to see you some time tomorrow. Between seven and eight."

She shook her head as she looked up at him, and said softly, "Don't go. Stay with me tonight. Please. I want you to."

For a moment he hesitated. "Are you sure?"
She nodded. "Yes. I'm quite sure."

• • •

Although Hoggart kept on his own two rooms in Fulham they moved into a good-sized flat together in Pimlico a month later.

It wouldn't be true to say that Eddie Hoggart had no illusions about the girl. But he knew what it was like to have to fend for yourself in a very tough world, and he knew enough about the world to know roughly how she had earned a living. But he didn't let his mind dwell on it.

A week after they had moved in together she had read a piece in the Evening Standard *that made her realise that whatever Eddie Hoggart's job was he knew how to get things done. The piece was about the arrest of a man named Sidney Arthur Cash. He'd been badly beaten up and when he arrived at the casualty department at Charing Cross Hospital the houseman in charge had found one-hundred grams of heroin taped to his stomach and had reported his find to the police. When he came to in a hospital bed he was charged with possession and intent to supply and a police guard was mounted on his room. Some instinct made her not show the piece to Eddie Hoggart and he never mentioned it to her. But she was sure that it was Eddie who had made it happen. And she knew then that he must be either a cop of some sort or a very influential criminal like Harry Gardner. A man who controlled other people without being personally involved in the things they did.*

As the months went by several people had noticed that Eddie Hoggart seemed unusually relaxed. Almost happy. And Hoggart himself was aware that the girl looked even younger. Away from her old life she seemed to thrive, and the old cynicism about people had changed to a self-assurance. Enough self-assurance to comment on his masculine habits and joke about his sudden absences. And to care enough to be on edge when he was late back home.

He had never said that she shouldn't get a job but as he left every aspect of looking after the flat to her, she assumed that he was happy for her to stay at home. He was generous with money and not fussy about her rather primitive housekeeping skills. His long years of living on his own showed in a few masculine habits that he still held to. He still washed his own underwear and was given to using her toothbrush and annoyed if she buttoned up his shirts after ironing them. When they made love, which was quite often, it was energetic and traditional. None of the fancy stuff required of her in the past.

Without either of them realising it or intending it they were leaving behind two lives that had no family background or support, and creating a new unit of their own. Because of their experiences it was a rather tentative creation. Wariness, natural distrust of all others, and an inclination to cynicism were their own frontiers, but both of them crossed the frontier cautiously from time to time and seemed to suffer no ill.

For Eddie Hoggart, having someone to protect acted as a kind of catalyst to the aggressive nature of his work. And for the girl, she was aware that for the first time in her life she was giving her care and affection instead of her body in exchange for security.

The following Christmas they were married at Chelsea Registrar's Office. The taxi-driver and an obliging passer-by were their witnesses. They spent the four days of the Christmas holidays at the Savoy.

* * *

There were congratulations from Fletcher and Renshaw and a few others at HQ and the marriage was recorded so that he could claim the marriage allowances and the extra insurance cover.

He guessed that there would be some sort of check on the girl but it wouldn't be a positive-vetting job. If a check had been done, nobody ever mentioned it to him.

CHAPTER NINE

Brigadier (Retd.) Sir Arthur Renshaw was a large burly man, straight-backed despite his age, balding with a bushy but trimmed moustache and alert blue eyes. He was wearing an olive green suit in a heavy Harris tweed and a pair of heavily welted brown boots. The last wisps of his hair lifted in the light summer breeze. He stood with his large head to one side as he listened to his son. When Tony had finished speaking his father looked down at his well-polished boots before he spoke.

"I don't understand you, Tony. I really don't." He paused and looked at his son. "It's your money." He shrugged. "OK. It's in a trust but that doesn't stop you from taking an interest in how it's doing. Poor Hawkins worries himself sick trying to make a few extra bucks for you."

"Well tell him not to father. I don't need any more money. I've already got all I need. More than I need, in fact. It doesn't interest me."

"Your grandfather would turn in his grave if he heard you say that." He sighed. "At least Charlie looks after his money."

"Charlie needs the money; he's got a wife and two kids, and a life-style to live up to."

Sir Arthur hunched his shoulders philosophically. "When are you going to get yourself a wife, boy?"

"I'm not interested in getting married. I like my independence."

"You've had some very nice girlfriends. Good backgrounds and good-looking and any one of them would jump at the chance of marrying you."

"I doubt it, pa. I like them all. But I don't want them hanging around every hour of my life."

Sir Arthur smiled. "You could be right, son. But your mother would like to see you settled down."

Tony laughed softly, "Is that why she's invited the Mercers over for dinner tonight? A nice moonlight walk with the sweet Mary?"

"I hadn't thought of that but you might well be right. How's the job going? Still knocking those bloody Reds for six?"

Tony smiled. "We bowl 'em the odd bumper every now and again."

"What do you make of this Gorbachev fellow? Think he'll last?"

"Who knows. If Maggie can last, he can. But battering down an old-established bureaucracy isn't all that easy."

"Do you want to join the shoot tomorrow?"

"No thanks. I'm going back to town."

"You lost interest in shooting?"

"Never had an interest, pa. I find it revolting, to put it mildly."

Sir Arthur laughed. "Mother used to say that. I thought she was just having a dig at me. Ah well . . ." he said, "takes all sorts. We'd better go and freshen up a bit for dinner."

• • •

There was a fallen tree near the edge of the lake and Tony Renshaw folded his jacket and laid it across the trunk before she sat down. Mary Mercer was twenty-two and very pretty. She had just heard that day that she'd graduated and her father was giving her a Mini. Metallic silver with stripes on it.

"Why are you looking at me like that, Tony?"

"The usual reason."

"Tell me."

"Because you're young and happy and very pretty. And you look like a Pre-Raphaelite painting."

"I thought Pre-Raphaelite girls were always lying dead in lakes."

"Only one," he paused. "What are you going to do now you've graduated?"

"I don't know—what would you suggest?"

"What did you read?"

"Economics."

"Well. If I were young and beautiful and I'd read economics, I'd want to compare all the theories with practice. So I'd go to the United States and Tokyo and see how capitalism works. Then maybe the Soviet Union and Cuba and check on how socialism works."

"Not get married and have children?"

"I've always felt that children are very unrewarding. Five or six years of pleasure and then they hate you, not because you do anything wrong but because in our society you're not a swinger unless you hate your parents. And as for marriage, well, we all know how that ends up these days. Marriage even starts off with a lie."

"Tell me."

"You promise to love someone for the rest of your life. That's crazy. It's not only crazy but it's patently impossible. I like

Swinburne's poetry, and Jerome Kern's melodies, and playing the piano, but I wouldn't promise to even like them, let alone love them, for the rest of my life. I used to like Frank Sinatra but I think he's a grinding bore now. I used to like Hemingway but now I think he's just a sweaty macho man who liked killing things."

"But like is different from love."

"If you don't like someone you aren't going to love 'em for long, sweetie."

"What about your mother and father and mine. They love one another."

"I wouldn't dream of commenting on your parents but my parents, well, they're like rocks that have been grinding against each other for a million years. They're worn smooth by sacrificing their original shapes. My mother hates many things that my father admires, but he's a good provider. My father suffers from fixed ideas of class and value and realises that my mother holds clashing views but has organised a good home for him and his children." He laughed. "They're a prime example of the vices and virtues of a hung parliament that everyone talks about these days."

"Don't you love them?"

"I admire how they've stuck together all these years."

"But you don't love them?"

"No. I don't even *like* my father."

"Why not?"

"He's a snob. He's a bully. And he's selfish. He's also quite fearless and physically brave. But that's because he lacks imagination."

"How long have you thought like this?"

He sighed. "Since I was about nineteen or twenty."

"Have you ever loved anybody?"

"I nearly did once."

"Didn't it work out?"

"Something diverted me away from it."

"Do you make love to girls?"

"You mean have sex with them?"

"Yes."

"Yes. I rather like that." He smiled and she smiled back at him.

"Do you want to have sex with me?"

"I rather hoped you'd let me."

"Is that why you brought me down here?"

"I'm afraid it is."

"Where shall we go?"

"There's a summer-house at the end of the lake. We could go there."

• • •

Hoggart stood on the slope of the hill and looked across the valley towards the ruins of Bayham Abbey and then turned to Yakunin.

"Let's sit in the sun for a bit." And he pointed at a spot between the rows of vines.

"Did you know a guy named Denikin?"

"I knew a poet named Denikin. He wasn't much good."

"I meant a KGB man with that name."

Yakunin frowned as he thought. "What directorate was he in?"

"I don't know."

"So why are you interested in him?"

"He's just been given a life sentence in the Soviet Union for espionage."

"Who was he spying for? Or was he framed?"

"I don't know. Not us anyway. Why would they frame him?"

Yakunin grinned. "Maybe somebody fancied his job. Or his girlfriend."

"Were you controlled from Dzerdzhinsky Square or from the new building on the Ring Road?"

"Neither. I was controlled from a special set-up in one of the Kremlin buildings."

"How often did you communicate with them?"

"After the first year when I was setting up the operation there was only one-way communication. Moscow to me."

"How?"

"Coded messages in the English section of Moscow's overseas service. They played Russian folk songs and the words in Russian were changed slightly. You'd have had to be a folk-song researcher to notice the changes."

"Why so little communication?"

"I was getting them far more than they ever dreamed of getting. They were happy to let me do it my way." The Russian smiled. "Like the Yanks say—I was cutting the mustard, and they didn't want to rock the boat."

"How often did you go back to Moscow?"

"Once a year for about three weeks at a time. Sometimes it was Vienna, not Moscow."

"What route did you take?"

"Sometimes via Canada, sometimes Mexico, and once through Tokyo."

"Who did you report to in Moscow?"

"Marshak. He's a lieutenant-colonel. One of the old school." Yakunin smiled. "He was very pleased with the results I was getting, but he didn't like me." He paused. "Not so much that he didn't like me. He didn't like my methods. Said I wasn't sticking to procedures." He laughed. "And of course I wasn't. The procedures had been laid down by people who'd never been in the field. People like Marshak himself. I got warnings but they left me alone." Yakunin shrugged. "His real name was Ulianov but the controllers all had working names. I found out his real name by accident. A bit of bad security on *his* part."

"Who was in charge of your radio staff?"

"Radchenko and later a guy I never met called Guchkov."

"Did you have any contact with the people who ran agents in England?" Hoggart said it casually but Yakunin turned quickly to look at Hoggart's face. For a moment he was silent and then he said quietly, "The same old routine. The one question that really matters, hiding amongst the chit-chat so that it won't be noticed. Yes?"

Hoggart smiled. "Yes. So what's the answer?"

Yakunin sighed and looked away as he started speaking.

"They consulted me sometimes when I was in Moscow. Told me about some problems and asked for my views."

"What kind of problems?"

"The problems of too much success. Like they had with me. Was it all too good to be true? All the checks and counter-checks said that it was genuine. But if the other side were playing games that's how they'd play it anyway. A little bit of disinformation wrapped up in a mass of middle-grade genuine information. A pearl in the dross from time to time. But always that worry on the receiving end. Was he our man or had he been turned again? The triple agent. And there's a problem if the man is right in the heart of the system."

"What particular problem?"

"If he's really at the top, the most important stuff you get won't be documents or facts but opinion. His opinion. But that's the part that really matters. What matters is his interpretation of decisions in a Cabinet meeting. His view of the Prime Minister's inner thoughts on a meeting with Gorbachev. The inner Cabinet's views on disarmament. Will public pressure make them sign a deal that gives us a secret advantage? Who in the opposition or the peace movements can most influence the media and public opinion? He could be genuinely mistaken in his assessment. Or he could be passing on what his controllers feed him."

"Did you have a solution?"

"I asked them to describe the man. His background. His life.

His work. Why was he helping us? Or why did he say he was helping us?"

"And?"

"They did all that." He shrugged. "He seemed OK to me. But they still weren't completely happy. Always the doubt. Always the worm in the mind. In the end I said the only way was to let me meet the person. Talk with him about everyday things. Just chat. And in the end I could be ninety-nine per cent certain. But they refused. Said nobody apart from his controller had ever met him. And that was how it was going to be."

"Tell me how they described him."

Yakunin grinned. "You're crazy if you think I'm going to tell you that until I'm satisfied about you and your people. Like I said, I don't want to end up face-down in the Thames. Whether it's the KGB who do it or your people, that's not how I plan for it to end."

"What can I do to convince you that we're playing it straight?"

"I don't know. But I'll know when it's right."

"Is it one of my people? An SIS man?"

"Forget it, Eddie. No more of this now."

As Hoggart drove up to London that evening he went over what Yakunin had told him. He had noticed that for the first time the Russian had called him by his first name. He was beginning to think that it wouldn't be too long before the Russian trusted him enough to tell him what he knew. Right now he would report to Renshaw, go home and clean up and take Jacqui out for a meal.

The wine shop was closed and Hoggart walked to the Monte Cristo. It was a long time since he had been there but nothing seemed to have changed. He stood at the bar and looked around. The barman was talking to a man sitting at a table in the alcove by the stairs. He saw the barman look towards him and then turn to say something to the man who looked across at him. He heard the barman laugh but the big man just went on looking.

When the barman walked across to the bar he was smiling. "Long time no see, skipper."

"I want a bottle of red wine. A claret. Something like that."

"I've got a nice Mouton Cadet. Four quid to members."

"OK. That'll do."

As Hoggart reached for his wallet the big man got up from the table and walked over to him, hands in pockets, and Hoggart noticed the well-cut suit. The man held out his big hand as he said, "Pleased to meet you. My name's Gardner."

"Glad to meet you."

"What'll you have?"

Hoggart smiled. "I can't stop, I just came in for a bottle of wine. Maybe some other time."

Gardner nodded amiably. "Jake tells me you married young Jacqui. How is she these days? Used to see her in here in the old days."

"She's fine."

And Hoggart reached for the bottle of wine and handed over the cash.

"Always thought she could make something of herself, that little girl, if somebody took her in hand." Gardner smiled. "Always felt she was a kind of Marilyn Monroe character. Needed a father figure."

For a moment Hoggart stared back at Gardner and then turned to the barman and said "Goodnight," nodding briefly to Gardner as he walked to the stairs that led up to the street.

He didn't mention the club or Gardner to Jacqui. He wasn't sure why. Something about the incident made him uneasy. The professional little red lights were blinking and distant warning bells were ringing. Like most SIS officers Hoggart had had to learn not to let his working attitude of constant suspicion and disbelief take over in his private life. They gave advice on it on early training courses. Despite the warnings and precautions, broken marriages and relationships were the norm. Sometimes a man resigned to save a marriage or a love affair but even that renunciation didn't always have its due reward. Men who went out one morning and didn't come home for a couple of weeks and offered no explanation of why they had been away didn't make ideal husbands and fathers. Not even good lovers. Merchant seamen at least came home with tales to tell and could be waved off and met in Southampton or Liverpool. And there were pals and the wives of pals who suffered the same partings and moaned at the owners' rules and regulations. But there was no such common cause for SIS men and it wasn't easy to bend a mind to the problems of a mortgage or a non-functioning dish-washer when you had flown back from identifying a bloated body in a West Berlin morgue. When enough personal relationships had failed, most men became loners. At least they were seen by others as loners, but most of them were loners from circumstances rather than choice. But Hoggart had been a real loner for too long to let vague feelings of unease disturb him too much.

• • •

Hoggart stood at the window. There had been one of those short, sharp summer thunderstorms and, as the sun broke through, rain dripped from the leaves of the beech trees and the gutter around the eaves of the roof. Yakunin was in a good mood. Relaxed and talkative. But Hoggart didn't want to risk sending him back to his cantankerous mood of non-cooperation. He turned and looked at the Russian. He was tuning from station to station on the small FM-only radio he had got for him. He especially liked listening to the police frequencies.

Hoggart walked back and sat opposite Yakunin at the small table. He took a deep breath before he plunged in.

"What's the relationship like between Gorbachev and the KGB?"

Yakunin switched off the radio, looked towards the window and then back at Hoggart.

"You know he's planning to re-organise them?"

"We've heard rumours but we thought it was just gossip."

"No. He's put a special committee working on it. He thinks the KGB is too big and uncontrollable. And he's right, of course."

"What does he want to do with them?"

"Separate all the functions. An organisation for internal security. Another for positive espionage. A legal section and a separate organisation for industrial and high-tech espionage."

"Will the KGB let him do that?"

"He gets on well with Chebrikov and the guy who heads the reform group in Mikyanov. He was a fellow law student of Gorbachev at Moscow University. There have been a few trials of strength already. Gorbachev has come out on top every time so far."

"Tell me more."

"Gorbachev threw out all the top brass in the Ukraine. KGB and party officials. They'd arrested a journalist who was going to expose the local corruption and abuses of power. The locals raised hell in the Politburo and lost. A few weeks later Gorbachev ordered the release of Sakharov and they started playing the bureaucratic game to hold on to him. Gorbachev ordered Chebrikov to go down to Gorki himself and get him out.

"A few weeks later there was the international peace forum in Moscow, and all over the world people saw the KGB men roughing up elderly demonstrators and foreign TV people themselves. That was done by the KGB hard-liners to embarrass Gorbachev. The KGB colonel who gave the order ended up in the Gulag himself. He's a tough cookie is Gorbachev. And the KGB is changing internally."

"In what way?"

"The new boys are much more sophisticated and well-educated. The thugs are still around but they don't control things any longer."

"Do people inside the KGB discuss these things openly?"

Yakunin grinned. "You're kidding. I only heard things because I was seldom in Moscow. They knew I was important but they didn't know where I operated or what I did. And I wasn't part of the Moscow set-up." He smiled. "I was safe. I just watched and listened—and it's not just the words—it's the silences that tell you what's going on."

Hoggart nodded. "Changing the subject, Igor, d'you want a girl?"

Yakunin smiled and shook his head. "Maybe some other time. Let's see how we go."

"Is there anything I can do to make you feel more secure?"

"Your people getting impatient?"

"No."

"Are you worried about something, Eddie?"

"No. Why?"

"I've noticed that when you're angry or annoyed with me there's a vein comes up alongside your left eye. It's there now."

"No. I'm OK." He paused. "You talked way back about a mole in SIS. Are you ready to talk about it?"

Yakunin smiled. "You think I'm conning you, don't you?"

"I thought at first you might be. I don't think you are now that I know you better." He paused. "That doesn't mean I think you're right. You could genuinely think you know, and still be wrong—or mistaken."

"I'm not mistaken, Eddie. What I know is hard fact, not gossip. I know the KGB guy who runs him." Yakunin paused. "I don't know his name or even his precise job but I know he's top top brass. He's the KGB's biggest success in this country."

Hoggart smiled. "When do I get it?"

Yakunin took a deep breath. "I'll know when it's the right time, Eddie. I don't know how but I'll know all right. OK?"

"OK. Let's go and get some fresh air."

• • •

Hoggart swore again as he typed one-fingered at the Olivetti portable, and Fletcher looked up smiling.

"I'll trade you a coffee and a Danish pastry for typing whatever that is."

Hoggart ripped the sheet out of the typewriter. "Done, my friend. I'll be back in ten minutes."

It was fifteen minutes later when Fletcher checked the type-written sheet against Hoggart's scrawl.

To: AR
From: EMH

Subject 1098 at location K19 has become more cooperative in the last two weeks. Considerable and useful information on the following has been established. (See separate individual reports.)

1. Personnel and locations of Department S cypher section, including relationship between Petrovsky and Head of Section.

2. Control and reporting system from KGB operations at UN to illegals in Canada.

3. Deception methods used against FBI and CIA during Walker operations. Analysis of operations and value to Red Navy.

4. Locations of two KGB safe-houses in Washington.

5. Names and status of four US nationals providing high-tech information to Soviet Union. (Locations LA and San Francisco areas.)

6. Location of transceiver used by subject in USA.

As reported previously subject makes frequent reference to identity of a senior member of SIS cooperating with KGB. This claim is frequently made by defecting subjects and has never led to any information of substance and has been assessed as a device for enhancing subject's importance and standing. However with improved subject relationship this claim is being hinted at more often. It seems possible that whatever subject knows will be forthcoming in the next few weeks.

When Hoggart came back with a tray and the coffees and pastries, Fletcher pointed at the sheet.

"Your handwriting is terrible, Eddie. You'd better check that I've transcribed it correctly."

Hoggart smiled and leaned over his desk to read the typed sheet.

"That's fine. Thanks."

"Is that for Renshaw?"

"Yes. I don't think he reads 'em but if I don't send in a report now and again he gets touchy."

"Sounds a strange set-up you've got down there."

"Yeah. He's a funny bastard. Cranky and bloody-minded. Full of his own importance. But I guess he's lonely."

"By the way, I've got four tickets to *Cats* for Saturday night. How about you and your old lady join me and Rachel?"

For a moment Hoggart hesitated. His normal instinct was to say no but something made him think again. He smiled and nodded.

"That would be nice. She'd enjoy that. I'll take us out to dinner afterwards."

"You don't have to, Eddie."

"I'd like to."

"Meet at the box office at seven, OK?"

"Great."

• • •

As Rachel and David Fletcher undressed he said, "What did you think of Eddie?"

"He looks more relaxed than he used to. She seems to have

done him a lot of good. Mind you he's still a bit too macho for me."

Fletcher laughed. "In what way?"

She shrugged. "It's hard to define. He looks like a spring or something—ready to uncoil. I'd guess that he's got a very short fuse and that he could be violent if he was crossed."

"All that from a nice quiet dinner in a Soho restaurant."

She smiled. "Maybe I'm exaggerating. Did you notice him when we left the restaurant and were looking for a taxi? He behaved like he expected one to appear especially for him. Like a gangster on his own territory."

"He had a pretty rough life as a kid. It probably comes from that."

"Rough in what way?"

"Taken into care. Brought up in an orphanage. That's what I heard on the grapevine."

"What do you think of Jacqui?"

"She's a doll. Every man in the place was giving her the once-over, but all she cared about was Eddie."

"She's very young for him."

"So what? She couldn't take her eyes off him. She obviously loves him. And that's what matters to a guy like Eddie."

"I suppose you're right."

"What's that mean?"

She laughed. "Nothing. But I hope he's good in bed."

Fletcher stared at her. "Why on earth do you say that?"

"You were right about all the men looking at her. But you're wrong if you think she wasn't aware of it. She was. Believe me. That little gal knows a lot more about men than your macho friend knows about women."

"You amaze me. How do you make that out?"

"Because I'm a female, honey. Do you want a drink before we go to bed?"

"I wouldn't mind a cuppa."

"OK. I'll have one too."

Fletcher lay on the bed, looking up at the ceiling. Thinking about what she'd said. Not about Hoggart and his Jacqui. But about her, Rachel. He wondered if he too knew enough about women.

CHAPTER TEN

Lensky had decoded the message from London himself. A despatch rider had brought it out to the dacha. They had already made careful plans for the eventuality once they knew for certain that Yakunin had defected to the British. But he had hoped that they wouldn't have to put the plan into action.

He walked down to the lake alone and sat on the fallen tree where he had sat with Ulianov. But then it had been Ulianov's problem not his. And even a few days ago it looked as if the plan wouldn't even be needed. But the message from London made it essential. Even now they had only a hazy idea of how much Yakunin knew. Maybe he was bluffing. Grinding the last concession out of his new friends. But they couldn't take the risk.

He would have to lie even to Halenka for his own security but he hated having to do it. They had estimated that it could take between two and six months, including the month in Paris before he went over. They had agreed a potential success rating of no more than 45 per cent despite his experience. And whichever way it had to go, it meant that London would revert to low-level material from now on. His star was waning already and when the plan was completed his value would be no more than middle-grade. If he did everything to plan they'd almost certainly let him keep his rank, but his duties would be routine and his status never exactly defined. He didn't dwell on what his fate would be if he failed. It wouldn't be Moscow deciding his fate if he failed.

He walked back slowly to the dacha and phoned Moscow. They called a meeting and two days later he had flown to Paris via Warsaw and Amsterdam with a diplomatic passport and a carefully constructed identity and background.

• • •

For a week Lensky had absorbed the names and functions of every member of the Paris Embassy and at the directorate of illegals in the big house in Passy. He was aware that because nobody knew why he was in Paris his presence was suspect, and resented by everyone from His Excellency to the chauffeurs who took him on strange unexplained tours of the city.

He checked the houses of all the senior officials and listened attentively to the gossip. He cultivated one particular driver and one of the telephone operators. From them he learned the secrets of the social lives of senior staff, including the ambassador.

In the second week he sat in as a silent observer at all operational meetings of the KGB staff in Passy. And in the evenings he visited the four main safe-houses in Paris. By the end of that week he had worked his charm on a pretty girl in illegals personnel. She had a room near the Gare St. Lazare where they spent most evenings together. As always with Lensky the love-making was only a small part of the relationship. He took her out for meals and to the cinema and they sat talking in small cafés in the squares of Les Batignolles. He was obviously amused at what she told him of the personal lives of KGB officers enjoying the freedom of the Paris operations. And when he made his final report to Moscow before leaving Paris he felt a twinge of conscience when he recommended that the girl should be withdrawn and classified as a security risk.

As if he were sitting an examination he spent the third week rereading his notes and memorising names and faces and in the fourth week he relaxed. He didn't want to overload his memory. That could cause confusion. And he needed to distance himself from the embassy and KGB people. He was going to defect and he must think like a defector. And behave like a defector. Two days before he was due to leave, Moscow bureau put on the pre-arranged scenario where he was called to the house in Passy and the director passed on a severe reprimand from Dzerdzhinski Square. He was to report back to Moscow immediately. After the meeting he made known to his girlfriend in personnel his anger and resentment of his treatment by Moscow.

• • •

It was a French passport and the name inside was Delarge, Jacques Delarge, and the immigration officer looked at it briefly and handed it back. He didn't compare the photograph with the face, but if he had there would have been no problem. It was a genuine passport except for its contents. A small favour to the Paris Embassy from an old friend in the passport office.

He picked up his only case and went through the green Customs exit and across the concourse to where the sign said "Trains." He was at Victoria Station an hour later and he took a taxi to the Reubens Hotel. Two days later he walked into West Central Police Station in Savile Row. A sergeant in blue shirt and pullover came over, smiling.

"Can I help you, sir?"

"Yes—I'd like to speak to your Special Branch officer."

The smile faded slowly and the eyes were suddenly professional policeman's eyes.

"What was it you wanted to discuss, sir?"

"I'd prefer to discuss it with the Special Branch man. It's Mr. Fowler isn't it?"

"Just a moment, sir."

The sergeant waved another policeman over to take charge of the counter and disappeared into a back office. The new man was younger and friendlier.

"You think Elton's going to sell them after all?"

"I'm sorry, I don't understand."

The young man laughed. "You're not a football fan. I meant Elton John selling Watford."

"I see. I'm sure he'll do whatever he thinks is right."

The phone rang and the constable answered it, listening intently and then replacing the receiver.

"Have you got any ID, sir? Driving licence—anything like that?"

"Would my passport do?"

"That would be fine."

He studied the passport carefully, checking each page and sometimes turning back for a second look. When he handed back the passport he leaned forward and pressed three buttons on the security lock control.

"Come on through, sir. Just push the door."

• • •

Fowler had never had to deal with a defector before and he stuck carefully to the drill and when the man with the French passport announced that in fact he was a Soviet and a major in the KGB he noted down the details impassively.

"What's your real name?"

"Belinsky. Sergei Belinsky. First Directorate, Department S."

"Where were you based?"

"In Paris."

"So why have you come here?"

The Russian smiled. "I speak better English than French and I was previously concerned with operations in the United States."

"Which part of the States?"

"New York."

"United Nations or illegals?"

"Illegals. No contact with our UN people."

"I'll need to check your bag and an officer will search you. Are you agreeable to that?"

Belinsky shrugged. "Whatever you want."

While the physical search was being carried out, Fowler phoned New Scotland Yard for further instructions and was told that the putative defector would be taken over by an officer from SIS.

Fowler found it strange that MI5 was handing over the Russian to its rival intelligence organisation. But the brass in Gower Street who dealt with these things were old hands and maybe the Russian was part of some inter-service deal.

•   •   •

It was 2 A.M. when Fletcher got the phone-call and he dressed quickly and left a note for when Rachel woke. An office car and driver drew up as he got down to the street and he shaved with a battery shaver as they drove to the West End.

He had signed for the Russian and taken him to the flat in the Sloane Street block. He'd given the Russian the option of a few hours' sleep before the interrogation started, but the Russian had shrugged and said he was happy to get the formalities over.

Belinsky was nothing like the usual defector. He seemed ready to talk about anything. Friendly and self-confident and what was more important he was obviously very well informed about the inner-workings of Dzerdzhinsky Square.

Tony Renshaw arranged for Fletcher to use a safe-house just

outside Southampton for de-briefing Belinsky. It was the first time that SIS had had to deal with two defectors at the same time. And both with all the extra evaluation problems that came with unknown "walk-ins."

The house was on a new estate of comparatively expensive four-bedroomed houses with double garage and mock-Tudor exterior. A full-time chauffeur-handyman lived in the two rooms over the garage. He was a man in his forties, tanned and well-built. An ex-SAS warrant-officer whose actual responsibility was the security of the premises and the occupants.

The Russian seemed very relaxed with a cynical amusement at his ex-colleagues in Department S. Archives checked on the names and details that he gave and where records were available they confirmed Belinsky's information. Renshaw had interviewed the Russian a couple of times himself and seemed satisfied that he was at least genuine.

After the second of the two interviews Belinsky had asked Fletcher who Renshaw was.

Fletcher smiled and shook his head. "I can't give you names of other officers at this stage, Sergei. You know the drill as well as I do."

"He speaks excellent Russian, anyway. Is he your boss?"

"Don't ask questions. That's my privilege. Maybe later on you'll be meeting other people."

"Are you married?"

"Why do you ask?"

Belinsky smiled. "You look like a married man."

"What do married men look like?"

"Solid citizens. Contented men."

"No, I'm not married, Sergei. Are you?"

"No. Unfortunately not."

"It's not fair in our kind of business, is it?"

Belinsky sighed and shrugged, but didn't reply.

• • •

As Hoggart came up the last few stairs and turned onto the landing he saw the man come out of the flat, standing at the door, smiling as he spoke to her. He saw the surprise in Jacqui's eyes as he walked up to them. The man had seen it too and he turned quickly towards Hoggart. It was the man from the club, Gardner.

"Hello, Mr. Hoggart," he said, amiably. "Nice to see you again." He smiled. "Just came to pay off an old debt. Never thought of it when I saw you at the club." He turned to Jacqui. "Sorry it's taken so long, my dear, but I lost track of you." Turning back to Hoggart, Gardner said. "She's got a great nose for a horse has this little girl." He grinned. "Thirty to one ain't bad." He paused. "Well, see you both around I hope." And he turned and made his way back down the stairs, whistling quietly through his teeth as he went. And the overt and exaggerated display of relaxation wasn't lost on Hoggart.

As he walked inside the flat she said, "He told me he'd met you at the club. Why didn't you tell me?"

Hoggart shrugged. "Didn't seem important." He looked at her. "Was it?"

"I suppose not."

"How did he find your address?"

"I've no idea. I thought maybe you'd told him."

"How long's he been here?"

"Five or ten minutes—he was in a hurry to go."

"What's he do for a living?"

"I've no idea. He's some kind of businessman. He's in the club a lot. Or used to be."

"I'll go and shave and we'll eat out."

"Don't I get a kiss?"

He kissed her on the cheek and she knew then that he hadn't believed her. Hoggart had noticed the two cigar butts in the ash-tray and also noticed that they had been removed by the time he came back to the sitting room.

While they ate dinner she had tried to establish some rapport between them but he had turned every attempt at personal chat to generalities. She was used to charming men out of their anger and black moods, but nothing like that ever worked with Hoggart. He was polite, but it was the politeness of a stranger not their usual kidding and chatting, no winks or grins and no affection. And they didn't make love that night.

• • •

The next day Hoggart stayed in London, phoning a man he knew in the Drug Squad who gave him an introduction to a colleague in Criminal Records. He sat in an office on the fifth floor at Scotland Yard and read through Gardner's file. He had no convictions but was a known instigator of big robberies. A planner not a participant. He laundered Mafia money through two gambling clubs that he owned that were mainly patronised by Arabs, and he had active connections in Chicago, New York, Amsterdam, and Marseilles. There was a list of overseas robberies that not only bore his hallmark but where some suspected participants were part of his London-based entourage.

He was married with two children with a large house standing in ten acres in Kent. There was a long list of known associates in alphabetical order and brief references to their roles, and further references to their personal files. The name Jacqueline Lovegrove had leapt out of the page but he had forced himself to read through the whole list. The bracketed reference beside her name merely said "Call-girl."

He stood up and walked to the window and looked out towards Westminster Cathedral and shivered as he watched the traffic turning into Parliament Square. Hundreds of times he had looked at confidential files that gave intimate details of peoples' lives, and read facts that the subjects thought were their private secrets without him being interested beyond whether the information served his purpose. Their lusts and weaknesses, their hypocrisies and deceptions, were a matter of indifference to him if they were not useful to whatever he was pursuing. So why the hesitation about checking Jacqui's file? And even that was an evasion. He wasn't hesitating, he was scared. Scared to learn the truth, scared for it all to come to a grinding halt. He swung round and walked back to the small table, checked the file reference number, and phoned down to Central Achives.

Ten minutes later a pretty constable brought in the file and he signed for it and handed back Gardner's file. When she had left he sat for several minutes before he finally opened it.

There were twenty-one pages. Records of regular court appearances for soliciting. A caution, a month's probation, and several twenty-five pound fines. There were reports of her living with three different men. Two of them convicted criminals. One of them a fence and the other had served four sentences for grievous bodily harm. The third man was Gardner, who had no convictions. He had not even been charged with anything. But there was a list of over twenty major robberies that he was suspected of initiating and planning. There was a list of bank accounts in five different tax-havens and an estimate of his assets as between two and three million pounds. But nothing that was not already on Gardner's own file. There was no suggestion that Jacqui Lovegrove was anything more than his mistress.

The rest of the pages were carbon-copies of the Probation Office interviews and the subsequent reports. When he had first heard about her from the barman at the Monte Cristo he had been hearing about somebody he had never even seen. And when eventually he had met her there was just a vague memory in his mind of a sad, and haunting, background. But what he now read was in the cold official jargon that he was used to in his work. But he wasn't reading about a suspect. He was reading about his wife. Cold, hard facts with explanation but no sympathy. Too involved and too set in her tatty life-style to be helped by authority. Not an uncommon story in the miserable, degrading back streets of London's slums. They would have seen it all before. Probably even trying to pluck these young brands from the burning before they found that their help was not only not wanted but ignored or resented. He felt a burning anger against the father and a different kind of anger that she hadn't had the sense or the guts to do something about it. But he knew all too well that with that sort of background you would never go to the police or anyone official. They were enemies, not saviours. He closed the file and sat with his head in his hands, his mind in a turmoil of conflicting thoughts. Eventually he went down to the CRO office and handed back the file. As he walked to the main doors he decided that he would drive down to the safe-house and Yakunin. And he was vaguely aware that there were two reasons for doing that. The first was that he had no idea how he would face Jacqui and no idea what he would do when he inevitably had to. The second was because he realised that he had no one he could talk to about his situation. He desperately wanted some wise advice but had no source of advice, be it wise or foolish.

As he drove out of the police parking lot he headed for Westminster Bridge and the route to the south.

● ● ●

He had played a game of chess with Yakunin in a silence so ominous that the Russian had asked him if he was angry about something. Without even answering he had left the room and walked up the path to the road. It was just beginning to get dark and at the road he hesitated for a moment and then turned right. He passed a pub called the Elephant and at the bottom of the hill he came to the entrance to the ruins of Bayham Abbey. Fifteen minutes later he saw the gaunt outlines of the abbey itself, the moon casting long shadows from the crumbling walls across the wet grass and piles of stone that had once been part of the abbey.

He sat down on the remains of one wall and looked up at the sky. A small cloud moved slowly across the face of the moon, an owl hooted somewhere off in the woods and a dog barked far away, the sound echoing in the ruins. Slowly and methodically he posed himself a series of questions in an effort to cast out emotion and bring some sense and logic to his troubled mind. After a few minutes he closed his eyes, shaking his head as he realised that he was shaping the questions to suit what he knew his answers would be. And he was doing what was professionally unthinkable. He was telling himself lies. It was nothing to do with him what she had done in the past. She'd done it because it was the only way she could survive. And maybe Gardner *had* only been paying off a gambling bet from the old days. He spat into the darkness with disgust. If he believed that he'd believe anything. Known associates. Jacqui Lovegrove brackets call-girl close brackets. It wasn't for her company. He'd got a wife and family. She'd been there to screw whenever he fancied her. Standing at the door of the flat, pretending he'd just arrived when in fact he was just leaving. Two cigar butts in the ashtray. How long did it take to smoke two cigars? None of it mattered. It was all in the past. None of his business. She didn't care about them or love them. She did what she had to do. To earn a living, to get by. She was his wife. For better or worse. Thinking about it wouldn't make anything better. Let sleeping dogs lie. Just get on with it. Keep yourself under control. Don't throw a good relationship away for nothing. He stood up slowly. The issue was settled and he walked back to the Frant road and headed for the safe-house.

As he closed the door to his bedroom he remembered the line in the senior probation officer's summary which said, "There is no doubt in my mind that the subject knows exactly what she is doing and will not respond to any help that we could provide.

Her little-girl appearance belies a calculating and exploitative character." He sat on the edge of his bed and cried. For himself and for the girl.

• • •

Hoggart had slept fitfully and it was barely light when he dressed and went down to his car. As he turned onto the A21 for London he knew what he had to do. Just go back as if nothing had changed, because nothing *had* changed. Like an idiot he had read some files. Long-ago history. He must forget all that and see her as he knew her now. Caring and warm and contented with her life with him.

An hour later he was entering the outer suburbs of London. He stopped at a roadside café for truck-drivers where he had coffee and buttered toast, and bought a bunch of dahlias from a stall alongside the café.

It was 6:30 when he parked outside the house and let himself in quietly so that he didn't wake her up. He drew the curtains in the living room, gathered up the flowers from the table and opened the bedroom door. There was only one person in the bed but it wasn't Jacqui. It was Jake, the barman from the Monte Cristo Club. He woke as Hoggart's big hand closed round his throat, his eyes popping, his hands scrabbling at Hoggart's wrist. Hoggart's face was only inches away.

"Tell me why you're here."

"Just having a kip that's all."

As his hand went to soothe his throat Hoggart's hard fist crashed into his face and his other hand grabbed at the barman's hair, wrenching his head back as blood gushed from his broken nose. His scream was cut short as Hoggart lashed at him again.

"Now tell me what you're doing here."

The man was shivering violently almost unable to speak as he gulped for breath. "She's with Gardner. She thought you were away on a job."

"When did she go?"

"He came for her about midnight."

"Where are they?"

"I dunno. I expect they're at his place in Hertford Street by the Hilton. You're tearing my bloody hair out, mate."

"Why are you here?"

The barman closed his eyes. "Why don't you ask her?"

"D'you want some more?"

The man opened his eyes and tried to shake his head.

"She phoned me to come round. It was my day off yesterday. She used to phone me when you were away. Said she was lonely."

"And you had your reward in bed, yes?"

The man sighed heavily. "I thought maybe you knew and didn't care."

"How long have you been doing this?"

"About once a week."

"How long? When did it start?"

"When she came out of hospital. We'd been doing it off and on long before you came on the scene."

"And you've been doing it ever since?"

"Only for the last couple of months."

"And Gardner?"

"She used to be his piece. Lived with him for a long time but he threw her out when he caught her screwing with the minder. He's been here regularly."

"Before he spoke to me the first time at the club?"

"Yes. He was only pretending he didn't know where she was. Having you on like."

Hoggart ripped back the sheets with one hand and wrenched the man's arm up his back with the other. And as the man's body curved back to ease the pain Hoggart pulled him off the bed, grabbing at the piles of clothes as he hustled him to the door. As he opened the door he said softly, "If I ever set eyes on you again I'll do for you. Understand?"

The man nodded and Hoggart shoved him naked towards the stairs and flung his clothes after him. When he had closed the door he leaned back against it, his chest heaving from the unaccustomed exertion.

• • •

"Here, drink this down and take this pill." Harry Gardner saw her hand shaking as she reached for the glass. Her whole body was trembling as she sat on the edge of the bed. When she had taken the Valium he said, "Tell me again what he said."

"He said not to come back—he'd had enough—he was going to divorce me."

"How did he know you were here?"

"I let Jake stay on at the flat. He must have threatened him, and he told him."

"You silly bitch. Why'd you do a stupid thing like that—leaving Jake there?"

"I didn't know he was coming back." She looked up at him. "What am I gonna do, Harry?"

"About what?"

"All of it?"

"Well you can stay here, kid. No problem about that. Do you want to let him divorce you?"

"No."

"Why not?"

"I love him, Harry."

"Oh, come off it, Jacqui. You wouldn't be screwing around with Jake and me if you loved him."

"D'you love your wife?"

"Of course I do."

"But you still screw me."

"So?"

She shrugged. "It's just a screw, but to him it's different. He doesn't understand that you can let somebody screw you and it's just that. Nothing to do with love." She shrugged. "To him it means I don't love him."

"D'you think he really will try and divorce you?"

"I'm sure he will. When that guy says he's gonna do something, he'll do it."

"You could bring a counter-petition for divorce against him."

"What good would that do?"

"Might calm him down so he doesn't drag my name into it."

"I'd have no reason to give for divorcing him."

"Old Foxy would soon dig up some reasons. D'you want me to have a word with him?"

"It's up to you, Harry. I'll do whatever you say."

• • •

Charles Stuart Fox had been Harry Gardner's lawyer for almost twenty years. From the early days Charlie Fox had been the chosen representative of the select band of top criminals who could afford his fees. It was accepted that he was quite prepared to do a deal with the cops and let an underling go down for a few years as part of a deal where the top man was not even charged. The victims were well taken care of during their time in jail and after.

His office in one of the small back-alleys off Fleet Street was untidy, dusty, and depressing. Some said it was like that intentionally to cut down the natural self-confidence of his more outrageous clients. Nobody had ever sent Foxy's costs to the Tax Master and only one had reneged on his bill. He'd gone down for seven years in the Scrubs on his next job. None of his associates on the bank robbery had ever been charged or interviewed. Rumour said that Foxy had sent him a Christmas card every year he was inside.

Foxy always maintained a rather old-fashioned appearance with brown three-piece suits and a gold fob chain across his stomach with a gold hunter watch at one end and four sovereigns in a gold case at the other. But those were his only overt extravagances.

As he listened patiently to Harry Gardner, his mind was going over the Theft Act, 1968, and when Gardner finished Foxy shoved his glasses up his nose and looked across at his client.

"Afraid you're wrong there, Harry. OK. Section forty-six *does* require that a search warrant can only be issued by a magistrate to authorise a constable if there is reasonable cause to believe et cetera, et cetera." He paused. "However under another statue any person can lay the sworn information—doesn't even have to be a copper."

Foxy stood up, opened his mall mahogany cupboard, took out two glasses and a bottle of Bell's whisky. Without asking he poured two drinks and sat down.

"What was the other thing, Harry?"

"I want you to handle a divorce thing for a friend of mine."

Foxy looked shocked. "You know I don't meddle in that side of the law, Harry. Never have and never will. All that filth and—no, I can't help you there. I'm sorry." He perked up. "I can give you a few names. Don't recommend them one way or another but you can see what you think of 'em."

"This isn't just a run-of-the-mill case, Foxy. Like I said, it's for a friend of mine. A very special friend. And money's no object."

"You tell your friend that he doesn't need to spend a lot of money these days."

"It's not a fella, Foxy. It's a young lady."

Foxy leaned back in his ancient chair and shook his head in apparent despair. "You'd better tell me all about it."

Ten minutes later Foxy poured them both another whisky, looking towards the window as if he wished he could escape. He sighed loudly.

"Why don't you just give her a thousand quid and one of my names and leave her to it? Be much cheaper that way."

"Because if I do that it'll be out of my control. I'll end up in the papers looking like either a baby-snatcher or a dirty old man, or both. And that'll mean big trouble from Hettie and losing face where it matters."

Foxy reached for his pad and ball-point. "What's her name, Harry?"

"Jacqueline Lovegrove."

"Address?"

"Same as mine. The Hertford Street address."

Foxy laid the pen down gently and said, "You'd better get her out of there fast, my friend."

"Why the hurry?"

"You said you'd checked on her way back and she'd had two court warnings for soliciting. Yes?"

"Yes."

"And you knew this before you took her on?"

"Yes."

"You had sex with her yourself, and she had sex with friends of yours, business friends. Sometimes at hotels and sometimes at your place?"

"That's right."

"You realise that it could be claimed that you were effectively running a brothel?"

"That's rubbish, Foxy. She wasn't paid by those people. It was just between friends."

"I don't remember the exact words, Harry, but there was a case under the Sexual Offences Act, 1956. Winter versus Woolfe. In the early sixties. It established that in law it is immaterial whether payment was received or not."

"So. Are you going to look after my interests or not?"

"You don't leave me any choice, Harry." He paused. "Yes, I'll take it on. Reluctantly."

"What do you think we can do?"

"Buy off the outraged husband to leave you out of it or put some sort of pressure on him. What's his job?"

"She doesn't know. There were rumours that he was an undercover man for the Drug Squad."

"You mean he's a copper?" The horror on Foxy's face was echoed in his voice.

"That was the rumour. I don't think it's true. But she doesn't know what he does."

"You mean a wife doesn't know what her husband's job is or where he goes each day?"

"I'm afraid not."

"It's hardly credible. Good grief. We'd better find out what he *does* do, my friend." He paused and looked at Gardner. "You'd better put me in funds, Harry, so I can get a proper investigator working on it."

"How much do you need?"

"Five thousand. To start with."

Gardner reached into his jacket pocket for his cheque-book.

• • •

Although none of Foxy's clients was a woman, his rather old-fashioned courtesy went down well with the ladies. They mentally cast him in an avuncular role, certainly not as a predator. His old mother, with whom he had always lived, had made sure that the few girls he had brought home for tea in his early days had been efficiently put off by her joking comments about her son's shortcomings. They had all recognised a very formidable opposition behind the woman-to-woman confidences. She was aware of the pictures and magazines in the locked cupboard in his study in the old Victorian house. And she saw them as insurance against any foolhardiness on the part of her only son. She knew nothing of his monthly visits to a young woman who had once worked for him as a typist and was now married. But she would not have been unduly disturbed at the liaison if she had known. Some of Foxy's more perceptive clients jokingly referred to him in private as "Mother's Boy" but even behind his back it was said with an amiable connotation.

When his elderly secretary Miss Purvis showed Jacqui Lovegrove into his office he fussed around her. Was her chair comfortable? Was the sun in her eyes? When eventually he settled back on his side of the desk he said, "Tell me about your husband. What's his job for instance?"

"I've no idea, Mr. Fox."

"Can I call you Jacqui?"

She smiled. "Of course."

"Do you mean to tell me that a pretty girl like you who must have had dozens of men wanting to marry her, actually married a man considerably older than her and never asked him what he did for a living?"

"I'm afraid so. I think it was something secret. But I've no idea what it was."

"What makes you think that?"

"He would be away sometimes for two or three days. And when he came back he never apologised or said where he'd been or what he'd been doing."

"He never talked about his work? That it made him tired or it was dangerous or that sort of thing?"

"No."

"Well now. First of all I'd like you to go away and make a list of everything—every asset—that you think might be yours or was part of the marriage. Furniture, property, leases, car—everything. And while you're doing that I'll see what I can find out about your husband's job and his resources. How about you come back and see me again this time next Wednesday?"

He hurried round his desk to open the door for her and almost bowed as she walked out onto the landing that led to the bare-board stairs.

• • •

It was ten days later when Foxy phoned Gardner who was about to retire for the night when the call came.

"It's Foxy, Harry. Are you alone?"

"No."

"The girl?"

"Yes."

"OK. Don't ask me any questions. I want to see you immediately."

"What about?"

"I said don't ask questions. It's not safe. Just do as I say. I'll be waiting at my office for you."

Gardner stopped the taxi by the Wig and Pen and walked the rest of the way to Foxy's office.

There was only a forty-watt bulb lighting the rickety stairs and Gardner cursed the dust from the walls and the banister as he made his way slowly up to the second floor and Foxy's office.

The drinks were already poured and as soon as Gardner was seated Foxy said, "I've got some bad news, Harry."

Gardner shrugged. "So tell me."

"You know what the little girl's old man does for a living?"

"No. What?"

"I've had him under surveillance for four days."

"Get on with it, Foxy, there's a good chap."

"He works at Century House."

"What's Century House?"

"It's the headquarters of SIS, the Secret Intelligence Service— MI bloody six. He's a bloody spy. And that explains why he knew so much about the girl that she hadn't told him."

"Jesus. No wonder she didn't know what his job was. Now what?"

"You're in for a right royal reaming if we ain't very, very careful, Harry."

"How much do they make a year?"

"Bound to be pretty high and it's all tax-free."

"Why tax-free?"

"So that no crafty little bastard in the Inland Revenue can sell a nice list of names to the Russkis."

"Doesn't sound like a big spender from what Jacqui's told me."

Foxy shrugged. "So what? The fact remains that that guy knows enough, or can use his resources to find out enough, to get you into court and give you a very nasty time. What we've got to bend our minds to is how to stop him."

"What do you suggest?"

"Nothing right now. I only got this stuff an hour ago. I wanna sleep on it and then we'll talk again."

"Maybe I should put a contract out on him."

"For Christ's sake. You just keep very quiet and don't make any waves while I think about it. If you don't—just remember you could be doing thirty years. If you don't want to do it my way then you'd better find yourself another lawyer." He paused and looked hard at Gardner. "You understand that, Harry?"

Gardner shrugged and stood up. "Give me a call some time tomorrow and we'll meet again."

* * *

It was two days before Foxy met Gardner again, and, as Foxy had intended, Gardner had had time to realise how dire his situation had become. He was used to fighting on his own ground with his resources of men and power behind him. And his own position carefully protected so that he couldn't be connected with any of the operations he planned so carefully. With Foxy checking over everything before it started there were no connecting strands to him. And to be under risk from a friendly relationship with a call-girl seemed incredible. His marriage, his status in the underworld, and even his living were all under threat.

He waved aside the glass that Foxy offered him.

"What have you got, Foxy—anything?"

Foxy looked solemn as he faced his client. There was just a faint element of *schadenfreude* in his mind as he looked at the deflated figure across his desk.

"I've had an idea that might work, Harry."

"What is it?"

"How much is it worth to you to get clear of all this?"

"Don't piss about, Foxy. What's your idea?"

"It's expensive and it's risky, so you answer my question if you please."

Gardner sighed. "I'll pay whatever it takes. What are we talking about—ten grand, fifty or what?"

"Could be twice that. I don't know yet. But I can't pursue it without having virtually a blank cheque from you."

"Level with me, Foxy, I'm not in the mood for guessing games."

"This man Hoggart isn't just looking for a divorce. He's got a grudge against you. You personally. He wants the whole world to hear what he thinks of you. Agreed?"

"Go on."

"So we look at the possibility of doing the same to him."

"What's he done that's criminal?"

"Nothing so far as I know. But he's an M16 man. And we all know what kind of games those jokers get up to, don't we? His bosses aren't going to like having him being cross-questioned in court about what he does. It's supposed to be secret. That's why they've got the Official Secrets Act."

"But we don't know what he does. He could be a bloody clerk or something."

Foxy smiled. "I know already that he ain't that. He's doing secret things."

"How do you know?"

"My chap's been keeping very discreet tabs on him. Hoggart's doing something at a cottage down in Kent. A place that's permanently under guard. At least two heavies. He's been seen twice with an oldish chap. Just walking around. But the last time he swears they were both talking Russian."

"The court wouldn't let you talk about that. It's nothing to do with a divorce case."

"It could be if it's handled right."

"How?"

"You'd have to leave that to me."

"It's too vague. You've lectured me a dozen times about how a court wants evidence, not surmises or opinions."

"So we get the evidence."

"How?"

"Again, you'd have to leave it to me."

"If this guy's in the spy business he'll spot your chap tailing him in no time."

"My chap's ex-SAS and ex-dirty tricks in Ulster. He's just as good as friend Hoggart. Maybe better."

Foxy was gratified to see the relief on Gardner's face.

"So how much, Foxy?"

"Like I said, I'm not sure. Could be a hundred grand. I can't afford to cut corners or I could end up doing time along with you."

For the first time Gardner smiled. "That'd be the day, Foxy." He sighed. "OK. Go ahead. Not a blank cheque but up to a hundred grand. But I'll want some sort of accounting at the end."

"Where's the girl now?"

"I found her a place by Victoria Station. The lease is in her name. She pays the rent. And I keep her funded."

"How? Not with cheques I hope."

"No. With cash."

"Good. Well, I'll contact you when I've got something to tell you."

CHAPTER ELEVEN

When Hoggart came into their office Fletcher was writing at his desk. He looked up. "Hi. I've not seen you for weeks." Then he paused. "Are you OK, Eddie?"

"Yeah."

"You look absolutely knackered."

Hoggart sat down at his desk and pulled an audio tape and a notebook out of his leather briefcase. As he turned the pages of his notebook Fletcher said, "How's the de-briefing going?"

Hoggart sighed deeply as he leaned back in his chair and Fletcher was shocked now that he could see Hoggart's face more clearly. The deep lines each side of his mouth, the usually ruddy skin pale and flaccid, the eyes bloodshot and sunken. He knew then that Hoggart was either seriously ill or something was terribly wrong.

"Slowly, but I think there's some progress."

"How long since you had a holiday?"

"God knows. Holidays don't interest me."

"Rachel and I are going to a small hotel we know in Devon at the weekend, why don't you and Jacqui come with us? Good food, peace and quiet, and a change of scenery. You'd like it, Eddie, you really would."

Hoggart looked towards the window, staring without seeing. When he looked back slowly at Fletcher he said quietly, "Thanks. But I can't. I got problems."

"Anything I can help with?"

Hoggart shook his head without speaking and turned back to looking at his notebook.

"Is it a work problem or private stuff?"

He could see the flash of anger on Hoggart's face as he snapped. "Forget it."

Fletcher persisted. "We're saving up to buy a house. I can lend you a bit if you need it."

Hoggart said quietly, "I'm sorry, mate. It's not money, but thanks for the offer." He took a deep breath. "How's your de-briefing going?"

Realising that Hoggart wanted to change the subject he said, "He's a strange fellow. Talkative but not informative."

Hoggart smiled. "What's that mean?"

"Full of KGB gossip which is quite useful, but dodges any questions about what he's been doing. Says he was directing an operation in the States."

"Any idea what the operation was doing?"

"He's hinted that it was a key operation and vague hints that it was a penetration of the US Navy."

"My chap was doing exactly that."

"I wonder why your stuff wasn't passed on to me?"

"Ask him if it was anything to do with the Walker family. Ask him what he knows about a KGB man named Yakunin."

"Is that your chap?"

"Yes."

"Maybe I'd better ask for your files to be released to me."

"Why not? Most of it's American material. Very little about us. Although he's hinting at revelations about a Soviet mole in SIS."

Fletcher laughed. "They all say that. It's part of their repertoire."

"I think it's more than that with this guy."

"If I don't get a release on your file maybe we could compare notes unofficially."

"That's OK by me."

"Renshaw is pretty sure my guy is genuine." He laughed. "He thinks he knows a hell of a lot, if I can only pin him down."

• • •

Harry Gardner felt that in Foxy's office he was at a disadvantage. Foxy was making up for all those times when he'd had to take orders and just do what he was told. And now Foxy was the one in charge, telling him, Harry Gardner, what to do. Friend Foxy was getting a bit above his station and needed to be brought under control again. It was for that reason that when Foxy called him for another meeting he told him to meet him in the lounge at the Savoy. Foxy was not an habitué of the Savoy but was not ignorant of the niceties required of its guests; nevertheless Gardner took the opportunity to open his campaign by pointing out that jacket and tie were essential. He had never seen Foxy not wearing a jacket and tie but the dig was irresistible.

Gardner deliberately arrived nearly ten minutes after the arranged time but Foxy wasn't sitting waiting for him. He arrived five minutes after Gardner. He looked pleased with himself as he made himself comfortable in the large leather chair opposite Gardner. Gardner ordered drinks for them and sat there impassively until they were served.

"What have you got to report, Foxy?"

Foxy smiled. "You'll like it, Harry. I think it's beginning to come together."

"Get on with it for Christ's sake."

115

"I've had a preliminary report from my investigation. It seems that he was right. Hoggart definitely works for M16—he calls it SIS."

"How's he know that?"

"He's followed him to Century House where all these chaps have their headquarters. He's fairly important because his office is on the ninth floor. He's something to do with the Russians."

"How'd he find that out?"

Foxy smiled. "He traced a girl who worked there until a few weeks ago. She's in pod and he's paying for an abortion. She's sweet on him. Thinks he's the White Knight come to rescue her. He's been very careful about not asking many questions. Seems like this Hoggart is a real tough cookie. Young Jacqui tells me he was in an orphanage when he was a kid. Went in the army and ended up in SIS. Got the equivalent rank of major."

"So what's the good news?"

Foxy smiled. "Seems young Jacqui went through his wallet one time when he was asleep. Found his bank book in it. How much do you think he's got in it?"

"How much?"

"Ninety quid. Ninety bloody quid. And if I use the law to make this divorce get put back again and again, he's going to have a bill with a lot of noughts on the end of it."

"That's his problem, not mine."

"You could make it yours and save a lot of trouble."

"How?"

"Pay him off."

"And if he refuses it's more evidence he's got against me in court."

Foxy smiled. "I ain't gonna let this go as far as a court, Harry."

"That's what you say. Stoppin' it's something else. How? Have you thought about that?"

"Of course."

Foxy was pleased at the surprise on Gardner's face.

"How?"

"I send his solicitor a new set of particulars which make clear that we claim his violence against Jake is typical of his behaviour." He paused. "Because he's trained to be violent. It's part of his job. His bosses won't like that."

"He may not tell 'em about what you've sent his solicitor. He may not even tell 'em he's getting a divorce."

"If he don't, then I do. A nice chat with one of his high-ups. Like I'm worried about what's going to come out. Land of Hope and Glory and all that. In the interests of security. Why don't they have a quiet word with our friend? No trouble in him getting his divorce. Just the irretrievable-breakdown formula. No detailed evidence against either party. And everybody can go away happy."

Gardner nodded slowly. "Maybe you've got something there, Foxy. Go away and try it."

Foxy found it hard to hide his resentment. He'd seen himself as hero not just a herald of good news. Never mind. Another grand on his final bill.

"Right, Harry. I'll put you in an interim bill in the meantime."

"How much is it so far, including the investigator?"

"Between four and five grand."

"OK. I ain't gonna argue with you." Gardner stood up. "Let me know when you've got something to report." He nodded. "See you."

Foxy walked back to his office barely aware of the rain. Trying not to dwell on how he might feel if he failed and he saw his client being done over by the other side in court. Whatever happened Gardner would come out of it badly. He was no better nor worse than the other big-timers who planned and organised armed robberies, but he'd be a laughing-stock for a few months and he'd hate that.

• • •

Cornish spoke very quietly but his eyes were on Hoggart all the time.

"May I ask why you came to me, Mr. Hoggart?"

"Your name was in the Yellow Pages."

Cornish smiled. "There must have been a lot of other names. Pages of them if I remember rightly."

"You're near where I work."

"Fair enough. Now for a few details."

Hoggart had given his own name and the address of his old rooms that he had kept on. Wife's name and unmarried name. A couple of suggestions of what might be her current address. Then Cornish put down his pen.

"Tell me why you want a divorce."

"Adultery."

"Could you outline the details for me?"

When Hoggart had finished speaking, Cornish was silent for a few moments and then he said. "What you suspect is that the first man, the barman, Jake, had sexual relations with your wife in the afternoon and then she went with Gardner, who she was with when you phoned that evening. Is that right?"

"That's right."

"What was the conversation between you when you spoke to her that night?"

"Gardner answered the phone. I told him I knew Jacqui was there and if he didn't put her on the phone I'd go round there. I told her about the barman and what he'd said. And I told her not to come back and that I was going to divorce her."

"What did she say to that?"

"Started crying. Asking me to forgive her. Said she was lonely because I was away a lot. It didn't mean anything. I was the only man she'd ever loved and all that crap."

Cornish said quietly, "You think she didn't mean it—about loving you?" He noticed the flash of anger and disbelief in Hoggart's eyes.

"For Christ's sake. She does it all afternoon with one creep and then for the evening with Gardner. She was just trying it on."

Cornish pursed his lips and then said. "How important was your sexual relationship with your wife?"

"I don't understand."

"Was it the most important part of your relationship?"

"No."

"What was the most important part?"

"She's had a really bad upbringing and early life. I felt I could help her."

"Tell me about it."

"She'd had an incestuous relationship with her lousy father and she'd ended up as some kind of good-time girl."

"But surely you didn't have to *marry* her to help her."

"In the end it seemed the only way to give her some kind of security."

"How long did you know her before you married her?"

"About a year."

"And it was a sexual relationship during that time?"

"No. Only for a few months."

"And you knew about her previous life?"

"Vaguely."

"But you knew enough? Or did she deceive you about it?"

"We never went into it." Hoggart shifted uncomfortably in his chair. "What's all this got to do with a divorce?"

"If you just want a divorce why not go for the usual formula of irretrievable breakdown? Why insist on the adultery charge?"

"So that Gardner gets his comeuppance."

"Is that important to you?"

"Very important."

"Do you know this man Gardner?"

"Not really. I've seen him around. I think he's a quite successful criminal."

"Can you prove this?"

"Not right now. I might be able to in a few days."

"Going back to when you first knew the girl. Did her old life-style offend you?"

"I didn't like it, but I understood. She did it to survive. It was the only way she knew." He paused. "Why are you asking these questions? It's got nothing to do with divorcing her."

"When somebody seeks a divorce, Mr. Hoggart, before the process drags its way through the court there is a responsibility laid on the solicitors concerned. They are officers of the court and the court requires them to examine the possibility of reconciliation. I must be frank and tell you that many solicitors ignore this responsibility. Experience tells them that it seldom works. But in some cases I should want, at least to try, to see if there was such a possibility. This is one of those cases."

"You'd be wasting your time, Mr. Cornish."

"You may be right. Nevertheless I want to ask you to come and see me again in two days' time. The same time as today. And in the meantime I'd like you to think calmly and seriously about the whole thing. The circumstances and the divorce petition. If you still want to go ahead, so be it. I'd be pleased to act for you."

"Does this mean you think my petition could fail?"

"It could. These things are never certain and if we go ahead I shall need to know a lot more. No, what it means is that I've had many years of dealing with divorce and family law and I recognise certain signs."

"What signs?"

Cornish smiled. "In divorce cases the difficult clients are the good honest people who have contributed little or nothing to the breakdown of the marriage. The easy ones are those men and women who are ruthless or feckless, amoral or immoral. They have lost nothing that they valued. All they want is out. They're seldom spiteful. They generally have their new lives to go to. New relationships. They're happy, so they make no difficulties either for me or their ex-spouses. The hard cases are the upright, decent folk who are shocked and angry at the perfidy or unfaithfulness of someone they loved or cared about. A large part of their world has been shattered. They don't deserve it and can't understand how it could have happened to them. They say they want justice but in fact what they want is revenge. And the only person who loses out is them. Tension, frustration, and big solicitors' bills."

Cornish stood up, offering his hand. "Come and see me again on Friday."

• • •

The Friday meeting with Cornish had not gone as Hoggart expected. In fact he had not given any thought to reconciliation. He knew exactly what he wanted to do. He wanted out from Jacqui and he wanted to damage Gardner as much as he could.

Cornish hadn't seemed surprised when he told him that he had not changed his mind.

"I've thought quite a lot about your case, Mr. Hoggart. And I'd like you to answer some things that came up in my thinking." He smiled. "They could be useful whichever way you decide to go. But I wouldn't be happy just to plunge in on your behalf without knowing a little more. Is that OK with you?"

Hoggart shrugged. "Whatever you want. But I don't understand why we're making such a meal of a straightforward situation."

"Well. You're the reason. You strike me as a rather unusual man. And you told me you had not discussed your divorce with anyone else because there is nobody whose advice you would trust. No friend who could advise you. Courts have a strange device called *amicus curiae*—friend of the court. That's the role I'm filling right now with you."

"Why do you think I'm odd?"

"I said unusual, not odd." Cornish paused. "You're unusual because you are obviously not only a very self-confident man, well capable of looking after yourself, but it strikes me that at the same time you are vulnerable. Your kindness to this girl. Your understanding of her background show more generosity and tolerance than most men would have.

"The only complaint you have is these new acts of infidelity on your wife's part. Most men would add a few traditional complaints. Laziness, nagging, rows, fights, insults, disparagement—you name it. But not you. Would it be fair to say that if these events had not taken place you would still be together?"

"Yes."

"I'd like to tread on some very thin ice for a moment and ask you some very personal things." Hoggart sat silent and Cornish went on. "From my legal experience I'd say that women who earn a living from sex are less likely to enjoy it than other women. It's a routine. A job that has to be done. They are very seldom sexually promiscuous. It's not an emotionally rewarding experience. Would you agree with me?"

"I suppose so."

"You told me that she's not only young but also very attractive. Was that why you married her?"

Hoggart shook his head. "No. Well, maybe. I'd have helped her anyway because I liked her. But I guess that without her being pretty I wouldn't have married her."

"That's what I thought. A straightforward honest appraisal. So . . ." Cornish hesitated for a moment. ". . . so what I want to ask is this." Cornish shook his head. "No. Let me say something else first. We are both what people call men of the world, so we know that the kind of sex that goes with money or favours does not indicate affection or even sexual satisfaction on the female's part. Agreed?"

Hoggart didn't respond but Cornish went on. "So my question is this—do a couple of acts of sex mean more to you than anything else your wife gave you—like love or caring or affection?"

For a moment Hoggart didn't respond then he said, "Do you speak French?"

"No. I'm afraid not."

"Well the French have a saying. Marriage is a castle. When the man commits adultery he goes outside the castle. When a woman commits adultery she invites in an invader." He paused. "I share those views, Mr. Cornish."

"So you'd like me to prepare a divorce petition?"

"Yes, please."

Cornish looked at his diary. "Can you see me next Wednesday at five?"

"Yes."

"I'll have a draft ready for you then."

* * *

Hoggart had arranged for a man to remove Jacqui's things from the flat the next day. He had decided to terminate the lease and go back to his old rooms. But he wanted to pack her stuff for the man to take away.

The flat had had no fresh air for several weeks and as he opened the window, the net curtain billowed round his face and he was aware of the noise of the traffic in the streets.

He stood, hands on hips looking around the bedroom. There was a teddy-bear and a rag doll on the floor beside the bed. She'd bought them in Berwick Street market. The dressing table had two bottles of perfume and an eau-de-toilette in a spray bottle and there was a thin layer of dust on the glass top. He opened one drawer after another and there were bits of cheap jewellery, neat folded piles of underwear, stockings and pantihose. And in a cardboard chocolate box were all the Christmas, Easter, and birthday cards he had ever given her. Two of each and three Valentine cards. There was a folded note in his handwriting reminding her to phone the plumber and the programmes from half a dozen shows he had taken her to.

He moved to the built-in chest of drawers and without thinking he opened them as if he were doing it in his job, the bottom one first. There was a card on top that said "Eddie's shirts" and a dozen shirts neatly piled, and a small sachet of dried flowers in the right-hand front corner. There was a drawer for his socks and underwear, a drawer for bath-towels and hand-towels, two drawers of sheets and pillow-cases, and one drawer that was empty.

The small kitchen was clean and tidy, with crockery and cutlery in a wire basket to dry and a small framed picture on one wall of pressed flowers that he'd bought her on a trip to some National Trust place.

He walked back to the living room and sat down heavily in one of the armchairs. A second-hand three-piece suite they had bought at an auction. For long moments he sat there, shivering with cold despite the warmth of the room. It had seemed indecent looking at everything. The things he knew nothing about. Strange, silent witness to her caring. Part of a life that she didn't expect to come to a sudden end. That must have been as much a shock for her as his on discovering her unfaithfulness. Lethargically he got out of the chair and checked the removal man's number. There was only an answering machine at the other end but he left a message to say that the move wasn't convenient the next day. He'd get in touch again in a few days' time. And when he had hung up he used the back of his hand to wipe the tears from his eyes.

• • •

The car forked right at the bottom of the hill turning away from the Hastings road and up through Lamberhurst village to the Down. Then right at the crossroads past the Swan and the northern edge of the vineyard. And a quarter of a mile further on Hoggart turned into the dusty track of the safe-house. He noticed that there was enough wind getting up to swing the

notice that said BED AND BREAKFAST. From time to time the FULL
sign was removed for a day or so just to keep up appearances.
The main sign provided an acceptable reason for the courtyard
comings and goings at the house, and the lower board was a
pre-emptive strike against genuine hitch-hikers and cyclists.

Some instinct made him turn to look back at the road as he
closed the door and he saw a blue Ford saloon which slowed
down and then moved off almost immediately. He vaguely
remembered a blue Ford a couple of cars behind him at the
Elephant and Castle roundabout. But his mind had been on
other things. Anyway blue Ford saloons were probably ten per
cent of the car population. Nevertheless he walked slowly back
up the slope to the road. The Ford was parked a couple of
hundred yards away with the bonnet up and Hoggart turned
back to the safe-house.

• • •

Foxy had agreed that it would be safer to have the meeting at
Gardner's place in Hertford Street. He had never been invited
there before and he was struck by the luxury of the apartment. It
had obviously been designed by a professional, and no expense
had been spared. It was meant to impress and Foxy was duly
impressed.

"A very nice place you got here, Harry. Must have cost you a
fortune."

Gardner shrugged. "All goes down to tax, Foxy. Sit down."

He pointed at one of the big armchairs and Foxy sank into it,
his hands clutching its arms as if he was afraid of sinking out of
sight. Gardner poured them each a whisky and handed a glass to
Foxy before sitting down facing him.

"What's it all about, Foxy? Why all the mystery?"

"Not mystery, Harry. Security. But first a small problem. The
date you gave me of the first time you had relations with the girl.
Are you sure it was the right date you gave me?"

"Yes, of course I'm sure. I checked my diary."

"You still got that diary?"

"Yeah."

"Well destroy it. Right away. Not tomorrow but today. As soon as I've gone."

"Why, for Christ's sake?"

Foxy took a deep breath. "I put a search on the girl's birth certificate. She was two months under-age on that date. If it comes to court we don't want any wrong dates flying about. Just a precaution, Harry."

"I can tear out any pages mentioning her."

"That would be even worse. If they thought you had a diary they'd subpoena it just to have a look-see. Missing pages would be nearly as damning as the entries." He paused. "OK?"

"Yeah?"

"Now to the important decision." He looked at Gardner's flushed face. "We got a choice, Harry. I've got a few shots left in the locker to delay things, but sooner or later they'll get me in court. I want to stop that from happening. Whichever way it went you'd be the loser. So . . ." Foxy paused, ". . . we got two ways we can pressure him. Physical or inside pressure."

"What inside pressure?"

"Well. I'm a solicitor. An officer of the court. I'm also a good citizen. Patriotic and all that. And I've got this piddling little case. But it means that to protect the interests of my client, Jacqui, I've got to show that this man's behaviour is what drove her to what she did. Not his fault of course. It's what he was trained to do, wasn't it? He's used to dealing with foreign agents and all that. Tough and ruthless and unfortunately given to violence in his private life. What a pity to see a man's career put in jeopardy just for a marital squabble. If they had a quiet word with him, it could all be smoothed over, quietly and calmly. Surely they'd agree that that was best for all concerned."

Foxy leaned back in his chair, watching Gardner's face for a reaction.

It was several minutes before Gardner responded. "Who's the 'they' you say you'll talk to?"

"I'll talk to his solicitor first. If I get no joy there I'll call M16. I got the number of the main switchboard from my chap. And I know who to talk to."

"Who?"

"Chap named Latham. Legal department."

"He'll say it's private, none of their business."

Foxy smiled and shook his head. "He won't. They can't afford to. They won't want all about what he does coming out in open court. Russians and all that."

Gardner stood up and walked over to the window, looking out, hands in pockets as his mind wrestled with what Foxy had said. Foxy wouldn't like the rough approach but he'd enjoy fencing with officials. But that didn't make it the right course. And if Foxy failed he couldn't return to rough stuff or they would know that he was behind it. But there was an alternative that Foxy hadn't suggested. Maybe hadn't thought of. And there was no need to tell him about it. He turned to look at Foxy.

"OK. Foxy, try it like you said. Won't do no harm talking to 'em."

Foxy nodded and struggled out of his chair. "OK, Harry. I'll start moving on it."

• • •

Foxy was at his most ingratiating as he held out his hand to Cornish.

"Do sit down, Mr. Fox. I understand you want to discuss the Hoggart divorce."

"That's right." Foxy smiled and shrugged. "I'd like to suggest a compromise, Mr. Cornish."

"Tell me what you have in mind."

"I think it would be better for both parties if we used irretrievable breakdown as the basis."

"My client wouldn't agree, Mr. Fox. And I don't see why he should."

"My client would agree to no claim for support, or some nominal sum, if the court insisted. No claims for assets of any kind. And she'd withdraw her cross-petition."

Cornish shook his head. "I'm afraid not. I've had very definite instructions from my client. I'll be sending you further particulars in the next few days."

"It would save him a lot of hassle about his character and his job."

Cornish looked surprised. "I don't understand."

"His governors wouldn't like all that stuff about his work coming out. Espionage and that sort of stuff."

Cornish took a deep breath, opened his mouth to speak and then closed it as he stood up and walked to the door.

"You'd better go, Mr. Fox."

Foxy got up and made his way to the open door. He shrugged as he left. "Don't say I didn't try, Mr. Cornish. Good day to you."

Cornish watched him until he'd walked through the outer office and into the corridor. Back at his desk he sat for several minutes thinking, until his secretary came in with letters for him to sign.

• • •

A man's voice answered the phone.

"Can I help you?"

"My name is Fox. I'm a solicitor. I'd like to talk with Mr. Latham."

"Which Mr. Latham?"

"Mr. Latham in Legal."

There were a few bars of harpsichord music and then a voice said, "Latham."

"Mr. Latham. My name is Fox. I'm a solicitor and a matter of security has come up in one of my cases. I'd like to talk to you about it."

"What kind of security?"

"National security. Espionage."

"Give me your number and I'll call you back."

Foxy gave his office number and ten minutes later the call came through.

"Latham. When can you call on me at my office?"

"I'm at your disposal, sir."

"What about four this afternoon?"

"Certainly."

"You know where I am?"

"Century House, isn't it?"

"Yes. I'll be at the desk."

• • •

Foxy was surprised when he met Latham. He wasn't sure what he expected but it wasn't the rather dour figure in the black jacket and pin-striped trousers. Latham signed in the book for Foxy and pinned on the identity card to Foxy's jacket and led him away. Latham didn't speak as they walked down wide corridors. Latham using several entry cards as they passed through a series of metal-framed doors.

The room he was shown into had bare, white walls and no windows. There were four chairs around a plain wooden table. When they were seated Foxy said, "Forgive me for asking, but is this place bugged?"

"No, Mr. Fox. You can speak freely."

"There'll be no record of any kind?"

"Not if that's how you want it."

"There's a man working here called Hoggart. Edward Hoggart. Do you know him?"

"Carry on, Mr. Fox. I'll just listen at this stage."

"I know he works here, I've had him checked out."

Foxy waited for a response but there was none and he went on. "There's a divorce case pending. Cross petitions. Not that his wife, who's my client, wanted it this way. But he's claiming adultery and several other things that I won't go into.

"So for the protection of my client I've got to put him in the box about acts of physical violence. I've got an affidavit from one of his victims to that effect. I'm going to need to establish his character, and I understand these chaps have special training in what they call unarmed combat. I'll have to establish that physical aggression is all part of his job. I understand that he's got something to do with work concerning Russians."

He waited and Latham merely said, "Carry on, Mr. Fox."

"I thought maybe you could have a word with him. Advise him of the wisdom of just keeping it to breakdown, etc."

Latham put his hands palm down on the table and looked at Foxy.

"Have you got copies of the two petitions and the affidavits alleging violence?"

Foxy reached for his battered brief-case, sorted through a bundle of correspondence, and handed over the photostats of the three items as he came to them.

Latham stood up. "Thanks for your time, Mr. Fox."

"You'll have a word with him, will you?"

"Let me show you out."

"Would you like my business card?"

Latham half-smiled. "I know your address and telephone number, Mr. Fox."

"Ah yes." He smiled. "I suppose I'll be on some blacklist from now on."

"I'm sure you won't, Mr. Fox."

Latham had been tempted to say that Foxy had already been on Scotland Yard's Criminal Records Office list for over ten years. But he just guided Foxy back down to the street doors.

Back in his own office he asked his assistant for the file on Hoggart E.

• • •

It was a week later when Latham interviewed Eddie Hoggart. He wasted no time.

"D'you know a chap named Fox, Eddie?"

"I don't think so. What's he do?"

"He's a solicitor. Your wife's solicitor."

Latham saw Hoggart's face flush with anger and noticed the muscles at the side of his mouth.

"I didn't notice his name. My solicitor's been dealing with all that."

"He came to see me last week."

"What about?"

"About the divorce. Wanted me to persuade you to limit your petition to irretrievable breakdown and your wife would withdraw her petition and make no claims for support or assets." As he saw Hoggart open his mouth to speak Latham held up his hand to silence him. "You could probably use him coming to see us as part of your case if you wanted to. He'd claim he was acting in the interests of the client, but the court wouldn't like it."

"And you said you'd look into it?"

"No way. I showed him the door. But I listened to what he had to say."

"What was that?"

"It was not so much what he said but what lay behind it. He'd call you on character. Claiming that your SIS training made your naturally aggressive. He's got a signed affidavit from some barman who claims you assaulted him." Latham shrugged. "What he's saying is that if you go on with your case he'll reveal anything he can about your work and to hell with national security."

"He can threaten all he likes. I'm going to have my pound of flesh."

"It's the chap Gardner you really want to do, isn't it?"

"Yes."

"Is he worth it?"

"He is to me." He paused. "Is this an official conversation?"

"Let's say official, but off the record."

"And the brass would like to avoid any publicity?"

"Your guess is as good as mine as to what they'd like."

"You've talked to them?"

"Very briefly. Just an outline. No details."

"And what was their reaction?"

"To leave it entirely up to you. But I think they wondered if you wouldn't be wiser to do it the quiet way. They don't want publicity and this bastard Gardner is obviously behind this. Ready to stir up all the muck he can to save his own skin."

"And meantime I'm suspended or on indefinite leave?"

"No way. This is the end of it. It won't be raised again. Just think it over. It's entirely up to you."

CHAPTER TWELVE

Mathews was not one of Renshaw's admirers. The languid manner and the deceptively casual approach irritated him to a barely concealed rudeness. But Mathews was running the Russian whose code-name was "Wheel." The Russian wasn't KGB, he was a Novosty journalist. A genuine journalist but the KGB used him when it suited them. He had been uncovered by MI5 two years earlier when he had been tapping out a message to Moscow in a code that had long been broken. The DF Section had spent a month pin-pointing the illegal transmitter and he and his radio had been taken in an early-morning raid.

At that time it seemed that he was not being used by the KGB to collect information but merely to transmit material passed to him by an actual KGB agent. The security people had interrogated him for three weeks and had realised that he was willing to cooperate in exchange for being allowed to stay on in London, ostensibly still doing his job as well as his duties for the KGB. He had a girlfriend in Barnes who was the attraction. Over the months after he was "turned" his radio traffic from Moscow increased, and in the end the Security Service reluctantly handed him over to SIS. They were the only agency who were allowed to run "turned" agents.

Mathews resented the fact that he had to keep Renshaw informed about "Wheel." On paper they were equal in rank and seniority, but he knew that in fact Renshaw rated higher in the opinions of the top brass. But a problem had arisen that meant Renshaw had to be told. He had outlined the problem and sat resentfully awaiting Renshaw's comments.

"What reason did he give, George?"

"Said that Moscow had ordered him to go back for discussions."

"Does their radio traffic support that?"

"Yes. I don't know whether Moscow has rumbled something but there's been very little Moscow traffic to him in the last two months compared with the usual weight. And the recall message gave no hint of what they wanted with him. They've changed codes every day and GCHQ say that's a sign that they're suspicious."

Renshaw nodded. "And you wonder whether we should let him go back?"

"Yes."

"We don't really have much choice, do we? If we let him go back and they suspect him they'll break him down and that's the end of the "Wheel" operation. But if we don't let him go back then the operation's over anyway. It's a bit of a Morton's Fork situation."

"A what?"

Renshaw said with a shrug, "A cleft stick. Either way it's not on. But of course, if he goes to Moscow and they're not suspicious, and he comes back, then you've a much enhanced operation."

"So do I let him go back?"

"I don't think you have much choice, George." And Renshaw stood up slowly to dilute his irritation with his colleague's obtuseness. Any "turned" KGB stooge had a potential value but it was obvious that Moscow had had enough of SIS's radio game with "Wheel." A pity, because "Wheel" had been useful. Renshaw smiled to himself. Useful to both sides in fact. He walked over to the window as Mathews left, looking down at the traffic in the street. He felt restless and it disturbed him. Watching the slow development of two defectors unsettled him. Yakunin obviously had something to say and he wished he knew what it was. He was a usually patient man but for a week or so he'd had this vague premonition of disaster.

Impulsively he turned and took his umbrella from the rack and checked the security safes in his office and headed for the lifts. He took a taxi back to King's Road and shopped at Sainsbury's in the precinct before going back to the flat.

He poured himself a whisky and took it over to the piano, opening the lid as he made himself comfortable on the ornate double stool. Almost without thinking he started playing one of Satie's Gymnopédies. For all their pretensions the French were basically Philistines. They derided all their musicians until they were almost at death's door. Satie, Ravel, poor sick Milhaud, and then their open hatred of Debussy. How on earth had such a bourgeois nation ever achieved a reputation for being romantic?

• • •

One of Mathews's watchers had witnessed the man code-named "Wheel" board the Aeroflot flight to Warsaw and Moscow. The Russian, Konstantin Bykov, settled back in his seat and closed his eyes. He was certain that the Brits no longer trusted him but he need worry no more. At long last Moscow had agreed to his return. Sooner or later Mathews would find out about the spare radio or the listening place at Cheltenham would get round to checking the transmission coordinates and breaking the code. It would be a shock for the girl but that was how it went in the business.

• • •

Bykov was right on all three counts. Mathews's rummage team had found the radio at the girl's house in Barnes the night Bykov left. The set was in the room he rented from her and was inside one of the loudspeaker enclosures linked to a cheap hi-fi unit. He was right too about the girl. Mathews had to send a car to take her in a state of hysteria to her mother's house in Wimbledon. The Russian had said he was going to Paris on business for three days. The third prediction proved correct at a meeting the next day at a special Government Communications Headquarters' lab in Store Street.

At the subsequent meeting it was Mathews's turn. Not to be shocked but to be beside himself with anger. Armitage, the GCHQ technical officer concerned, had put over the bad news as tactfully as he could, pointing to the radio set and the two cassettes of tape.

"It's quite a sophisticated set. Our code-name for it is 'Combine' and the Russians call it Soyuz 4. The message is recorded at normal speed and then you press this copy button and it's re-recorded at very high speed. A transmission that would normally take six minutes is transmitted in fifteen seconds." He looked at Mathews's face. "That's why there's no chance for us to use a direction-finding net. There's no way of even hearing a transmission, let alone locating the source."

"What about the code?"

"It's high-grade code. A variation on their ambassador's code. Based on a new version of one-time pads. I won't go into it. It's very complicated. But we broke it a few months ago at our Hong Kong base."

"What are the contents of the messages like?"

Armitage pursed his lips and then took a deep breath. "The subject was being instructed by Moscow on his collaboration with SIS. I'm afraid he was a triple-turn operation."

• • •

Renshaw seemed to take the news philosophically when Mathews told him. Just a supercilious lift of his eyebrows and a half smile as he said, "I shouldn't give up."

"I don't understand. Give up what?"

Renshaw laughed softly as if the answer and its logic were obvious. "They might make the same mistake that you did. They might not realise he's been blown and they might risk sending him back. Then it'll be your turn again."

"They wouldn't dare risk it. Neither would he."

Renshaw shrugged. "Have it your own way, my boy. But if I were you I'd get the girl on one side and get her back at the house in case he tries to contact her. He could well risk a telephone call even if it's only to find out if you've found the transmitter." Renshaw laughed. "Work your charm on her, old chap. She'll be feeling let down and lonely."

A light dawned slowly on Mathews's face. "You could be right you know. You could . . . I'll see what I can do."

CHAPTER THIRTEEN

Ulianov had never wanted to be in charge of the operation and having to share responsibility with Sostov bordered on humiliation. The whole thing had been done in a hurry. KGB ground-rules ignored and far too much reliance on Lensky's improvisations. They were like some small-town amateur dramatic society who were sure it would be all right on the night. But it wasn't all right, it was a shambles.

The stuff coming back from London was useless. Vague reassurances that all was going to plan but it needed time and patience. There was no plan. It was one of those wild-goose chases that the new men seemed to indulge in at the slightest pretext. Rules, they said, were there to be broken, rules were inhibiting progress. In Ulianov's opinion *glasnost* didn't apply to the KGB. They had built up their world-wide power and success on careful and meticulous planning, not wild bursts of misplaced and risky enthusiasm.

It had become like some crazy chess game where they were

sacrificing piece after piece to protect the king without noticing that white hadn't even lost a pawn. And now Sostov had cut their only line of communication by bringing back Bykov. If they were getting too little before, they would be getting nothing now. Playing blindfold. Yakunin gone, Lensky at risk, and now Bykov out of the game. And Sostov hadn't even consulted him before withdrawing Bykov. Did that mean that somebody higher had initiated it or approved it? And did that mean that they were telling him that his days were numbered?

Tomorrow was the evaluation meeting and Chebrikov was sending his own man to report back to him. It would probably be one of the new boys. In the old days they would have just cut their losses and called the whole thing off. Maybe close it down for a couple of years and then revive it. He and Sostov were supposed to come up with a solution and Sostov couldn't be found. The bastard had probably worked out another crazy scheme and didn't want him to have the chance to lobby against it. Or maybe it was so good he didn't want to share the bouquets. Ulianov felt tired and old, and a little bit scared.

• • •

The meeting had started at 8 P.M. and went on long past midnight. There were six others there and Ulianov realised that there had obviously been other meetings to which he had not been invited. Chebrikov's personal representative had not come just as an observer, he had come with a mission. A plan that Ulianov had to agree had a great prize if it came off, but a plan that was far too risky. Ulianov knew what the game was. If he and Sostov wouldn't go along with it he could expect immediate retirement with a reduced pension and Sostov, who was only a captain, would end up with some Frontier Police unit on the Chinese border. He felt a twinge of sympathy for his rival. They both knew that if they accepted the plan and it went wrong it would be *their* plan and they would carry the can. Chebrikov's man hadn't even given his name. The others had stayed silent, sometimes scribbling on their pads when he or Sostov were pointing out the snags.

Chebrikov's man was looking at Sostov, his chin thrust out aggressively.

"I don't understand your reasoning, comrade. Have you any indication that they have realised that Bykov was doubleturned?"

"There's no way we could have any indication either way."

"I read a report that acting on your instructions Bykov phoned the girl. She made no mention of the radio having been discovered. She accepted his explanation about having to extend his time because he had to go to Berlin. She exchanged a lot of love chat with him. Don't those things amount to some verification?"

"The British could be using the girl to lure him back."

"She didn't contact him, he contacted her."

"She didn't know how to contact him."

"If they were working her, they would have found some way round that." The man turned to Ulianov. "What do you think, Comrade Colonel? Are you scared of the risks too?"

Ulianov shrugged his big shoulders. "It's not a question of being scared, my friend, it's a question of assessing the risk and what we get if we succeed."

"You're absolutely right, Comrade. So what is your assessment of risk and reward?"

"If we send Bykov back, there are three possible scenarios. The best is that they don't suspect him. He told the girl *and* his controller that he was coming back. And he comes back. The second is that they pick him up the moment he lands and that's the end of the story. Or it could be that they know everything but say nothing. They go on with him as if nothing has happened and the information we get back has been fed to him by them, without him knowing it."

Chebrikov's man nodded. "But if it's scenario number one then we can keep our man in London in place."

Sostov said quietly, "Is he all that valuable? We are taking a lot of risks and hazarding our own citizens just to protect that man."

Chebrikov's man looked with open disdain at Sostov and then turned to Ulianov.

"The man in London is vital." He paused significantly. "And that comes right from the top." And he jabbed a finger at the ceiling to emphasise the point. He paused again and looked at Ulianov and then Sostov. "You understand, both of you?"

Sostov nodded but Ulianov said, "How long before he goes back?"

"How long will you need to brief him on Yakunin?"

"Not more than a week."

"Make it three days. And two days preparing his cover story. Any problems and you contact me in the Directorate office. Ask for Yevgeny." He took a deep breath as he stood up to leave, pausing to look at Ulianov.

"You are in charge, Ulianov."

• • •

Bykov was scared and he made no effort to hide his fear. But a lot of promises and a lot of vodka had at least got him into a state where he could absorb the briefing on Yakunin. There were forged documents to read and photostats of false internal memos and reports. All created to destroy any credibility Yakunin might have established with the Brits. The briefing was thorough.

Moscow had said that they had had the house in Barnes under surveillance and there was no indication that the girl was not carrying on quite normally with her job at the garden centre where she worked as a secretary. There had been few visitors and all had been checked and found to be old school friends. She seemed to have settled down to her solo existence and two men were redecorating the ground floor of the house. Bykov gradually overcame his fear as he was swept along in the routine of the operation. The man who called himself Yevgeny had come to the airport himself and had shaken his hand when they called the flight to Paris.

The next day the photographs were taken of him in Paris at several obvious tourist places. The following day he flew to Heathrow. He went through the trade-craft procedures they had taught him to throw off any watchers but he had seen no sign of anyone following him. He booked into a small hotel in Bayswater.

CHAPTER FOURTEEN

Martin Crowther had been Deputy DG of MI6 for over ten years. Passed over twice for promotion when his superiors had retired, he showed no resentment, neither did he feel any. He loved his life with SIS's strange mixture of intellectuals, technicians, and contrivers, and in turn they had an affection for the rather rotund man in Harris Tweed suits, brown brogues, and club ties. And inevitably SIS cashed in on this affection. Nobody could better pass on the tidings of a passed promotion or sideways shift without causing resentment than Martin Crowther. He had been a victim too and they knew it. A very senior victim who accepted his fate and who obviously took it for granted that as adult and sophisticated men they would accept their disappointments with equal fortitude.

In fact, Martin Crowther would have hated the responsibilities that went with the top job. He loved his role as smoother of ruffled feathers. The old hand who could recommend a solution to some current problem that had been tried and proved years before in similar circumstances. The wisdom was imparted with anecdotal humour laced with self-deprecating laughter at what fools they'd all been in the old days not to have grasped some solution more speedily. Many called him "Uncle" Martin without realising that the avuncular attitude, although entirely genuine, disguised a wealth of experience in dealing with a wide variety of people and problems. What was more, he had a genuine admiration for his colleagues at all levels in SIS, from the penetrating academic minds to the human ferrets whose street-sharpness was the backbone of many top-secret operations.

Nobody was really certain about what Martin Crowther's role had been before he became the DG's deputy but there seemed to be no area of SIS's wide remit that he was not familiar with. His function as a sort of internal roving ambassador was far from putting out a valued retainer to grass, and his talents had been used as a two-way safety valve. Standing between authority and recalcitrant talents on one hand, and providing advice in a relaxed and unofficial manner to men in charge of operations that were in danger of coming apart on the other. He had never been trained for those functions nor was it even suggested that this was his official mission. He was just a man who had been around a long time and knew the funny ways of all the levels of SIS.

It was to Martin Crowther that Latham handed over his notes and the potential problem of Hoggart's divorce and the threat of revelations in court. As it happened, Crowther knew Hoggart quite well, and had actually sat on the board that had first considered him for a career in SIS. After reading the notes he realised that there wasn't enough material to pass even an opinion and he wasn't in the habit of rushing in like a bull in a china shop. He'd have the little solicitor chap, Foxy, checked out before doing more than letting it all swill around his mind like the tea-leaves in a teapot.

* * *

She had gone back to calling herself Jacqui Lovegrove and she had a large room in an old house not far from Victoria Station. For several weeks she had gone out only to buy a few things to eat, and cigarettes. Night after night she had cried herself to sleep and in the daytime she wrote countless letters to Eddie Hoggart. None of them had been posted. She knew there was no point in trying to explain things to him. She had done what she had done and that was all that mattered to him.

She had never told him how lonely she felt when he just disappeared for days on end. She had felt that it wasn't right to complain about a man's job. But she still wondered why he didn't ever explain. And when he came back that was all that had mattered. She was too happy to complain. But what she had done was so stupid. No straight man would have put up with that. She must have been mad to even think of it. But it was the only way she knew to make the time go by quicker when he was away. It didn't take more than a couple of hours to make the flat tidy and go shopping and to the launderette. And it was in the launderette that she'd met that bloody Jake again. He'd said she'd looked "down" and had made her laugh with his silly jokes and take-offs of the people she knew from the club.

Gradually it worked out that they had met twice a week at the launderette. Just chatting and larking about. Then one week she'd gone with him to have coffee at an Italian café, and it was there she'd met Gardner again. It had seemed an accidental meeting but she knew later that it wasn't. Gardner didn't come there every time but his visits gradually became more frequent. Then that fatal time when Eddie had been away for a whole week. With no phone calls and the loneliness had turned to fear. Fear that he may have been hurt or even killed. She wouldn't leave the flat in case he phoned and Jake had taken her wash to the launderette and brought it back. He'd said she looked as if she'd been crying and that made her cry again. He'd put his arms round her as if to comfort her. But it had ended on the bed. It had meant no more to her than the usual way that things ended when a man had been kind or had done her a favour. It hadn't been more than three or four times and once with Harry Gardner at his place in Mayfair. She had £7,000 left in her bank account and she would have gladly given all of it to turn back the clock. She had never seen Jake or Gardner after he'd said she had to leave his place and she bore neither of them any grudge. She had obviously caused trouble for Gardner and she had only let Jake do what any club girl would do for a friendly barman.

After five weeks on her own she knew that staying in her room was making things worse. She got a job in a nearby store on the cosmetics counter and the company of other girls and customers kept her mind occupied. Several men had tried to date her but she had refused. She'd had enough of men.

• • •

Harry Gardner sat with a half-empty bottle of Bell's whisky and a full glass on the low coffee table in front of his armchair as he read slowly through the notes from Foxy's man who had been tailing Hoggart. He hadn't bothered to read them before but now that he'd absorbed them he wondered if perhaps Foxy was right. There was nothing that they could prove but still there was mud to be thrown around. Maybe he should hold his plan for a few days. Anyway he'd sleep on it.

• • •

As Gardner swung his car between the big double doors an old man in a cap pointed towards a wooden shack. But Gardner drove on past the shack and nosed the car between two huge piles of rusting car bodies. He got out of the car and made his way through heaps of rusty gearboxes and the skeletons of cannibalised engines to where a man was standing at the door of the shack.

He was a huge man in an oil-stained white cotton shirt and torn denim trousers tucked into cowboy boots with poker-work designs up the sides. He stood with his big arms folded across his chest and made no move to acknowledge Gardner's presence.

"Hello, Rocky," Gardner said.

"What d'you want this time?"

"Let's go inside I want to talk to you."

"What about?"

"Don't play silly buggers, mate. I told you. I wanna talk to you."

"So talk here."

"What's biting *you* today? I want to talk inside. Stop sodding about."

Slowly and reluctantly the man turned and walked into the shack. He pointed to a wooden bench but when Gardner saw its condition he just stood, hands in his coat pockets, looking at the man.

Rocky Miller was a man of many parts, none of them very impressive. At one time he had been a moderately successful all-in wrestler and now he called himself a promoter and manager. The well-rehearsed bouts at his promotions were designed to appeal to audiences who enjoyed the crudest display of brute force and violence. At one time Gardner had been his backer but Miller's private life had been more than he could take. He didn't object to what he did so much as his overt indifference to the consequences. Foxy had defended him on a dozen or more charges ranging from GBH to rape. Only massive pay-offs and favours repaid had kept Miller out of jail. The scrapyard provided a steady income and the extra came from stolen vehicles and, from time to time, as a minder for leaders of gangs involved in armed robberies. He had always blamed Gardner for withdrawing support from his wrestling enterprises.

"I've got a job for you, Rocky, if you're interested."

"How much?"

"It'll add up to about five hundred nicker."

"What is it?"

Gardner walked slowly over to the cracked window that looked over the scrapyard. You had to make it look like a contest to interest Rocky. He turned and smiled.

"I'm gonna put my money on you, Rocky. It won't be a walkover but I'm betting on you winning." He saw the interest in the man's blue eyes. Gardner looked down and slowly pushed a rusty bolt aside with his well-polished shoe before he looked up again. "It's just one chap. You and him. But he's good. And he's well trained."

"Who is he?"

"Are you interested?"

"Course I am."

"You still got that blue suit I gave you?"

"Yeah."

"Meet me at the club tonight. Eight o'clock. I'll tell you what it's all about." He smiled. "There'll be some entertainment after we've done a deal . . . OK?"

Miller nodded and looked pleased. "The young one . . . eh . . . the blonde."

"I'll see what I can do."

• • •

Rocky Miller didn't drink anything alcoholic. Not, he maintained, for reasons of health or propriety but solely because he had never liked the taste of either beer or spirits. Gardner had talked to him for an hour, carefully and slowly going over all the necessary details. Description, name and places. When he had gone over it all several times he had made Miller repeat all the salient facts again and again.

"You gotta remember, Rocky, this ain't no amateur you're dealing with. He's a professional. Knows all the moves. No need to do a lotta damage. It's just to let him know he'll get no place until he does a deal." He paused. "You understand all that, don't you, pal?"

Miller nodded. "Yeah. When's the first installment?"

Gardner handed him an envelope. "Used tenners. Don't undo it here."

"And the girl?"

"You go up the stairs by the bar and at the top of it says 'Gents.' Turn right and it's the door at the end of the passage. She's waiting for you."

"How long do I get?"

"As long as you like, but no rough stuff. Her name's Penny."

Miller grinned. "You finished now, guv'nor?"

"Yeah. Keep me in the picture. Phone me. But don't say anything, just yes or no that you've done it and I'll send you the next installment."

• • •

The envelope had contained no covering letter, just a business card stapled to the first page. The business card of Fox and Partners, Solicitors and Notary Public. And it was delivered by hand by a cyclist from one of the Fleet Street messenger services.

Latham was in two minds whether to read it or just pass the stuff straight over to "Uncle" Martin. But he'd want some sort of legal comment sooner or later.

The top page was headed, "Hoggart v Hoggart—Draft petition (not yet filed)." On the last page it listed supporting documents. A notarised statement from a Jack Gordon Nelson employed as a barman. It gave details of an alleged violent assault by the defendant. There followed several extracts from newspaper articles and books covering the training of soldiers and others in what was described as "Special Forces." Certain passages emphasising toughness and methods of dealing with opposition had been side-lined. There was also a pseudo-psychological assessment of the characteristics of soldiers carrying out covert operations in Northern Ireland.

The petition itself was four pages outlining the petitioner's unhappy married life. Unexplained absences of the defendant without explanation. Domineering attitude. Fear of violence. No social life. Confined to a small flat, a virtual prisoner. Lack of affection. Vain attempts by the petitioner to improve the relationship.

The petition went on to claim that the training and work of the defendant was the root cause of the defendant's intolerable behaviour.

There was a page of notes which recorded that an application would be made to the courts for the defendant's employers— MI6—to provide details of his work during the term of the marriage and his current work status and pay.

He sighed and slid the papers back in the envelope. It was a blatant fishing expedition. The court wouldn't like it. But they might let it go through because of the woman's complete lack of knowledge of her husband's work when she married him and subsequently. It was a long shot but they could claim that if she had known what his work was she wouldn't have married him in the first place. Marriage by deception. He wondered how Hoggart would react when this little lot came through the post. Anyway he'd make brief notes for "Uncle" Martin and pass the baby to him.

*   *   *

It was two days before Martin Crowther got the papers and Latham's notes. He read everything several times and then locked it all in his safe. He realised something that wouldn't have occurred to Latham, who saw things solely from a legal point of view. These people didn't have to get to court before their pressure started working. A lead to a newspaper would be enough. It was just to show them the shape and colour of the threat, not an actual intention.

• • •

When Hoggart got into his car at the safe-house he switched on the ignition and the engine turned but didn't fire. He tried it several times before he gave up and asked one of the guards to check the car for him and if necessary call a garage to get it fixed.

Yakunin was already asleep when he looked in and Hoggart walked back to his room and checked his notes on the day's work with the Russian. He had checked the files on the Walker case that the FBI had passed to SIS. Either they had intentionally omitted a lot of information or the information he had got from Yakunin showed that they had missed a lot of the earlier part of Yakunin's operation. Renshaw could decide whether to pass them the additional information.

It was an hour before the guard knocked on the door and came in.

"Have they fixed the car?"

"I checked it over myself." He paused. "It was this." And the guard held out a neatly cut half of a large potato, the smooth wet surface of the cut stained with what looked like soot. He looked up at the guard.

"On the exhaust?"

The man nodded. It was an old device from way back in SOE days in the war. You clamped a potato or a clump of earth into an exhaust pipe and the engine couldn't breathe. It not only stopped a quick getaway but it meant a long delay going over all the more usual causes of engine failure before the real cause was discovered.

Hoggart looked at the guard.

"Any footprints? Any indications?"

"No, sir. Do you want me to contact Forensic?"

Hoggart shook his head slowly. "No. It's not worth it." He

took a deep breath. "You'd better ask for the guard detail to be doubled up."

"I was called away to the phone. A wrong number. But I was not patrolling outside for about seven minutes. Whoever did it must have had an accomplice for the phone call. It was from a call-box. I heard the tones and the coin go in."

"Log the incident but leave it at that."

"Can I say that was your orders, Mr. Hoggart?"

"Yes. Of course."

It was after midnight when Hoggart got back to his place in Pimlico. As he undressed slowly he wondered what the motive had been. Whoever was responsible, he knew by instinct that it was nothing to do with his work.

• • •

Martin Crowther shook out his wet umbrella on the steps of his club, grateful that Sir Graham had not insisted on meeting at the Reform. He found the Reform a bit solemn for his taste. He preferred the more convivial company of creative people: musicians, writers, and journalists.

Sir Graham was already sitting there in the main lounge reading the evening paper. He looked up when Crowther stood in front of him and then patted the seat beside him.

"I took the liberty of ordering myself a whisky, Martin." He smiled. "The other one's for you."

Crowther lifted his glass in salutation and sipped modestly before putting it down.

"I've got a problem, DG. It's nothing to do with SIS really, and yet it is. I felt I'd better have a word with you before I dealt with it."

"Sounds ominous."

Crowther smiled. "Not really. It's about one of our chaps involved in a divorce case that's getting a bit messy from our point of view."

"Tell me."

Crowther outlined the facts, carefully and without expressing an opinion apart from Latham's brief legal comments.

For long moments Sir Graham sat looking through the big open doors to the bar and then he said quietly, "I didn't hear what you were saying. Too much noise in the bar. Whatever it was, settle it yourself."

"But . . ."

"No buts, Martin. Just teach the cheeky bastards a lesson."

"Right, sir. Let's go upstairs and have a bite."

"Lead the way, my friend. Isn't that V. S. Pritchett over there? Don't know how he does it. Looks younger every time I see him."

Sir Graham nodded to the author as they walked by. "Nice to see you, Victor."

The author obviously had no idea who was addressing him but he smiled back. "Thank you very much."

• • •

Martin Crowther had one of the larger flats in Dolphin Square and it was there he talked the next day with the Director of Section R, responsible for clandestine operations. They had talked for four hours without reaching a decision. And finally Crowther had said, "Would it help if I had a word with the DPP or the Solicitor General?"

"For Christ's sake, no, Martin. Can you imagine what the Director of Public Prosecutions would say if you told him we were contemplating interfering in a civil divorce case?"

"But this is a man involved in highly sensitive intelligence matters whose attitude is likely to cause us severe embarrassment or even endanger his present operation."

Basil Moody was exasperated, and showed it. "It doesn't matter a damn, Martin, what the embarrassment or security problem is so far as the DPP's concerned. All he could do was warn you that you could end up in the dock yourselves. It's just not on." He paused. "If we do anything we just have to make our minds up and get on with it."

Crowther shrugged. "So who do we go for? The girl or this man Gardner?"

"Well get this straight first, Martin. There are a lot of things that my section can do that are within the law. But to consult the Attorney General or the Solicitor General or even those things would be madness."

"I'm concerned that both the girl and Gardner are merely citizens. They aren't part of our normal format."

"So why are you talking to me? You're talking to me because some seedy solicitor is blackmailing you to protect one of his clients who just happens to be a top league villain who has managed to escape the law. So far. He isn't merely a citizen. He wants to play games and he don't know the rules, old friend. If you want me to straighten him out it's legit as far as I'm concerned."

"Tell me what you've got in mind."

Moody grinned and shook his head. "You know better than that, my friend. You just press the button and my remit takes over."

"I don't seem to have much choice, Basil. You'd better go ahead."

"OK. Can I have copies of everything that you've got?"

"Of course."

• • •

Foxy was on the phone when his secretary came into his office and waited for him to finish his call. But he put his hand over the phone and said, "What is it, Miss Purvis?"

"There's a gentleman to see you, Mr. Fox."

"I don't remember any appointments this morning. Who is he?"

"He won't say."

"Tell him to go away, or make a proper appointment."

"I think you should see him, Mr. Fox."

"Why?"

She shrugged. "He looks kind of official. He said he'd wait however long it takes."

Foxy looked puzzled. "Better wheel him in then."

He had a last few words on the phone before Miss Purvis brought in his visitor. And Foxy knew at once that the visitor spelled trouble. Not because of his appearance. He was a man in his early forties, a rather chubby schoolboy face and a self-confident smile as he sat down without being asked. But Foxy had met barristers like that. Looking like overgrown schoolboys, easy smilers and as crafty as you could ever wish to meet.

"I didn't get your name, sir."

"I didn't give it, Mr. Fox. But it's Harris."

"What can I do for you Mr. Harris?"

"A couple of things actually. I want to see all the documents you have on the premises of Gaylord Overseas Limited. And while I'm here I'd like to look at your own books covering the last eight years." The man beamed. "Inland Revenue, Mr. Fox. Here's my card."

Foxy took the card reluctantly, glancing at it only briefly before he placed it on his blotter.

"What's all this about, Mr. Harris?" Foxy said quietly.

"Well every now and again we stick a pin in the list and wherever it lands we do a special check covering eight or ten years. Your clients Gaylord Overseas came up this time. So here we are."

"We."

"Yes. My team are having a coffee over the road at the moment. They'll be over here in a few minutes. Meanwhile I have to warn you that any attempt to conceal information is a very serious offense."

"Why *my* books? I put my returns in every year."

"They're usually a bit late, Mr. Fox." He smiled. "We thought we might as well give you a whirl at the same time."

"I'll have to get permission from my clients before I can let you go ahead."

Harris shook his head. "This is the registered office of Gaylord and you're down as the company secretary. We don't need any permission." He paused. "But you can accompany my two chaps who do the search at your home. Two others will be going to do the search simultaneously at your colleague's house."

"My colleague?"

"Yes. Mr. Gardner, isn't it? Hertford Street, Mayfair?"

"You mean you're going to search Harry Gardner's place?" Foxy looked aghast.

"Yes. It's his company that's the main subject of the check."

"Does he know?"

"I'll be going round there myself when my chaps are settled in here."

Foxy shook his head slowly. "I can't believe it."

"It does often seem to come as a shock to the people concerned."

"How long will all this take?"

"It looks like several weeks. Your clients seem to have a whole network of subsidiaries and associates."

"And what about my work? This is only a small place."

"You just carry on, Mr. Fox. Once we've got what we need, we can use your outer office."

• • •

"Well you got your bloody answer, didn't you, Foxy?" Gardner was beside himself with anger as he waited for Foxy's reply.

"It could be just a coincidence, Harry."

"Coincidence my arse. One of us—yes, but both at the same time—they're telling you to get stuffed. And me too."

"So what do we do?"

"You do nothing and pray that the bastards don't find anything."

"I've been very careful, Harry. Most of it's in the Cayman Islands set-up."

"Wanna bet?"

"On what?"

"On how much they screw me for." He paused, sucking his big yellow teeth. "I reckon mine'll be a hundred grand and they'll do you for fifteen."

"On what grounds?"

"Don't be so bloody naive, Foxy. They'll do us because they want to. That's what this thing's all about. It's their answer to your little games with them. They're teaching you a lesson, Foxy. And I'm bloody payin' for it."

"What d'you want me to do? I could tell them she's changed her mind and there won't be no trouble."

"I'll still be in trouble," and Gardner tapped his chest to emphasise his point and his frustration. "I'm back to square one with Hoggart out to ruin me."

"So what do you want me to do?"

"Give 'em another dose, up the stakes. Show 'em we ain't scared."

Foxy nodded his agreement without any idea of how he could raise the stakes.

• • •

There had been a note in her pay-packet on the Friday night giving her a week's notice and she had gone straight to the store manager's office a few minutes before closing time. She had asked for an explanation and had been shown into the manager's office.

He sat at his desk looking at her and then pointed to a chair. When she was seated he said, "I'm sorry, Jacqui, but it's group policy."

"What is? I don't understand."

"Your dismissal."

"I still don't understand. What have I done?"

The manager sighed. "I think you know, my dear."

"So tell me and give me a chance to put it right."

"You've got a police record. And you didn't mention it in your application form. There's a question about it. You just crossed it through."

"How did it come up?"

"I've no idea. Maybe head office did some checking."

"But all that was years ago."

"Maybe they would have ignored those old offences but you gave a false declaration on the form. It says on it quite plainly that if any negative information is concealed it means instant dismissal. At least they've given you a week to look around." He stood up. "Try one of the smaller places that doesn't have formalities."

As she walked home she wondered who had tipped them off. She was sure it wasn't just a check by the head office. They'd had weeks to do that. She probably could get a job, but it wouldn't be as well paid and it wouldn't be easy without a reference. She'd thought at first it might be Harry Gardner but it couldn't be him, he'd given her the reference for the store. But who else could it be? She had no enemies. She had got on well with all the girls at the store.

By the time she had made herself a cup of tea the thought that she had tried to dismiss was the only one left. But she found it hard to believe that Eddie would do something like this. He wasn't that kind of man.

• • •

Eventually she plucked up the courage to phone Harry Gardner. He seemed very cold at first but when she told him what had happened he told her to meet him in the café at Victoria Station, which was within walking distance of her room.

He was waiting for her at one of the tables, drinking a coffee with a hot chocolate already waiting for her. He told her what had happened with Foxy and him. When she didn't seem to grasp the implications he spelt it out.

"It's your chap Hoggart. That's what it's all about."

"Eddie? But what's Eddie got to do with tax and VAT?"

"He's put 'em up to it just to do me down. If he can't do it one way he's going to do it another."

"But Eddie wouldn't harm me that way. He may not care about me anymore but he wouldn't do a thing like that to me."

"I wouldn't count on that, Jacqui. They're not doing all this harassment without him knowing."

• • •

Two nights later she had gone to their old place. Walking on the other side of the street. It was dusk but there was already a light on in the flat. She walked to the end of the street, smoked a cigarette, and then walked back. The outer door was open and she walked up the stairs still trying to work out what to say to him.

At their door she stopped and pressed the bell. She heard it ringing inside but nobody came to the door. She waited for a few moments and then rang again. But there was still no response. She had kept her key to the flat but was reluctant to use it. Almost without thinking she turned the knob on the door. The door swung open and she saw that the lock had been forced open. Splinters of wood still gaping from around the lock itself. And what she saw made her walk inside.

The whole place was a shambles. Everything smashed. Furniture, crockery in pieces, carpets covered in some sort of mess. For a moment she thought that maybe Eddie had done it in a fit of anger when he threw Jake out. But then she saw the message scrawled in lipstick on the mirror. It said, WHO LOVES YA EDDIE BABY.

CHAPTER FIFTEEN

Hoggart and Yakunin were munching sandwiches in the sun as they talked.

"When you were running Walker for the KGB did you understand all the stuff about submarines that he passed to you?"

"As soon as it was obvious that John Walker was going to be valuable I was brought back to Moscow. Then sent down to the Naval Academy at Frunze for a crash course on submarine communication and missile guidance systems. And a week on detection systems."

"And that was enough?"

"Once I was actually working him. Moscow sent me instructions on what they wanted. I didn't need to understand the technicalities."

"How did you keep contact with him?"

"Mainly dead-drops. Sometimes we met, but not often in the USA."

"Where did you meet?"

"Mexico twice, Vienna twice, and a few times in Washington."

"Where were the dead-drops?"

"Usually wherever Walker was stationed. US Navy towns. Norfolk, Virginia, for the months before the FBI picked him up."

"What kind of drops did you use?"

"Mainly in rural areas. Trees, telegraph poles, trash bins where he could leave messages in 7-Up cans. For the last series of drops the sites were in Washington, DC, and Montgomery County, Maryland."

"Who worked out the drops?"

"I did."

"How elaborate were they?"

"I took weeks working them out. Photographs of key routes and the drop itself. Anti-surveillance checks. Route maps. Procedures. Timing for every section of the route. Traffic conditions. Cover story. Vehicle changes. Everything to make it safe."

"And you reckon they'd never have got him if he hadn't been informed on by his wife?"

"He'd been active with me for years." Yakunin shrugged. "But he was a fool in his private life. Young girls on the side and all that. I warned him time and time again but he was too arrogant to take any notice."

"How did you know they'd got him?"

"I was driving a hired car and I saw an unmarked car pass me three times in half an hour on the route Walker was supposed to follow. Then I saw a helicopter flying low over the area and I knew it was all over."

"What did you do?"

"I went back to a room I rented in Washington, packed my things, and went to San Francisco. I got rid of my radio and codes and documents on the way. I rented a room there and sent a report back to Moscow through the consulate in San Francisco."

"What made you decide to come over to us?"

"I hung around there for two months without any contact

from Moscow. And finally a meeting was arranged with the head of illegals in New York. Nothing but abuse and insults that the operation had folded. Not a word of thanks for all those years of hard and successful work. They questioned all my living expenses. Told me it wouldn't have happened if I had followed the orders for illegals in US of A. Rules written by desk men. Never been to the USA. Never been active field agents."

"Who did they say the criticisms came from?"

"They said from a senior man named Ulianov but I don't believe them. He was stupid, yes. But not that stupid."

"Can you remember what kind of car the FBI were using when you saw them pass you three times that day?"

Yakunin looked at Hoggart. "You disappoint me, my friend. You're checking on me. Checking on something you know already."

"I'm checking on you, yes. But not on something I know the answer to."

"Maybe I haven't got a good memory. Maybe I don't recognise the different models of American cars. What then?"

Hoggart shrugged and smiled. "OK. Let's forget it."

Yakunin smiled back. "The FBI vehicle was a Chevy Cherokee."

"Is there anything you want, Igor?"

"I'd like a few more books and maybe newspapers. Russian ones." He laughed. "I would never have believed I'd miss reading *Pravda*. But I do. Not because of what it says. Just homesickness." He laughed again. "Homesickness for God knows what. I'd hate to go back."

"Why?"

"Oh, all the intrigue, the back-stabbing. The fighting for position. The jealousies, the hatreds. The little cliques of influence. The wire-pullers. The corruption."

Hoggart smiled. "I'd bet there's people in Langley who think the same."

"But not in London?" Yakunin was smiling.

"Maybe I'm not sophisticated enough or important enough to have noticed it."

Yakunin smiled. "Her Majesty's loyal servant."

"I'll see what reading matter I can get you."

• • •

At Century House Hoggart had taken a bundle of *Pravdas* and current Soviet novels from the library and had checked with Malins who was the current SIS/FBI liaison officer and asked him to check on the car. Malins wasn't hopeful. The FBI had got little kudos for their capture of Walker and his network. But a lot of criticism for not having uncovered him years before. The British security services were used to that sort of treatment. No praise for making an arrest, just a tirade of criticism from the media for not doing it earlier.

The next day there was a reply from the FBI on his desk. The principal vehicle used in the final arrest of Walker was a Chevrolet Cherokee.

The other note on his desk was in a sealed envelope addressed to him. It was sent to him at his office address by his solicitor because he had not been contactable by phone at his home address and the letter he enclosed was marked "Urgent."

The envelope addressed to him was typewritten but the word "Urgent" was obviously an afterthought and written by hand. It was addressed to him care of his solicitor and marked PLEASE FORWARD. The postmark was Victoria.

He opened it and read it. Screwed it up angrily and threw it in the waste-paper basket. Ten minutes later he retrieved it, flattened it out and read it again.

Dear Eddie,
   I don't know if it is OK to write to you because of the divorce business but here goes.

Have you bin to our old place recently. I was there last week hoping to speak to you. It is all smashed up and bin broken into. It was not me you can be sure.

I lost my job because somebody tole them about the fines I got way back. Since then I get promises of jobs but never hear no more. So I think somebody is doing it deliberate. I am really sorry about what happened. I was a fool. But if you don't give me a chance to work I will be in a bad way.

Hoping this finds you OK.

Your loving

Jacqui.

P.S. They even tore up the new curtains I made.

For long moments Hoggart sat there thinking about the letter. Why did she seem to connect the damage to the room to her not getting jobs? Break-ins were part of normal life in central London. Why was it significant in some way to her? And maybe she didn't have the necessary qualifications or experience for the jobs she applied for. It looked as if she had not taken the easy way out and gone back to her old life at the clubs. And she obviously wasn't living with Gardner. But what on earth made her think he was stopping her from getting work? He hadn't even known where she lived until he got this letter.

He folded up the crumpled letter as well as he could and slid it into his jacket pocket and twenty minutes later he was at their old flat. The door was off its hinges leaning against the wall on the first-floor landing. There had obviously been further visitors. The place had been stripped and the remaining fixtures like the bath and wash-bowl had been smashed in pieces. What hadn't been stolen had been vandalised. But for some reason the mirror had been left and he stood looking at the message. Jacqui would have seen the message and would have realised as he did that it was not initially a break-in, but a warning. He didn't have any doubt who the warning came from. Gardner must be really scared to react so crudely.

He turned away from the shambles and walked down the stairs. The flat no longer had any significance for him. It was just two rooms he had once lived in. Gardner had probably thought that he still lived there. He'd have to contact the landlord and the supply companies, gas, electricity, and the phone. He ought to have done it before but he hadn't wanted to be reminded of the place. He looked at his watch and realised he had only an hour before he had to attend the bi-monthly meeting of the group.

• • •

Hoggart had passed a photograph of Yakunin to Fletcher and a week later they had met in their shared office at Century House.

"Have you got a couple of minutes, Eddie?"

"Yes, of course."

"I showed the photograph of your guy to Belinsky."

"Did he recognise him?"

"Yes. As soon as he saw him. I hadn't told him who it was but he said it right away, Igor Yakunin."

"I didn't have much doubt about his identity. Did he say anything else?"

"Yes. It's a bit disturbing."

"Tell me."

"He said that Yakunin was a fantasist—imagined himself as a kind of James Bond figure."

"What was his job?"

"Apparently way back he was in their scientific section. Worked on miniature radios and surveillance equipment. But about five years ago he had some kind of breakdown and was in hospital for about a year. A psychiatric hospital."

"What was wrong with him?"

"A kind of schizophrenia."

"Go on."

"He was discharged and worked in the same section on equipment used in clandestine operations. A couple of years ago their guy running illegals in New York wanted a specialist technician for servicing and modifying equipment and your boy Yakunin was sent over there. Had a German passport and a cover as a German technical journalist.

"For the last six months he worked on the Walker case as a technician and according to Belinsky he made a cock-up of the whole operation. Walker was arrested by the FBI.

"Yakunin was ordered back to Moscow and obviously realised he was in trouble and did a bunk. They think he defected but they're not sure. If he did they think he'd have gone over to the Americans rather than us because he's never been in the UK." He paused. "In fact they were just going to retire him on the grounds that he was mentally unstable." He shrugged. "I'm sorry to be bringing bad news."

"Do you think he's telling the truth?"

"I think so. He didn't take it very seriously. More amused than critical. But I think with me showing him the photograph he's rumbled that we've got Yakunin."

"You didn't tell him that we'd got him?"

"No. Not a word. I implied that we were doing a random check on him himself using a picture from our archives. He didn't seem all that interested either way."

"What stage are you at with Belinsky?"

"Well, Renshaw and the others have accepted his identity. And I'm spending most of my time on building up information on the whole staff at his Directorate. Down to cypher clerks, secretaries, telephone operators and typists. He's a bit vague in places and I think there are areas where he's holding back. Renshaw thinks he's probably holding out so that he can drive a better final deal when we've finally finished de-briefing him. What we've been able to check on fits OK, but previously we'd got very little on the internal structure of any Directorate. It looks useful. How about your chap?"

"I don't know, after what you've told me."

"Does what Belinsky said fit at all?"

Hoggart shrugged. "It's hard to say. There are markers both ways. The story he gives has the same background as Belinsky gives but different interpretations. It'll mean starting all over again. Checking his story from a different angle. But I've got a good relationship with him now and that's taken a long time to establish. I don't want to spoil it."

"Does it matter all that much?"

"Well I've got the hints of something special he's going to lay on the line when he's ready."

"About what?"

"A KGB plant in high places in SIS."

Fletcher smiled. "At least Belinsky hasn't tried that one on me."

"Well Yakunin may be wrong, but I'm convinced that he thinks he knows something big. Big enough to be scared to tell me until I've passed some test of his."

"What are you doing tonight?"

"I was going back to the safe-house."

"Rachel is playing in a quartet at Smith Square tonight. How about you and Jacqui come with me? I've got spare tickets already."

Fletcher wondered what he had said that so changed Hoggart's face and demeanour and then Hoggart said stiffly, "We've split up."

"Oh, my God. I'm sorry. I had no idea. Is there anything we could do to help you, either of you?"

Hoggart shook his head. "No. It's over and done with."

"I know you're not a man for friends and all that, but you'd better know that I'm your friend. Any time. Any place. You just whistle and I'll be there."

Hoggart picked up his brief-case and hurried from the room. Near to tears and angry for being so.

• • •

The dark blue Saab seemed to come out of nowhere and the first Hoggart knew was the clash of metal against metal as it ground the length of his car. He saw the driver of the Saab wrench at his wheel to send him onto the narrow pavement and crashing into the concrete post of the bus-stop. He was aware of sparks flying as the Saab ground and clattered its way along the crumpled body of his car before it sped off up the hill and away from the village.

He had had to wait for the police and fire brigade to cut him free, and the police, after taking a breathalyser test, had insisted on taking him to the Kent and Sussex hospital in Tunbridge Wells.

The police had phoned their HQ at Cranbrook who had phoned SIS transport and Hoggart had been taken into casualty where they had treated his wrist and X-rayed his legs, arms, and ribs. The jagged cut on his jaw had been stitched with a local anesthetic when he stubbornly refused a general anesthetic. Two hours later an officer from SIS surveillance had taken over from the police who had been asked not to log the incident beyond a "damaged only" report.

Rawson from Century House sat on his bed in the private room in the hospital.

"You feel fit to talk, Mr. Hoggart?"

"Yeah," he sighed. "I'm OK."

"Tell me what happened."

Hoggart told him what he could recall and Rawson said, "Did you see the driver?"

"Just a vague impression. I may be wrong but I think he was wearing a balaclava."

"You turned right into the village off the A21?"

"Yes."

"There are some shops there on the corner. Did you notice any cars parked there?"

"There might have been but I didn't look, I wasn't aware of them. There was not much traffic around so late."

"Are you working on anything at the moment that could be connected to this in any way?"

"No."

"Where had you come from?"

"I'd had a snack in the cafeteria at Century House and I drove straight down."

"Where were you going?"

"Lamberhurst village."

"Have you got property there, Mr. Hoggart?"

"Kind of."

"What's that mean?"

"I'm based there at the moment."

"I'd better check it out before you go back. This looks deliberate to me."

"There's no need. I'm based at a safe-house there. It has its own security people."

"D'you think it was an accident?"

"No. I'm sure it was deliberate."

"Why are you so sure?"

Hoggart told him about the vandalising of his flat and the message on the mirror and the potato clamped on his car exhaust pipe.

"Sounds like some boyo to do with cars. Any idea who it could be?"

"I don't know who's actually doing it but I know who's giving him his orders to do it."

"Who?"

"A man named Gardner."

"Not a guy named Harry Gardner?"

"That's him. Big-time criminal but no convictions. How come you know him?"

He saw Rawson hesitate and then shrug. "As it happens we've been looking him over."

"What's that mean?"

Rawson smiled. "We've been keeping an eye on him for Malins's people. I think they're giving him the treatment."

"Why?"

"I've no idea. You'd better get some sleep."

"Can you drive me up to the crossroads in Lamberhurst?"

"You need a good night's sleep before you go anywhere."

"I'll phone for a taxi, if you can't do it."

"You're crazy, Mr. Hoggart, but if that's what you want, so be it."

Hoggart had walked slowly from the crossroads to the farmhouse. There had been a light shower and although Hoggart didn't notice it, there was a sweet smell of honeysuckle from the hedgerows.

• • •

They had sent a girl with the polygraph machine. The new ones were much smaller, in a fitted plastic case like a camera bag with velvet lined compartments for the bits and pieces. The girl was in her mid-twenties, pretty and friendly, trying to take the tension out of the situation. Not that Yakunin looked particularly tense. He never looked completely relaxed, but that was what you expected from a defector. He sat in what had become "his" chair watching the girl calibrate the recorder and plug in a small dot-matrix printer. The record no longer depended on the eye of the operator on a swing needle. There was a digital read-out to indicate current fluctuations and the whole session was recorded on the printer for subsequent detailed analysis.

When the girl had taped the four sensors into place she sat down and waited for Hoggart to indicate that he was ready.

When he nodded to her she started her routine questions to calibrate the instrument.

"Can I have your name please."

"Yakunin. Igor Yakunin."

"Are you quite comfortable, Mr. Yakunin?"

"Yes, thank you."

"What's your favourite food?"

"Piroshkis."

"Your favourite flower?"

Yakunin wasn't a flower man and it was several seconds before he said, "*Margaretka*."

When the girl looked at Hoggart he said, "Daisy."

She nodded. "I'm all set, sir, if you are."

"OK."

Hoggart turned to look at Yakunin.

"Have you ever done all this stuff before, Igor?"

Yakunin shrugged. "Many times. But in my own language."

"There's a built-in allowance in the programme for that."

Yakunin shrugged. "So go ahead—do I love my mother more than my father?"

Hoggart smiled. "How old are you, Igor?"

"Fifty-two in October."

"Why did you go to the British Embassy in Washington?"

"To defect."

"Why?"

"I was recalled to Moscow when Walker was arrested. I didn't want to go back."

"Why not?"

"They wanted somebody as a scapegoat. I knew it was going to be me."

"What did you expect to happen in Moscow?"

Yakunin shrugged. "An internal trial. Dismissal without pension. And maybe a couple of years in a labour camp."

"How did you get into the United States?"

"German passport via Toronto and Buffalo. Supporting documents from a German press agency, which was a front organisation for the KGB in Hanover."

"Where did you report?"

"To head of illegals in New York."

"And what was your task in the US to be?"

"To run the Walker network."

"Right from the start?"

"Yes."

"Did you have special training before you left Moscow?"

"I did a course on operating an agent. Dead-drops, brushes, codes, payment, surveillance avoidance. The usual stuff."

"And radio?"

"I knew that already."

"When were you last in hospital?"

"Just before I left Moscow."

"What were you in for?"

"For my teeth. They took out my Russian fillings and put in German ones."

"How long did that take?"

"About five days."

"If you have the choice what would you like to be? Ignore whether you are qualified or not. What would be your ideal way of earning a living?"

"Making films. Being a famous film director."

"What kind of films would you make?"

"Thrillers, spy stories, James Bond."

"If you told lies apart from having to in your work, what area would you tell lies about?"

"Sex."

"Why that?"

"Most people would lie about sex."

"What aspects of sex?"

"What they would really like to do—their fantasies."

"Did you lie to Walker?"

"Sometimes."

"What about?"

"How Moscow would treat him as a People's Hero if he ever had to escape from the States. That sort of thing."

"Did he speak Russian?"

"No. He tried to study Russian but he wasn't capable. He wasn't intelligent."

"But he was working on very high-tech equipment."

"Men like that have an aptitude for technical things. But they're not intelligent despite that. I don't know why. They build their own short-wave radios, scanners, and TV scanners, but they speak their own language worse than I do. If they go in the armed services they do fantastic work by instinct but in other ways they are just ignorant. Foul-mouthed, drunkards, womanisers."

"Did you have enemies in Moscow?"

Yakunin smiled. "Everybody has enemies in Moscow. Me and Gorbachev together both." He shrugged. "It's part of the system."

"Who would you say was your main enemy in your own directorate?"

"You can't talk about enemies like that. I was away for years. The guy who's not there is the one who takes the blame for everything. He doesn't even know it. They gave me a good time whenever I was back for a few weeks, but I wouldn't trust any of them. It's a jungle and you have to accept that to survive."

"No friends? Not even one?"

Yakunin grinned. "There's an old Arab proverb that the Russians sometimes use, "Fear your enemy once. Fear your friends a hundred times."

With a break for a snack at midday they had questioned and answered for over six hours before Hoggart felt that he had enough.

• • •

The next day Hoggart discussed the polygraph reading with the operator.

"It's a very steady reading, Mr. Hoggart." She smiled. "In fact the only real deviation was when I asked him about his favourite flower."

Hoggart laughed. "I think it was probably the only flower he could think of. And you'd classify all the rest of his responses as stable?"

"Yes. But we have had recent reports that the KGB are giving agents, especially illegals, special training in reacting to polygraph tests. He said he'd had lots before, but I think the training only began about a year ago, and from the notes you gave me he hasn't been there in that time."

"Can you let me have a written assessment routine in the next couple of days?"

"Yes, sir."

"Thanks for your help."

• • •

Hoggart contacted Fletcher who had come in from the safe-house where Belinsky was held. He had played him the tape of the questioning and they had spent the whole day discussing it. Playing back sections again and again. But there was no disputing the result of the polygraph test.

"You know, Eddie, it's like those sine waves you see on oscilloscopes. Two of them, out of phase with one another but exactly the same shape. Matching but never coinciding. Hospital treatment? Yes. But for his fillings and not for a breakdown. I'd say he *did* run the Walker operation himself. Maybe it was the guy in New York who had it in for him and misinformed Moscow to make sure that he didn't carry the can himself when Walker was caught.

"Even Belinsky's comment about Walter Mitty had an echo in him wanting to be a film director. Even his answers about where he'd tell lies was another marker. Sex fantasies. Could be other fantasies too."

"Did you give Belinsky a polygraph test?"

"No. Renshaw wouldn't sanction it."

"Why not?"

"Said it wasn't justified. He was talking and cooperating so why rock the boat. I think he was right."

"So why did you apply for a test?"

Fletcher shrugged. "I guess I thought it was all coming too easy." He smiled. "And I'm always suspicious of charmers. And Belinsky's a real charmer."

"Do you put daily progress reports in?"

"Yes. To Renshaw. Do you?"

"Yes."

"What made you ask?"

"When I applied for a test he just signed the forms without asking for any grounds."

Fletcher smiled. "You've been at this game much longer than I have. Maybe he just accepts that you know what you're up to and I've still got to work my passage."

• • •

Although Hoggart had kept on the lease of his old flat while he was married, he had never gone back there after they lived together. But now the marriage was over he had moved his few personal belongings back to the old place. He made no attempt to make it a comfortable home. It was just a place to sleep and change his clothes. A base and nothing more.

There was a letter for him that night at the flat. A two-line note from his solicitor saying that he wanted to contact him urgently. It was dated three days earlier and postmarked the same date. He phoned Cornish early the next morning.

"There's something I need to discuss with you, Mr. Hoggart, as soon as possible. When can we meet?"

"I'll come this morning if that's convenient."

"I'd rather meet at your place, if possible."

"I see. Well come round this morning."

"I'll come straight away. How do I get there?"

Hoggart gave him directions and hung up. Cornish had sounded cold and almost aggressive and he wondered why an obviously busy solicitor should want to meet away from his office. He tidied the place a little and ten minutes later he was letting Cornish into his flat.

Cornish looked around the room briefly as he sat down and opened his briefcase. With a folder in his hand he looked at Hoggart.

"Did you wonder why I asked to see you here rather than at my office?"

"Yes, I did."

"It's because I've got a problem, Mr. Hoggart. I'm not sure that I want to continue as your solicitor and I thought we ought to have a talk before I decide."

Hoggart nodded. "That's OK with me."

Cornish looked at him intently. "Does the name Rawson mean anything to you?"

Hoggart shook his head slowly. "No."

"What about Malins?"

"D'you mean Phil Malins? And yes, Rawson does mean something. I didn't connect it until you mentioned Malins."

"They work for the same government services that you work for?"

"Yes."

"Would it be fair to describe them as involved in what journalists call 'dirty tricks'?"

"Malins would prefer it described as clandestine operations."

"I'm sure he would."

"What have they got to do with my divorce case?"

"Are you telling me you don't know already?"

"Look, Mr. Cornish. I don't know what you're on about but quite frankly I don't like your attitude. What is all this, some kind of interrogation?"

"Did you know that your wife was in Charing Cross Hospital?

"No. What's wrong with her?"

"She took an overdose of drugs. An attempt at suicide."

"When was this?"

"Two days ago."

"Is she OK now?"

"More or less, but still in a very distressed state."

"How do you know all this?"

"I need to go back a couple of weeks. Your wife came to see me. Quite wrong of course. She gave a false name and I was very critical of her contacting me. But as you know she's not aware of the niceties of the law, and she poured out her story before I could stop her. But I warned her that not only would the court frown on her contacting me but it would also seriously criticise me for listening to her. And that she was doing great harm to her own case. "But . . ." Cornish shrugged, ". . . nothing I could say stopped her rather sad little story."

"I still don't understand what it's all about, Mr. Cornish."

"I'm relieved to hear that. Very relieved. Let me go on." He took a big diary from the folder and checked several pages before he looked back at Hoggart again. "When you originally came to me I tried to pour a little oil on the troubled waters. But it clearly wasn't going to work because the divorce wasn't really aimed at your wife but the man Gardner. You wanted him exposed in court, in public. Unwise and not to my liking but that's what you wanted.

"Since then the other side have used every legal device for stopping the case coming to court. I've done what I can to counter their moves but they are all legal so I haven't made much progress.

"What your wife told me is very disturbing and if I'm honest I have to say that I suspected that you were part of it. And quite frankly I'm not only shocked but deeply disturbed at what's been going on. Seemingly without your knowledge but nevertheless concerning you."

"Please get to the point, Mr. Cornish."

Cornish said coldly, "Your wife is being harassed by your colleagues in SIS."

"I don't believe it. Why on earth would they do that?"

"Believe it or not, it's a matter of fact. Their main target is Gardner but she's getting similar treatment. Much milder in her case but enough to bring her to attempted suicide." Cornish paused. "And if it's any consolation to you I understand that Gardner, tough as he may be, is at his wits' end on how to deal with the situation."

"I'm glad to hear it. How did you get all this information?"

"From your wife mainly. A little from others."

"Why did she come to you? Why not her own solicitor?"

"She came because of her concern for you."

"For me? How?"

"Would I be right in thinking that you have been harassed yourself in the past few weeks? An incident with a car? Your old premises vandalised? Yes?"

"Yes."

"That was done at Gardner's instigation in an attempt to frighten you off."

"How do you know that?"

"He told your wife."

"She's still knocking around with him then?"

"Not at all. He threw her out when the divorce started and she hasn't seen him since until a meeting with him last week. She got herself a job as an assistant in a chain store. She was sacked after a few weeks. Offers of other jobs were withdrawn days later. He told her that he was out to get you. It seems he hinted that he would even have you killed if necessary. He told her about the harassment he'd had over tax and so on. And told her that they were obviously doing the same to her. Stopping her from getting jobs and the like. A few days later she took the overdose because she thought that with her out of the picture everyone would be off the hook. She thought it was all her fault."

"Was it a serious attempt?"

"According to the doctor it looked determined enough. But a girl from the store where she had worked called on her and the door was open and she found her, and called for an ambulance."

"How did Gardner find out about Malins and Rawson?"

"He didn't. I found out myself. Made some enquiries."

"How did you find out about Jacqui?"

"They found a note addressed to me."

"Why to you?"

"I think she felt I was the only person who was concerned about her."

"I still can't really believe it."

"Does it sound possible?"

"Oh yes. It has all the hallmarks. They'll deny it, of course. That's always the official line."

"Even to you?"

"Yes. They'll see me as an outsider."

"Can you stop any further harassment?"

"Of Jacqui yes, but the more they harass Gardner the more I'd like it."

Cornish said, "I've given up hope of you ever taking my advice, but I strongly advise you to get this divorce over as quickly and simply as possible. It's getting out of hand and affecting too many people's lives, including mine."

"Do you want me to find another solicitor?"

"Not unless you want to. With what's gone on you wouldn't find it easy."

"You've got a strange idea of justice, Mr. Cornish. This man commits adultery with my wife. He tries harassing me. My wife sleeps with two other men just for the hell of it, but you talk like I was the guilty party."

"You're my client, Hoggart; all I've tried to do is see that you keep your nose clean as far as the court is concerned." He stood up, gathering up his papers and putting them in his case, then he said, "I apologise if I seemed biased. I'm not. But I was very moved by your wife's dilemma. She's stupid in many ways, but nobody except you has given her much of a break in a pretty grim life. And although people say that suicide is the coward's way out I don't agree. I think it takes a lot of courage or a lot of love. Once Gardner had told her that he was ready to have you killed she realised that not only did she have no idea what had been going on behind her back but that she was on the wrong side." Cornish stood up. "I must get back to the office."

As he stood at the open door Cornish said quietly, "I'll keep in touch."

* * *

Seething with anger, Hoggart went straight back to Century House and checked on the internal directory the location of Malins's office. A secretary in an outer office tried to stop him but he was already past her, flinging open the door of Malins's office. They had never met and Malins half rose from his chair and then sat down again. Hoggart noticed that the man with Malins was Rawson, whom he had met when the Saab smashed up his car.

Malins was a big man with heavy shoulders, a barrel chest and thick hairy arms exposed by his rolled-up sleeves. He had a smooth moonlike face with big blue eyes. And despite Hoggart's violent entrance he smiled amiably. He recognised violence and knew every way there was to deal with it.

"I assume you want to see me. I'm afraid I don't know you."

Rawson leaped in. "This is Mr. Hoggart, Phil. I went down to see him in Tunbridge Wells—remember? He'd had a car accident."

Malins held out his big hand. "Do sit down, Mr. Hoggart."

Hoggart ignored both the hand and the invitation."

Almost speechless with anger he said, "I want to warn you, Malins. Lay off my wife or I'll take your outfit apart."

Malins glanced briefly at Rawson who shrugged his ignorance.

"I don't understand, Mr. Hoggart. I think there must be some misunderstanding." Then quietly. "Do sit down and tell me what it's all about."

"Your people have been harassing my wife, Malins. And you bloody well know that."

Malins looked at Rawson. "Do you know anything about this, Peter?"

Rawson shook his head and looked at Hoggart. "I can assure you that it's not true, Mr. Hoggart. What makes you think that has been happening?"

"When you spoke to me in the hospital we talked about a man named Gardner. Do you deny that?"

"No. We did talk about him briefly."

"And you said Surveillance were watching him for Malins's people, who were turning him over."

Malins looked quickly at Rawson, who ignored the look. "Yes. I did. But what the hell's that got to do with your wife?"

"You've been harassing her too. Stopping her from getting jobs. The usual stuff that you people go in for."

Malins interrupted. "I can assure you, Mr. Hoggart, that your wife is not part of our business with Gardner or anybody else."

"So why is she in Charing Cross Hospital recovering from an

overdose because every time she goes for some piddling job she doesn't get it?"

Malins looked at Rawson and their glances held for several moments before Malins looked back at Hoggart. He said quietly. "Is your wife's name Jacqui, Jacqui Lovegrove?"

"That's her unmarried name, yes."

"For Christ's sake sit down, Hoggart. I can't think with you looming over me."

Hoggart sat reluctantly, staring at Malins.

"I had no idea she was your wife, Mr. Hoggart. I had a list from Central Records of known associates of Gardner, and, by some incredible mistake, that name—Jacqui Lovegrove—was on the list."

"Did you stop her getting jobs?"

"You know that I shall deny this in other circumstances, but bearing that in mind, yes, we did put mild pressure on her."

"Like what?"

"We gave certain information to her employer which caused her to be dismissed. And we've done the same when she has gone for other job interviews. We've done nothing beyond that, I assure you."

"Did they tell you why they wanted Gardner worked over?"

"No. Unless it's relevant we seldom get told. We are given certain parameters of pressure to work in and we get on with it." He paused again. "Let me say that we had been notified of Jacqui's attempt and we crossed her off our list immediately."

"You reckoned you'd done the job, eh?"

There was anger in Malins's eyes as he said quietly, "You're in the business, Hoggart. You know better than that."

"What's the state of the game with Gardner?"

"Why are you interested?"

"Because I know why you've been put on to him."

"Then you know more than I do. Maybe I could be told."

"Because I'm divorcing my wife for her relationship with

Gardner and I'm giving chapter and verse of the things he's been doing that I've learned about. His solicitor approached our legal department to get them to stop me. He threatened to expose the work I do in SIS." He sighed. "They sent him off with a flea in his ear but it looks as if they went behind my back and handed it over to you."

"And Gardner's been marking your card to get his own back."

"Yep."

"His solicitor was a chap named Fox?"

"Yes."

Malins gave a half-smile. "If it's any consolation he's a pretty unhappy man right now. Entertaining a special team from the Inland Revenue."

"And Gardner?"

"Inland Revenue and a few more little touches." He smiled. "Can't seem to leave his car anywhere without it gets clamped. Malins sighed. "I'm sorry about all this, Hoggart. I really am. Nothing personal, just a classic cock-up. Is there anything I can do to help?"

"Yes. Ring the hospital and find out how she is."

"Why don't you ring them?"

"I'm in the middle of divorcing her."

Rawson dialled the number, and Hoggart and Malins sat in silence as he made his way through the hospital system to the Ward Sister. He listened and asked a few questions and then hung up and looked at Hoggart.

"Medics never seem to give you a straight answer but as near as I can make out she's just about holding her own. You heard me ask for their prognosis but she wouldn't give out. Said medically the prognosis was that their seemed no brain damage but the psychological response was negative. Whatever that means." He paused. "Would you like me to go round and take a look at her?"

"No thanks."

Malins said, "If it's any consolation, Gardner is in real deep. According to what Inland Revenue and Customs and Excise tell me he's certainly going to be bankrupt by the time they've finished with him. And a good chance of not less than ten years inside. And that's apart from what we'll be doing. He's a very desperate man, my friend, believe me. His solicitor chap, Foxy, is singing like a bird to the investigators. Harry Gardner's finished."

Hoggart stood up and without saying any more he walked out of the office.

Rawson said, "Poor bastard. What with her and bloody Gardner harassing him he must wonder whether he's coming or going."

"What else did they say at the hospital?"

"Touch and go. Not sure she'll make it."

"You saw the background on her?"

"Yep."

"Why one earth does a chap like Hoggart marry a girl like that?"

Rawson grinned. "Why do any of us marry the women we marry?"

• • •

At the weekly meeting with Renshaw, Hoggart and Fletcher had to report on the progress, if any, that they had made with the two defectors. And that day Fletcher had raised the question of Belinsky's future.

Renshaw raised his eyebrows. "What have you got in mind? Or more to the point, what has *he* got in mind?"

"I've only talked in generalisations so far. Obviously he wants to be released. He is a useful reference point because he knows so much about the personnel of both First and Second Directorates but he doesn't seem to know much about actual operations."

"Would you rate him as having been cooperative?"

"Yes."

"What could he do if we released him? How would he earn a living?"

"I think he's hoping for some kind of financial reward. A lump sum and some kind of retainer."

"Doing what?"

"He could be a useful member of the reading section. World Service might be interested or I could sound out Radio Free Europe and the Voice of America."

Renshaw shrugged. "Soviet observers are ten a penny at the moment."

"I think he could look after himself if we gave him a pension and a bit of capital."

"How much?"

"Enough to buy a cottage or a flat, say five or six thousand a year basic pension, and help in getting him a job of some sort."

Renshaw looked at Hoggart. "What do you think?"

"I don't know enough to pass a sensible comment, sir. But it already costs a packet to keep him in custody."

"We'd have to put him under some sort of control and surveillance if we let him out. That would cost almost as much."

The three of them sat in silence for several minutes and then Renshaw looked at Fletcher.

"Let's put it on the back burner until we've heard what Hoggart has to say." He looked at Hoggart. "How is it?"

"Well, as you know, I've been concentrating on the nuts and bolts of the Fowler case in the States. I'd say we know more about how the operation was run than the FBI do."

"What makes you think that?"

"I've read their long report on the whole case. There seems to be a lot they don't know about how it was run by the other side."

"We've had approaches from the FBI through liaison and from State via the Foreign Office about your chap. But I've not even admitted that we've got him."

"I can't see any disadvantages in cooperating."

Renshaw leaned back in his chair. "I can. Especially after the contradictory information that Belinsky gave us about him. We don't want to end up looking gullible after they've done him over and find that he's been making half of it up as he went along."

"You think Belinsky's right, sir?"

"Who knows, old chap? I wouldn't trust any of them. They live on lies as you well know." Renshaw smiled. "That's why I'm always glad to leave it to the professional beavers like you two." He stood up as if he were bored by it all and then said crisply. "Start making plans for releasing Belinsky, Fletcher. And Hoggart—just keep grinding away as you have been. If the Americans keep on at us it might mean sending you to Washington for a few days." He laughed softly as he saw Hoggart's face. "There are worse places to be in autumn than Washington, DC, my friend."

"Not if your hosts are the FBI, sir. I've had some before."

Renshaw smiled and waved them towards the door.

● ● ●

Hoggart heated up a Marks & Spencer Individual Steak and Kidney Pie and followed it with rice pudding laced with generous spoonfuls of blackcurrant jam. He watched an old black-and-white Charlie Chan film on Channel 4 and tried not to think about anything. He was only half way through the rice pudding when he gave up the struggle, putting down the spoon and walking over to the battered leather armchair.

Hoggart had never been an introspective man. Neither his life-style nor his work had burdened him with indecision. Things had to be done and you got on and dealt with them. But for once his brain and instincts provided no solution. He couldn't even identify the problems. What to do about Gardner led to anger at what his own people had done without even consulting him. And that led him to what to do about Jacqui, and his mind raced away to evade any answer. There was no answer because there wasn't a question. And then Yakunin on permanent alert for some deception, some clue to deviousness and all the time the hint of revelations to come if only he proved a worthy recipient. And then a quickly fading flash vision of Jacqui in the hospital bed when the drug hoodlum had beaten her up. And all she'd wanted as proof that she was a human being and not just a body, was that he'd tell her his real name. And now all these people, intertwined, circled his bruised mind like vultures circling a corpse in the desert.

He wondered what it was about him that had made it such a shambles. And he wondered what it was that compelled him to let it continue, and even get worse. He knew that he only had to do what his lawyer advised and everything would be calm again. And everyone concerned could get back to their tatty lives. But he could no more bring himself to do that than he could forgive and eventually forget what they had all done to him.

He tried to think of someone he trusted who he could talk to. He had never needed a confidant before, and he could think of nobody whose advice he would respect. Nobody but someone like himself would understand. He didn't understand himself. He just knew. You didn't back off when you were in the right. He hadn't read the Bible since he was at school but he remembered that somewhere it said "An eye for an eye." And he shared that view of life and justice. Another man might have wondered why he had no friend in whom he could confide, but not Hoggart. Despite what the poet had written, Hoggart *was* an island unto himself.

Eventually he fell asleep in the armchair and slept through fitfully until the next morning. He washed and shaved and then washed down his body before putting on clean clothes.

On his office desk there was a stiff-backed A4 envelope marked "Private" and with his name scrawled on it. He opened it and there was a photograph of a man and a handwritten note from Fletcher saying that the photograph was of Belinsky. He tucked it back into the envelope and put it on top of the Russian newspapers and books that he had forgotten to take down to the safe-house.

He was about to leave when a call came through from the safe-house to say that Yakunin had retired to bed with a heavy cold. They had given him the usual medical reliefs but he wouldn't be fit to talk for a couple of days.

CHAPTER SIXTEEN

Bill Altieri read slowly through the collated reports from sources covering the KGB. The CIA had more information now from the Soviet Union since the reorganisation at Langley had highlighted the holes in the system's networks that had previously prevented the diverse and apparently insignificant pieces of the intelligence jigsaw being made available to all who might find them useful. The problem was in allowing the widest possible distribution of information without compromising the security of either its content or its sources. The borderline cases went to Altieri, a man with many years of experience of covert operations.

All day he had read and come to some decision, making three piles of reports. The largest batch were for onward distribution. Half a dozen documents were for very limited distribution and about the same number were put in a tray for second thoughts.

He made it a firm practice to re-read and make a final decision on the doubtful cases the same day. It was not only a question of the documents' urgency but decisions on one day's referrals were always in danger of being clouded by the next day's load.

When he looked at his watch it was already 5 P.M. and he stretched his arms and stood up, walking along the wide echoing corridors to the cafeteria. He had two coffees and a beef sandwich, and phoned his home to say that it looked as if it would be at least a couple of hours before he left.

The decision pile had already been removed by his assistant and the restricted pile was covered by a typed page of reference numbers awaiting his signature. He signed and pressed the button on his internal telephone as he reached for the batch of undecided reports.

An hour later there was only one item still needing a decision. It was a report from the senior CIA officer in Moscow. Several times he had typed five-digit codes into the desk VDU display, checking on names, dates, and archive references. The problem was not so much the distribution but whether it should be passed to London. All the computer references led back to London. Unlike many senior CIA officers, he was no Anglophobe, but in this case London had shown minimal cooperation when the original problem had arisen. They had not even admitted that they had the man, but there was strong evidence to that effect. And, if that was the case, they must have known that the information the man had must be of vital importance, not only to the CIA but even more to the FBI.

Finally Altieri phoned Langford, who was CIA/SIS liaison.

"How do we stand with the Brits at the moment, Jack?"

"At what level?"

"Top end. Who owes who?"

"I'd say we're all square at the moment. Both parties uncooperative."

"Any advantages for us in a friendly gesture?"

"Not that I know of. What area?"

"You remember a Brit named Charlton got sent to the Gulag for a long stretch?"

"Not off hand. Tell me more."

"He was tried for espionage along with a KGB guy. Spying for the Brits. The Russian got a life sentence."

"I don't really recall it, Bill. What have you got?"

"It's not very specific but it looks as though it might have been a cover for something else by the KGB." Altieri paused. "And the data base indicates that there's a vague link to the KGB guy who was running the Walker network over here."

"What's the link?"

"We think he defected to the Brits. It's a bit of a tangled connection but there might be a useful trade for us."

"I should go ahead then, Bill. At least we'll be able to assess their attitude to genuine cooperation."

"OK."

Altieri read the report again to see if anything should be deleted before he passed a copy on to SIS liaison. Bailey, the SIS officer, was an old friend of Altieri and the CIA man was anxious to see Bailey's reaction to the gesture. Altieri decided that there was nothing that needed to be deleted except the code references and internal details, but as a precaution he had it rewritten by one of the specialists so that the original text could not be used to identify the code.

• • •

Bailey had just come back from a routine briefing trip to London but he had not been briefed on the two defectors. The meeting with Altieri had been cordial and London would be pleased at the sign that there was a thaw in the frosty relationship with the CIA. Not that the paper that had been passed over to him appeared to be of major importance. But it was a gesture and that was enough. He read it through one last time before sealing the envelope and marking it for the Diplomatic Bag. It seemed very vague.

As instructed after the trial of DENIKIN and the British journalist CHARLTON an attempt was made to establish some details of what they had been involved in. As reported previously there were a number of rumors concerning the case. The rumors ranged from the reported execution of the Soviet concerned to suggestions that only the man CHARLTON had actually been jailed. This led us to endeavor to check on the status of the Soviet involved.

An extensive operation indicates that the Soviet concerned was a KGB officer whose working name was LENSKY, a married man in his early forties with a daughter. Parallel enquiries elicited that he was a much respected and senior officer employed on special duties with Directorates 1 and 2. We have not been able to establish what his special duties were but he seems to have worked somewhere in Moscow other than KGB HQ either at Dzerdzhinski Square or at the new building on the Moscow Ring Road.

However a check was made on his family circumstances. The check produced information that his wife and child had left the family apartment before the trial started. At this point our inquiries ceased to be productive. However we recently received a report from YEREVAN that the wife and daughter were living in favorable conditions in a villa at the edge of the town. They seem to have all the usual privileges of KGB next-of-kin. Our evaluation here is that the trial was some sort of contrivance but the motives elude us. It could possibly have been merely a warning to the British about their clandestine operations in the Soviet Union or something much more sinister.

As there seems to be no immediate relevance so far as Langley is concerned we have not pursued the matter further. There are several further rather tenuous leads if anyone wished to pursue the matter but we propose letting the matter close unless we hear otherwise from HQ.

There was an oblique suggestion from two sources that the trial was related in some way to a recent KGB defection to the British of a KGB man named Yakunin (see Walker), but when the hint was pursued both sources clammed up. Bearing in mind that the KGB man we suspect of having defected to London was solely concerned with operations in the USA these suggestions seem ill-founded.

There was no addressee and no signature.

CHAPTER SEVENTEEN

Hoggart spent the day reading the routine sitreps that had piled up on his desk and was surprised when Renshaw phoned and asked him to go over for a drink.

Renshaw suggested that they have a drink at his place in Chelsea and Hoggart could think of no reasonable reason to decline the invitation from his boss.

It was strange to see Renshaw in his own surroundings and although Hoggart was always ill at ease with even modest wealth, he was taken with the sparseness and the obvious signs of Renshaw's taste, interests, and character. He was used to the senior man's unintentionally superior manner at work and was surprised at the man's charm and the natural way he made him feel at ease.

"Which would you prefer—fruit juice, tinned I'm afraid, but the real thing, Perrier, or what about a decent coffee?"

"Coffee would be fine, sir, thank you."

"Let's not bother about sirs and misters. You know my name and I know yours. We're not at the office. Just two chaps relaxing."

Hoggart was amused at Renshaw's description of what they were doing. He was far from relaxed.

Renshaw had brought the Cona on a tray with cream, milk and sugar, and a cup and saucer. When he had poured himself an apple juice he sat down, smiling as he looked at Hoggart.

"You look like a cat at the Kennel Club, Eddie. Are you worried by the outward signs of a bit of money?"

"No. I hadn't . . . I'm not very good on social occasions."

"Why is that, do you think?"

"I don't really know. I guess I've got a closed mind."

"That's interesting. You wouldn't like to live in a place like this?"

"Of course I would, but I'd feel guilty all the time, knowing I didn't belong."

"Is this just inverted working-class snobbery?"

Hoggart smiled. "It could be but I don't think it is. It's just lack of sophistication."

"But a lot of our chaps come from working-class backgrounds and they take to the good life like ducks to water."

"Maybe it's just that the good life, as you call it, doesn't interest me."

"You had a tougher start in life, of course, than most men do. That's bound to make a difference."

"That was a long time ago. Water under the bridge."

"I don't think that sort of thing is wiped out just by time. Only self-confidence can keep it in the background."

"Sounds like you've been reading my 'P' file?"

"You're right. I have. Nothing I didn't know before but it's as well to be reminded."

"Why?"

"Because I'm worried about you."

"You mean the trouble about my wife?"

"Yes. But other things too."

"What other things?"

"Just you as a man."

"What's that mean?"

Renshaw filled his glass again and leaned back in his chair.

"When the divorce thing is over, then what?"

"I don't understand?"

"What's your life going to be like? Where are you going to find your pleasure, or even some happiness? Maybe you've got it all planned out."

Hoggart shrugged. "I shall just carry on as usual."

"You never get lonely?"

"No. Do you?"

Renshaw smiled. "I've got many friends and lots of acquaintances. I've got my music and I've got my boat." He paused. "But I feel lonely sometimes."

"Why don't you get married then?"

"You feel that might be a cure for loneliness?"

"Could be."

"Was it for you, before this lot blew up?"

"I certainly wasn't lonely with her around."

"Did you ever wonder why you married her? You'd left it quite late in life."

"I was wondering about that only last night."

"And what did you conclude?"

"I think I just drifted into it."

"I disagree entirely."

"Tell me why?"

"You were treated very callously when you were a child. You were brought up in an orphanage and only a strange quirk of fate in the shape of a kind-hearted old man saved you from ending up in the same back-streets that you came from. And out of all that you developed a strong antipathy to injustice. Particularly to

197

people who were defenceless. You cared about lame dogs. Not all lame dogs, just those who came from back-streets as you did.

"I took the liberty of reading the girl's record in the CRO files and every line I read was one more marker of why you married her." Renshaw paused. "You're a man who most people see as a very self-confident loner. But you're not, my dear Eddie." Renshaw smiled. "You, my friend, are a born romantic. Some romantics try to play God—rescuing chronic alcoholics or hardened criminals or whatever. But you were more modest, you only played the White Knight.

"In your job you're one of the most determined and persistent men I've ever known. You never give up. But when you played the White Knight you gave up at the first hurdle. Out of sympathy and, I suspect, some affection, you married her. I'll bet she never even asked you to marry her—am I right?"

Hoggart nodded. "Yes."

"So you put her in a race that she was neither bred for, nor trained for. And you weren't a lot of help either. You just watched from the grandstand and when she fell—that was it. Off to the knacker's yard. All her life she only knew one way to pass the time or please a man." Renshaw wagged a finger at Hoggart. "And you knew that, Eddie, before you even tangled with her. Yes?"

"Why are you saying all this?"

"Somebody has to say it, my friend. And too few people know the facts—thank God."

"And you want me to do what they all want—my solicitor, her solicitor, Gardner, SIS legal—and then there's no trouble for anyone?"

"Not at all. How you deal with the divorce is up to you. But what worries me is what sort of life you will have when it's over."

"The same as I had before."

"Oh, Eddie, don't kid yourself. You know as well as I do that it won't be the same."

"Who asked you to talk to me, the DG?"

"Nobody. So far as I know he doesn't know anything about this business. He's got enough on his plate without involving him in our domestic problems."

"What do you suggest I do?"

Renshaw was silent for a few seconds then he said quietly, "When you go back home tonight imagine that the divorce is over. Gardner had been brought down in public. He's finished. And you're a free man. And then think of what you're going to do with the rest of your life. Is chasing a few Soviets and squeezing a few more Yakunins all that you want? I don't know. Maybe it is. But at least think about it."

"What made you talk to me like this?"

Renshaw unfolded his long body and stood up. "Firstly because you're a good chap and secondly because I think it's all been affecting your work."

• • •

When Hoggart went down to the safe-house Yakunin was still in bed, restless and pale, a heap of used tissue beside the bed, aspirin and cough linctus on the cupboard under the small barred window.

They had talked desultorily for a few minutes, then Hoggart put the Soviet newspapers and books at the end of the bed before he left and went to his room.

He was deeply asleep when one of the minders came in and shook him awake.

"The Russian wants to talk to you. Says it's urgent."

"What time is it?"

The man looked at his watch. "Three-fifteen."

Hoggart sighed and wrapped a blanket around his naked body, one end trailing along the floor as he made his way down the passage to Yakunin's room.

The light was on and Yakunin was sitting on the edge of the bed.

"What is it, Igor? Why aren't you asleep?"

"Is it some sort of trick?"

"What?"

And then Hoggart noticed that Yakunin had the photograph of Belinsky in his hand.

"This photograph, why was it with the books and newspapers?"

"I forgot. I just wanted to ask you if you recognised the man."

"And if I do? What then?"

"Nothing. It's just a routine identification."

"Why do you lie to me?"

"Come off it, Igor. You didn't ask them to wake me in the middle of the night just to accuse me of lying to you. What's biting you?"

"You know who he is of course?"

And Hoggart saw that Yakunin's hand holding the photograph was trembling. Yakunin was scared and Yakunin hadn't been scared at any time before.

Hoggart sat down beside Yakunin on the bed, still clutching the grey blanket around him.

"What's it all about, Igor?"

"You call this man Belinsky—why?"

"We understood that that was his name."

Yakunin said quietly. "Have you got this man?"

"You know I wouldn't tell you even if we did have him."

"So let me tell you something." Yakunin paused. "If you have this man then you and I are finished. No more cooperation of any kind from me."

For a few moments Hoggart was silent and then he turned to look at Yakunin's face.

"What if I tell you the truth? Whichever way it is."

"If you haven't got him there's no problem. But if you

have . . ." Yakunin shrugged. ". . . then we are all in deep deep trouble."

"We have got him, Igor. We've had him for some time."

"And he defected, yes?"

"Yes."

"And he's cooperating in every possible way?"

"More or less."

"He gave this name—Belinsky. And you just believed him?"

"No. We checked on him every way we could. His background, his career. The people he knew in Dzerdzhinsky Square."

"Where did he say he'd been operating?"

"In Paris. We checked on that too."

"His name is not Belinsky. Except maybe as part of a cover-story for his defection, he's never worked in Paris. He's been once to the United States but apart from that he's never been out of Moscow."

"Why are you so worried about him?"

"Why did he say that he defected?"

"I've never talked with him but from the transcripts he seems to be saying that he'd had enough of the KGB and Moscow." Hoggart half-smiled. "I think he just wanted a better life in the West."

Yakunin shook his head slowly. "Whatever it was it wasn't that. First of all he was a totally committed Soviet and apart from that he had every privilege and luxury in Moscow that he could get over here."

"Who is he?"

"His name's Lensky. Yuri Lensky."

"How come you know so much about him?"

"He was a very important man but very few people knew of him or what he did. There were just a handful of men who did his kind of job. And they did it with the greatest secrecy."

"How did you know about him?"

"Because I worked for one of them myself. The guy I told you about—Ulianov. He and Lensky worked closely together. Ulianov covering the States and Lensky covering special operations in Britain."

"But you said he'd never been outside Moscow apart from one visit to the USA. How could he control an operation here from Moscow?"

"It wasn't just a routine operation. It was a special. He was full-time on it."

"What was the operation?"

"I told you way back that if they discovered that I knew about this operation they would kill me. D'you remember?"

"Yes."

"You thought I was exaggerating, didn't you?"

"I thought it was possible."

"It wouldn't have taken them long to find out that I knew a lot about it." He paused. "They've sent Lensky over to kill me before I talk."

"How can they be sure that you haven't talked already?"

"They'll know everything that you and I have talked about. Everything. They'll know I haven't talked."

"So talk now, and they're too late."

Yakunin looked at Hoggart. "They'd still kill me. For revenge. And they'd kill you too."

"Why me?"

"To stop you from passing on what I'd told you." Yakunin put his hand out and touched Hoggart's hand as it clutched at his blanket. "If you value your life, my friend, you won't report to anybody what I've just told you. You wouldn't live a week."

"And who would kill me?"

"They have men here—you know that already. Not just Russians, but others. Arabs, Iranians, Irish. People who'd kill for money or support for some revolutionary organisation."

"How would they know what we've talked about?"

"They won't if you don't repeat it. But if you do they'll know within two or three hours."

"But how?"

"I told you. They have an agent in place in your organisation."

"Who is he?"

"I don't know. I know a few things about him but I don't know his name."

"How long has he worked for Moscow?"

"At least ten years. Probably much longer. He's the most valuable source they have."

"Don't tell me any more right now. Let me think about this."

"If you report on it I shall deny it. All of it. You understand that. It would be my only chance."

Hoggart stood up, nodded to Yakunin and walked slowly back to his room. He slept soundly to mid-morning and felt refreshed.

As he shaved and washed, the gloom and confusion of the last few weeks seemed to have gone. He felt alert and alive again, his mind on what Yakunin had told him. All his experience tended to make him feel that Yakunin was telling the truth as he knew it. And a long, drawn-out, apparently routine de-briefing was beginning to come alive. At last he was dealing with a problem that he was trained for, not the sludge of law cases and dirty tricks.

• • •

Hoggart had taken Yakunin to the main room in the farmhouse and as they settled down at the old-fashioned oak table the Russian sensed a difference in the atmosphere. He listened carefully as Hoggart talked.

"Let's change the set-up, Igor. It's not a de-briefing any longer. I'm not going to report what you told to anybody. You and I are going into partnership to find out what the hell is going on and who the mole is in SIS. OK?"

"Is OK with me."

"The chap who's de-briefing this Lensky showed him your photograph and Lensky said you had a reputation for fantasising your role in KGB operations, and that you played only a minor part in the Walker operation. What's your answer to that?"

Yakunin shrugged. "I've been over it in detail with you. How could I have known so much if I wasn't in charge? Who did he say was actually running it?"

"The head of illegals based in New York."

"Well I suppose as the senior officer on the ground he was senior to me. I reported to Moscow and all the documents from Walker went back through our embassy in Washington using the Diplomatic Bag. But the man in New York was only an administrator as far as I was concerned. When Moscow wanted to kick my arse it was he who did it. My expenses and salary came from him. But that's all he did. I don't think he was there to get involved in any operations, not just mine."

"So we know Lensky was lying. Why?"

"To devalue anything I said, to make you suspect me of being unreliable. Just the usual low-grade KGB defector bullshitting his way to a better pension deal for defecting."

"But if you really were so important, Moscow could leave you to rot away with us. They aren't going to send a top KGB man just to put down a nonentity. So either what you know is very important or he's here for some other reason."

"And how did they find out I was with the British? All my work had been in the States. They'd expect me to defect to Washington, not here. That was part of the reason why I defected to you people. How many people know I've come over?"

"A dozen or so people know I'm de-briefing a KGB man but only seven know your name."

"So which one of the seven passed the good news back to Moscow?"

"Not that easy. Seven who know officially but someone could have got through our security."

"Like who?"

"A telephonist. A typist. A clerk. Accounts people. They wouldn't know much but they could provide clues that experienced people could put together."

Hoggart hesitated and then said, "It could help if you told me more about the man—the mole."

"I don't know his name."

"What *do* you know?"

"He's SIS and very senior and he passes information on SIS's anti-KGB operations. And he's senior enough to know about top government thinking."

"That could cover twenty or thirty people, Igor."

"I've seen a picture of him. I'd recognise him."

"I'll see what I can bring for you to look at. I'll have a look at Lensky too. But he's not officially any concern of mine and there's tight security round him. Just as there is here for you."

• • •

It had been a routine meeting between the National Security Agency and GCHQ. Neither NSA's HQ at Fort Meade nor GCHQ's HQ at Cheltenham had been used. The meeting had taken place in Paris.

The two agencies seldom behaved as rivals. They may not have passed all the information they gathered to their collaborators but on the whole they worked as if their interests were identical. They faced the same technical problems of electronic surveillance and the same problems of evaluation. If you eavesdrop on every radio and telephone signal in the world and record it, you're going to have the problem of evaluating what you get.

A combination of mathematicians, cryptographers, and intelligence officers ground down the residue to nearly manageable proportions. The brotherhood of shared skills and problems and their solutions made for a friendly if cautious relationship between the staffs of both sides. The relationship was the only intelligence operation where phobias and prejudices were instantly recognised and removed.

The meeting had been mainly an exchange of information on a wide range of Soviet codes and talks by technicians on the latest developments in systems analysis techniques that would rationalise some of the problems of using check-word combinations to throw up signals traffic that might be significant.

Malone had taken Boyd to one side during the buffet lunch. Malone was NSA and Boyd was GCHQ on more or less permanent loan to MI5.

"Are you still doing special radio surveillance?"

"Yes."

"Who's looking after London area?"

Boyd smiled. "Are you fishing?"

Malone laughed. "No, I just wanted to check something with you."

"Go on then."

"We've got a dozen tapes of high-speed radio transmissions with a code so complex we're sure it must be a clandestine transmitter."

Boyd frowned. "What's that got to do with London?"

"The transmissions are in the London area."

For a few moments Boyd was silent. Then he said quietly, "What are you trying to tell me?"

"I assumed that you would know already."

"We've no record of a clandestine transmitter apart from the Soviet Embassy itself. And they are only technically illegal because they operate without our permission. What's the one you have in mind?"

"It's based in a block of flats in Putney—almost in Wimbledon, on the south side of the Common. It's low-powered. About two watts. But it's very directional and beamed to Belgium. Bruges. I imagine it goes on to Moscow from there."

"What kind of traffic?"

"High-speed Morse. Random times. Two- or three-second bursts."

"What's the content?"

"No idea. That's why I brought it up. Thought you might have broken the code. It's beating our guys at the moment. It was only because of the code that we took so much interest in it."

"Where did you monitor it?"

Malone laughed. "A mobile and let's say somewhere in Mayfair."

"Your embassy?"

"Maybe."

"Can I have tapes?"

"Of course. Send one of your people over if you like, and he can see what we've done so far. Could save you going over the same ground again and wasting your time."

"That's very generous of you, Mike."

"Not really. We want to break this damn code before they change it."

"What frequency was it on?"

"It was tucked in one of your Cellnet bands. I think it was about nine four three point four megacycles. It had a beat laid over it while it was on. A pulse beat." He grinned. "We've got a little box that can erase beats."

"Let me do some checking and I'll get back to you."

"Soon?"

"Tonight if possible. Can you give me the location in Putney?"

"Yep. As soon as you OK it."

"It would help to know it before I checked."

"In case it was one of yours?" Malone grinned.

"No way. It's not ours."

"OK. Flat Seventy-two, Marlow House, Putney Heath." The American looked quizzically at Boyd. "Mean anything?"

"No. Not a thing. I'll see you later, Mike. I'd better get cracking."

• • •

Boyd hadn't needed to go to Fort Meade. A talk with the head porter at Marlow House had started the rot. Ex-sergeant major Macrae had drawn himself up to his full height as he said, "I'm sorry, mate, but you ought to know better. We never discuss the tenants under any circumstances."

Boyd had shown him his warrant card and that was enough.

"Number seventy-two, sir. That's a Mr. Botha, a South African. Some sort of businessman. Don't spend much time here. He's abroad most of the time."

"Is he here at the moment?"

"I believe he is. Was here yesterday. Saw him meself."

"Any way you can check?"

"I could check if he wants an evening paper."

"I'd be glad if you'd do that."

Macrae was back in five minutes, looking suitably solemn.

"Don't want a paper but he's there. Leavin' tomorrow he says. New York this time. He asked me to call him a taxi to take him into town at eight."

Boyd looked at his watch. That would give him two hours. He had used the phone in the porter's lodge. When he was finished he turned to Macrae and gave him four five-pound notes.

"Don't call a taxi. There'll be one coming for him bang on time. OK?"

"Yes, sir." He hesitated. "This is all above-board, isn't it?"

"Of course it is. Don't worry about anything. Nothing's going to happen. He just gets a different taxi, that's all."

• • •

By 10 P.M. Boyd knew the worst. Mr. Botha was Konstantin Bykov, code-name "Wheel." No wonder there had been no transmissions from the house in Barnes. The little bastard was operating out of Putney with a different transmitter and some high-tech code that operated in such short bursts that they were almost immune to detection. He already had a warrant for searching both the flat in Putney and the house in Barnes. With a little bit of luck he wouldn't need a warrant for Bykov. The taxi had taken Bykov to Kew and the surveillance team had trailed him back to Barnes. And the cheeky bastard had called himself Mr. Botha.

The rummage team had found the transmitter under the floor-boards in the Putney flat but there was nothing else to incriminate him. Boyd had gone with a Special Branch officer to the house in Barnes. It was just after midnight when they arrived.

It was the girl who answered the door.

"Miss Gartside?"

"Yes. Who are you? What do you want?"

"This is a signed warrant which allows me to search this house."

Boyd held out the warrant and the girl glanced at it before starting to close the door.

"There's some mistake. I'm going to call the police."

But Boyd's foot was in the door.

"This gentleman with me is a police officer. I think it would be wiser to let me come in and talk to you."

"Has he got any proof he's a policeman?"

Kimber showed her his Special Branch card and still hesitating she opened the door and let them in. Kimber closed the door and Boyd smiled and whispered, "It's OK," and then in his normal voice he said, "Where's your friend?"

"He's asleep in bed."

"Show me his room."

"Tell me what it's all about. Are you sure you've got the right house?"

"In the bedroom upstairs?"

"Yes."

The front bedroom was empty and in the second Bykov was putting on his trousers. He didn't look surprised. He'd probably heard the doorbell and their voices in the hall. He looked up at Boyd and said in good English, "Who the hell are you?"

"Don't worry about me, Comrade Bykov. I'll look after you. Hurry up and get dressed."

"My name is Botha. I'm a South African national and I have a South African passport."

"You're a cheeky bugger, Bykov. Mr. Botha wouldn't like you using his name."

"Am I being arrested?"

"No. You're just coming with me to answer a few questions."

"Going where?"

"You'll spend the rest of the night in Wormword Scrubs and after that we'll see how it goes."

"I demand to see my lawyer. It's my right."

"Of course you can see your lawyer but not unless I arrest you. And at the moment you're just being detained for questioning."

"About what?"

"About espionage."

"I am working for British Intelligence."

Boyd laughed. "You sure are, sunbeam."

CHAPTER EIGHTEEN

It was 10 A.M. when Hoggart got the call from Renshaw asking him to come up to his flat in King's Road. He had tried to get out of it so that he wouldn't break his new-found rapport with Yakunin, but Renshaw was insistent.

Hoggart had left his car at Tunbridge Wells Station and taken the train to Charing Cross and a taxi to Renshaw's place. He could hear music as he stood at the door. It was Fauré's Requiem but he didn't recognise it. No kind of music interested Eddie Hoggart. He pressed the doorbell and Renshaw answered it almost immediately. As if he'd been waiting for the bell to ring. He was dressed in a black polo-necked sweater and cavalry cords.

"Come in, Eddie." Renshaw pointed to the sofa. "Do sit down."

As Hoggart made himself comfortable Renshaw walked over to his hi-fi and switched it off. When he came back and sat in the armchair facing Hoggart he leaned forward and said quietly,

"Eddie, I've got some upsetting news for you." He paused. "Jacqui's dead. She slashed her wrists in the middle of the night. She was dead when they found her. I went over to the hospital to do what I could. There'll be an inquest of course." Renshaw reached into his jacket pocket and pulled out an envelope. "She left a note for you. They wanted to keep it and hand it to the coroner but I insisted that you have it on the undertaking that it would be made available for the inquest."

Hoggart reached out for the envelope but Renshaw made no move to hand it over. "I took the liberty of reading it, Eddie. I wanted to be able to help. It's a sad little note from a sad little girl. But nothing more than that." And he handed the envelope to Hoggart who took it and opened it, taking out the single sheet of paper, unfolding it and reading it slowly.

Saturday night

Dear Eddie,

Please forgive me but I've got to the end of my tether as they say. I seem to have caused everybody so much trouble. I'm truly sorry for what I done. I did love you proper but I spoilt it all. Take care of yourself.

Love,

Jacqui.

For a long time Hoggart didn't look up and Renshaw waited silently. When Hoggart folded up the note and looked up at Renshaw his face was pale and drawn.

"It must be a terrible shock, Eddie. And very sad. But you're not to blame."

"So who is to blame?"

"A lot of people. But you're not one of them. You gave her the only bit of security that she ever had. And the only genuine affection."

Hoggart sighed. "So why didn't it work?"

"Because she was doomed, Eddie. Doomed from the start. Doomed by that old pervert, her father who started her on a path that inevitably ended in tragedy." Renshaw paused. "She didn't stand a cat in hell's chance of getting away from that. Neither did you. However hard you tried."

"I didn't try hard enough, Tony, that's for sure."

"No matter how hard you had tried, it would have made no difference. She was imprinted as a kid with the basic idea that all that mattered was her body. That was the password to male approval. People think that girls like her are motivated by their sex-drive. It's not true. Sex becomes meaningless for them. Nothing to do with love or even pleasure. Just a ritual to gain approval."

"Who could have helped her? A psychiatrist?"

"Before I spoke to you last time. About the divorce, I had a word with a psychiatrist friend of mine. A woman. She'd dealt with several similar cases and the prognosis was . . ." Renshaw shrugged. ". . . to say it was poor would be exaggerating. It goes through drink and drugs and ends in tragedy."

"Why did you bother to find out about her?"

"To see if there was anything I could do to help you."

"Why?"

"You really want to know?"

"Yes."

"Because you and the girl—in my opinion—were like a pair of book-ends. Your backgrounds were almost exactly the same. You'd ended up in ways that looked very different. But deep down you weren't. You were like a couple of lost souls. You survived because of your work and she was lost because of that bloody father of hers. He's the villain. Not her and not you." He paused. "And I want you to survive, Eddie."

"Why?"

"Because you deserve to survive. So. Will you take some advice from me? Or shall I shut up?"

"What's the advice?"

"Don't go back to the safe-house. Let him stew for a bit. Forget work. I've got a beautiful boat in a beautiful spot. Use it for a couple of weeks. Get off the treadmill and rest that mind of yours."

"Where is she being buried?"

"Leave it to me, Eddie. I'll take care of all of it for you. And I'll do it with affection. The way you'd have it done."

"I've never been to a funeral."

"Don't start now. I find them barbaric myself. But I'll be there, don't worry."

"It seems uncaring not to go."

"Rubbish. That poor soul is out of her misery. You going would be no better than an act of masochism. Just leave it to me."

"Are you sure?"

"Of course I am. Did you come by car?"

"No. Train."

"OK. I'll drive you down to the boat and show you how things work and I'll get somebody to drive your car down in a couple of days' time. There's shaving gear down there and food in the galley."

Hoggart stood up. "You know I'm very grateful. Not just for the practical help but for you bothering at all. It's very unexpected and undeserved."

"Rubbish."

* * *

When Hoggart was alone at last on the boat the temporary relief of escape from responsibility was swamped by his thoughts. He was tortured by the thought of her lying in a hospital bed and writing the note. It must have taken a lot of courage to write it and be aware that when he got it she'd be dead. He shook his head like a dog coming out of water to put the thoughts from his mind.

He looked at his watch. It was still only 8:15 P.M. and he put on his jacket and left the boat to walk up to the phone box he had seen by the boatyard. He dialled the safe-house number and asked to speak to Yakunin and explained that he wouldn't be able to see him for a few days.

Yakunin sounded icy cold as he said, "They stop you already?"

"No. Nobody's stopped me from anything."

"So why aren't you here. Whatever you're doing can't be as important as what we were discussing."

For long moments Hoggart was silent and then he said quietly, "I lied to you, Igor. I *am* married. My wife died last night."

There was a short silence and then Yakunin said, "I'm sorry, Eddie. Very sorry. God rest her soul. I'll wait for you to contact me. Forget me for a few days. *Do svedanya.*"

"*Do svedanya,* Igor."

• • •

On the Tuesday morning a driver had brought down Hoggart's car and, after driving the man back to catch a train from Chichester, Hoggart had wandered round the picturesque old city that was dominated by its magnificent cathedral. Almost without thinking about it he found himself sitting in the small Lady-Chapel in the cathedral away from the visitors. He closed his eyes and sat with his hands covering his face, his head bowed. He wanted to pray for her but no words came into his mind. Just thoughts of them eating together in some cheap café. A vision of the clothes and sheets so neatly placed in their drawers. The cards from him in the envelope. And he stood up suddenly, ashamed that for a brief moment he had thought that he was free now of a terrible burden of responsibility.

He drove back to the boat and walked up to the Lock Stores and ate hungrily, and realised that he had eaten nothing for almost three days. As he walked back to the boat he thought of Tony Renshaw and the harsh things he had said about him in the past because he was upper-class and so casually efficient. He might be all that but he was the only man who had cared about him and his feelings since the old major had died. Renshaw wasn't all that much older than he was but he seemed to have a self-assurance about the whole of life. He was self-assured himself, but only about his work and his own survival. But Renshaw seemed to have thought about all the world's problems and knew exactly how to deal with them. He knew that he would never be like that but he was grateful for the other man's unexpected kindness.

• • •

On the Saturday morning Hoggart drove back to London, bathed and changed and took a taxi to Century House. He was surprised to find Fletcher in their office. Fletcher looked harassed but he looked up when Hoggart came in and as the door closed he said quietly, "We were both terribly sorry about the news, Eddie. Rachel told me to give you her love." He paused. "Anything I can do to help?"

"Thanks, no. Why are you here on a Saturday?"

"Everybody in the whole damn building seems to be dumping files on my desk."

"You and I had better have a talk."

"What about?"

"Your guy and mine."

"D'you want to talk now?"

"When are you going home?"

"Rachel's away with her parents in Bath for a few days. I can talk now if you want."

"D'you want to go out or stay here?"

"Would you mind if we took this stuff back to my place and talked there? Or maybe you're doing something?"

"No. I'm not doing anything."

Fletcher noticed the flat voice and was sorry for the man.

• • •

Boyd had reluctantly passed Bykov over to Mathews's team, angry that GCHQ had only been asked to monitor radio transmissions out of the house in Barnes. Just common sense ought to have told them that he might be using some other location. It proved once again Boyd's pet theory that more intelligence was lost because of lack of inter-service communication than for any other reason.

Nevertheless, when he got a call from Malone to say that NSA's cryptographers had broken Bykov's code he was in no mood just to pass over the news to Mathews's people. It didn't look very interesting anyway, and nobody was going to get any kudos from the revelation.

He delayed for a couple of days and then phoned Mathews.

"I've heard from CIA, Mathews. They've broken Bykov's code but it's not going to help you."

"Why not? That's for me to decide."

"You're welcome. You got a pen and paper handy?"

"What for?"

"So you can take down the details."

"That'll take too long. Can't you send it over and I'll read it through?"

"It's only four words."

"That's crazy, you told me that there had been daily transmissions over several months."

"That's right."

"So how come there's only four words?"

"Because every transmission was the same. Just four words repeated three times."

"What were the words?"

"You ready?"

"Yes."

"OK. Starts—asset safe and secure—ends."

"And that's all?"

"Yep."

"Any significance in the transmission times?"

"No. It's been checked. It's based on six P.M. GMT and the date. The date is the time in minutes after the hour. Six zero one for the first of the month. Six three zero or one for the last day of the month. It's a very low-level set-up and used quite often for routine regular contacts."

"Will you be sending me something in writing?"

"Yes, if you want."

"Yeah. I do." He paused. "And thanks."

"You're welcome."

• • •

Fletcher laid out the files side by side on the divan while the water boiled for their coffee.

"It's only instant, Eddie, I'm not a kitchen expert."

"That's fine for me."

When the mugs of coffee were ready Fletcher sat down facing Hoggart.

"How're you getting on with Yakunin?"

"I was doing fine but I've been on leave for a few days."

"Of course." Fletcher paused. "One of the files has got a request from CIA to interrogate Yakunin about the the Walker operation that he ran."

"That backs up his own story against your guy's version."

"That's what I thought."

"Why don't I see your guy with you and you come down with me to see Yakunin?"

"At least we'd get a second opinion."

"He says your guy's real name is Lensky, and he was really scared when he saw his photograph. Got me up at three in the morning to tell me that Lensky was very important. He wouldn't tell me what his work was but he said he felt his life was in danger. And mine too."

Fletcher pursed his lips. "Sounds a bit over the top. Especially about you. The Walker operation was a success for the KGB so why should they want to knock him off? Or you?"

"My impression was that it was something else, not the Walker case."

"Any idea what?"

"He's been on about a 'mole' in SIS. Whenever we make some progress he brings that up and it all grinds to a halt."

"Have you tried to pursue it?"

"Yes. But I have to go pretty cautiously because he's so prickly. Says he's waiting to see if we are to be trusted."

"How's he going to decide that?"

Hoggart shrugged. "Who knows? He just says that he'll know. When he saw the picture of your guy he was really scared. He wasn't faking it. I'm sure of that."

"Which safe-house are you using?"

"The one at Lamberhurst."

"Where's that?"

"In Kent. Just outside Tunbridge Wells."

"We could go to my safe-house near Southampton and look over Belinsky or Lensky, whatever his name is, and come back through Lamberhurst."

"What about your back-log of files?"

"They'll have to wait. If Belinsky is lying then he's a plant and the sooner I know the better. Let's go now. We'll take my car."

• • •

Belinsky was wearing a silk dressing-gown when Fletcher introduced him to Hoggart whom he referred to merely as "a colleague."

Belinsky held out his hand and when Hoggart took it the

Russian held it in both hands before releasing it and pointing to one of the armchairs.

"Do please make yourself at home, sir. Your colleagues have been very kind to me." He grinned. "Not that I shan't be very grateful to be a little more independent."

When they were all seated in their chairs, Hoggart said quietly, "Tell me about what you were doing before you defected."

Belinsky smiled. "You've read my de-briefing reports, I'm sure."

"Only very briefly."

"I see." The Russian's eyes were intent on Hoggart's face as he said, "What particular aspect of my previous work would you like to talk about?"

Hoggart recognised the attempt to narrow the field of discussion and to fish for the area where there might be some doubts in SIS minds. But his face was impassive.

"Just you tell me what you think will most interest me."

The Russian smiled and leaned back in his chair as if Hoggart had put him at his ease but Hoggart noticed the white knuckles of Belinsky's hands on the arms of his chair.

"Ah well. Before I came over I was working in Paris. Not at the embassy but at the house that was the HQ of KGB illegals in France. I was a kind of trouble-shooter between the bosses of various departments." Belinsky grinned. "I expect you have it too in SIS. Rivalries between sections or individual heads. Then persuading one section to share its findings with another. That sort of thing."

Belinsky looked at Hoggart. "I must apologise for not offering you a drink. We have a good selection. What can I offer you?"

"Let's just talk, shall we?"

The Russian smiled. A charming smile. "I wish that I'd had men as conscientious as you are, Comrade. I'd have counted myself as very lucky." He laughed. "I might even have stayed."

"Why did you come over?"

"Ah now. I suppose we all think our reasons for escape are ours alone." He paused. "A bit of a fruit salad really. Disenchantment. A fondness for the West. Family problems. That sort of thing."

"What about freedom and democracy?"

Belinsky shifted in his chair, settling comfortably.

"You know I've never really believed our chaps who go over to the West claiming freedom and democracy as their reasons, or motives."

"Why not?"

"Quite frankly I think it's an excuse. Rationalising." He grinned. "Maybe they think it pleases their new masters. I think that with the CIA people it actually works."

"And what were you disenchanted with?"

"The restrictions. The narrow minds. The petty rivalries between old men. That sort of thing."

"And the family problems?"

"A very dull marriage. Lack of sympathy from my partner. A wish for a release from the restrictions of marriage."

"What sort of background did your wife come from?"

The Russian looked surprised. "What a strange question." He paused for a few moments. "She was working-class, the same as me. A very ordinary lady. Pretty, but not sophisticated."

Hoggart changed over to Russian. "What kind of friends did you have?"

"In Paris or in Moscow?"

"Both."

"In Paris, none. My job made me enemies not friends. In Moscow it was fellow officers. People I'd done my training with."

Hoggart stood up and looked at Fletcher, reverting to English. "I'll have to go, it's getting late." He turned to Belinsky. "Thank you for talking to me so frankly."

"Not at all. I enjoyed our little chat."

CHAPTER NINETEEN

In the car as they drove along the A27 to Brighton, Fletcher said, "What did you make of him?"

"I think he's phoney."

"Why?"

"First of all, instinct. I didn't like all that charm. It was condescending. He's made himself too much at home."

"I think he's genuinely a charming sort of chap."

"I'm not saying it isn't genuine. I'm saying I think he's using it very deliberately."

Fletcher smiled. "You sound like you talking about Tony Renshaw. All your working-class prejudices coming out."

"He claimed his wife was working-class and so was he. But did you notice his accent when we were speaking Russian?"

"My Russian's not good enough to detect accents, Eddie. Regional dialects, yes. But not accents."

"He's got an upper-class Moscow accent and he's had it a long long time."

"Well, he's top brass in KGB."

"So what? Have you ever heard Gorbachev speaking? His accent's the Moscow equivalent of *EastEnders*. Lensky has the same accent that Andropov had." Hoggart smiled. "And his mates in the Politburo saw it as a drawback."

"What else don't you like?"

"His cover-story."

"It struck me as being frank and honest. Not making himself a hero or an instant democrat."

"That's what's wrong with it. It's too good to be true. Not just the story but the laid-back attitude. It's absolutely tailored to suit a Brit audience. A marvellous piece of work. Whoever worked it out ought to get a two-grade promotion. Most SIS officers would agree with your assessment. And that's what it's meant to do. It's a frank chat between friends in leather armchairs in some posh bloody club. We're all chaps together. The boring wife. The rivalries, the feuds between the old China hands. Instant appeal. Instant mutual identification."

"Didn't anything ring true?"

"Yes. Just one thing. An important thing."

"What's that?"

"What rank did he say he was?"

"Major."

"He's bullshitting us, David."

"Go on."

"No friends because of his job. Let's check on Central Archives when we get back. Not under Belinsky but under Lensky. I'll bet anything you like that he's not only at least lieutenant colonel but that the reason why he doesn't have friends is because he's not allowed to because his job is too high-powered, too important to risk his operational security outside the operation itself." Hoggart paused. "Did you check on him as Belinsky?"

"Yes. His story fitted well with what he's told me."

"In the light of what I've said would you say it fits a bit too well?"

There was a long silence and then Fletcher said quietly, "You could be right."

"You know how to test it?"

"No."

"Has he told you in the de-briefing anything of substance that wasn't on his SIS file?"

"Only about personal relationships in the KGB in Paris. I had those checked on. They fitted and quite a lot of it was news to our people in Paris."

"A little present from Moscow, David. Gift-wrapped. Nice and handy for checking on in Paris. You couldn't check on much of his Moscow story, that's for sure."

"You really are a cynical bastard, Eddie."

"But you wouldn't fancy putting a hundred quid on me being wrong, would you?"

"No. I'm worried, Eddie. How about we give your guy a miss and see him tomorrow so we can go back to Century House and check on the Lensky file?"

"A good idea. I haven't had time to check on it since Yakunin identified the photograph."

• • •

They signed in at Century House just after midnight and there was a girl on duty in Central Archives. They had both shown their passes and the girl had tapped in the name Lensky and watched the computer screen, which was turned away from them as they stood at the counter. A few moments later she looked at Fletcher.

"There are three Lenskys registered. What is the forename?"

Fletcher looked at Hoggart who frowned. "He told me but I can't remember it."

Fletcher turned to the girl. "Tell us what you've got. Just enough to identify the person."

The girl looked at the screen. "Lensky—Igor Alexandrovich. Captain GRU based in Samarkand." She looked up but Fletcher shook his head and the girl turned back to the screen. "Lensky, Michael Davidovich. Rank not known. Mathematician attached Cypher Section, KGB Irkutsk." Again Fletcher shook his head. Then she said, "Lensky, Yuri Fyodorovich. Lieutenant Colonel KGB. Duties unknown."

Fletcher said quietly, "That's the one. Can I see the file?"

The girl shrugged. "That's the only information on the file."

Hoggart said, "We'd still like to see it."

"It's out for updating."

"When's it due back?"

The girl tapped the keyboard. "It's been out for two months and there's no date for return."

"Who's got it?"

"Can I see your ID cards again?"

She checked both IDs using the terminal and handed them back. "I'm sorry but you're not cleared for that information. Either of you."

When she saw their surprise she said, "I can assure you that what I gave you is the only information on that file."

As they went down in the lift Fletcher said, "Looks like you're right, Eddie."

"I'd like to know who's fixed that file. Once they've got a name there should be a whole raft of information. Especially on a half-colonel in the KGB."

"I'd like to know who initiated that file and who pulled it out."

"And why." Hoggart said quietly.

"Let's get some sleep first."

• • •

There were five different files that Fletcher had to check. Not read meticulously but scan for information from other sources that might be useful for other members of Rawson's team to read. It was a routine duty that only came round every thirteen weeks. Most of it was irrelevant and that made the task all the more unpopular. The file covers had the blue stripe that classified them as Top Secret and they carried the title of their contents. GCHQ LIAISON, CIA LIAISON, KGB UPDATE, MOSCOW EMBASSY, and MISCELLANEOUS.

Miscellaneous was mainly internal. Postings, new boys and retirements, new pension arrangements and new internal security measures. Moscow Embassy was not much more than a collation of rumours and gossip gleaned from diplomats and journalists based in Moscow. But a rumour could harden into a fact and the file gave fair warning. GCHQ Liaison was almost entirely technical and only intended as information not calling for action from Renshaw's staff. Fletcher scanned them conscientiously, signed the acknowledgment forms, and ticked off the items for distribution.

As always he kept KGB Update and CIA Liaison until last. They tended to be both extensive and useful.

Fletcher looked at Hoggart, who was lying stretched out on the divan, his eyes closed, one arm trailing down to the floor, the other across his chest, and then Fletcher picked up CIA Liaison.

There was an itemised list of contents with individual names and organisational acronyms in capitals and the name "Yakunin" had instantly leapt up off the page. It was Item 20 and Fletcher turned over the pages and flattened the file so that he could read right up to the margin.

By the time Fletcher had got to the second paragraph he looked again at the source details. It had come from Bailey, SIS's liaison officer with the CIA at Langley, and it had been officially handed over to him by a William Altieri, a senior officer in the CIA.

A note from Bailey said that despite the inconclusiveness of the report from the US Embassy in Moscow the fact that Altieri had passed it over was probably intended as an emollient gesture to improve relations between the two intelligence organisations.

Fletcher took a deep breath and went back to the beginning of the report again. And as he read through it slowly he felt a mixture of burning anger and apprehension at what it all meant. Anger that despite years of experience he had been so smoothly and efficiently deceived. Hoggart had been right. His cynicism justified, his intuition uncannily accurate.

He looked across at Hoggart's prone figure on the divan. From what he had heard Hoggart had been having a very rough time. Nobody knew the details but the death of his wife must have been burden enough. And yet through all that, Hoggart's thinking was better than his own. Maybe having his calm background and contented existence made him too vulnerable. Not enough tension. Not enough adrenalin. Maybe you had to trade being good at the job against a comfortable personal life. Or what could be worse, maybe the other way around. And Fletcher knew in that moment that he wouldn't trade his Rachel for being better at his job. And he knew too that he wasn't in the same league as Hoggart. He wondered if it was because he didn't choose to be, or that he just hadn't got what it takes. Whichever it was, he'd better wake Hoggart and break the good news. The intelligence machinery had ground away and had just spewed up a lot of pieces of the jigsaw puzzle.

He stood up and looked down at the sleeping figure on the divan and then put his hand on Hoggart's shoulder and shook him roughly. He was awake instantly, sitting up and swinging his feet to the floor in one quick movement, rubbing his eyes as he said, "Have you finished your reading?"

Fletcher gave him the open file. "Read that, Eddie."

Hoggart read the report slowly and then turned his head to

look towards the window. His face was calm and he was obviously lost in his own thoughts.

After a few minutes Fletcher said quietly, "What do you think?"

Hoggart took a deep breath and turned his head to look at Fletcher. "We've got a lot to do, Dave. We'd better get on with it."

• • •

Fletcher and half a dozen others had read the National Security Agency's report of Bykov's radio traffic but nobody found it of any interest, let alone significant.

CHAPTER TWENTY

They had talked for nearly an hour and finally Fletcher had said, "We don't seem to have as much as I first thought."

"You've got to separate it into two parts. What we know and can prove or substantiate strongly, and what we know because of our experience but can't prove."

"So what d'you reckon we've got?"

"Well we know that your guy is a plant. False name, false background. We know his real name. We know he's KGB, and we know he's a lieutenant colonel. So we've got a lot of pressure we can put on Comrade Lensky.

"Then we've got my little pal, Yakunin. He hasn't told me all that much that helps us, but we know that on the whole he's been telling the truth. He ran the Walker spy-ring in the States. So we've got something to trade with either the FBI or the CIA." He paused. "And now we know that Lensky's here for some special purpose. He's not just a routine plant. You don't risk sacrificing a guy like Lensky just to get yourself a double-agent. Maybe Yakunin will come clean now we've got some news for him."

"D'you think he'll play?"

"Well he's very scared. If he's scared enough he'll want to make sure we're on his side."

"Have you got any ideas on what Lensky's here for?"

"Not that I'd say out loud at the moment."

"Why not?"

"Because it's only intuition, and once you start down that road you can get tunnel-vision trying to fit the facts to your thinking. And when the facts don't fit you can start rationalising and discount them." Hoggart smiled. "Somebody once said that the only enemy a beautiful hypothesis has is one small contradictory fact. And it's true. I've done it myself." He shook his head. "When we find we ain't got no facts we'll start dreaming dreams, but not until. Meantime we grind away. And this time at least there's two of us."

"Who shall we tackle first?"

"Yakunin," Hoggart said without hesitating.

"Why not Lensky? We've got enough on Lensky to fix him already. Maybe twenty years in the nick for espionage. But if he's here for something vital he'll settle for that. He'll have known before he was sent over that that was a highly possible scenario. And we'll never know what he was really here for." Fletcher paused. "We could offer him some sort of deal."

"We could. But he wouldn't accept it."

"What makes you think that?"

"He's a proud bastard. Sees himself as a classic hero. He'd almost like to be made into a martyr. The guy who wouldn't talk."

Fletcher smiled. "Are you sure you aren't just letting your working-class prejudices take over again?"

"You quite liked him, didn't you?"

"I suppose I did. He's likeable. Intelligent. Lively. Sophisti-cated."

"I agree. He's all those things. But inside all that charm there's a steely conviction that what he believes in is right. He's a Soviet, that guy. Don't kid yourself that he isn't."

"When shall we see Yakunin?"

"I'll go down today and try and get back to where I was with him, and you come down tomorrow."

"OK. How long do you think it will take?"

"No idea. We'll just have to play it by ear."

• • •

After the first few days of trying to get some sort of information out of Bykov, Mathews had virtually given up trying. Nobody seemed particularly interested in Bykov. They could put him away for seven years on the false documents and illegal entry but Mathews was determined to break the man if he could.

In the end he had come down to a "good guy—bad guy" scenario using Langham, one of his assistants, as the good guy. They had assessed Bykov as essentially a weak character who was sticking out for fear of what his masters in Moscow might do about his failed mission. He had no idea what his mission was all about. All he had to do was check the sign and transmit the same text at the appointed time. And that was all he knew. And that was what he had done. They'd told him the code was special and unbreakable and they were obviously wrong. But he knew who'd get the blame, and he wasn't going to give them any excuse for leaving him to rot in some British jail. They'd promised that if he was arrested and didn't talk they'd get him out. Or at least do an exchange.

Langham had brought him a packet of Gitanes that he had asked for and when he'd lit one and inhaled deeply, Langham said, "I think the boss is going to send you back."

Langham saw the fear on Bykov's pale face as he said, "What do you mean, send me back?"

"Send you back to Moscow."

"Why should he do that?"

"Don't you want to go back?"

"Not until after the trial."

"Why not?"

Bykov just shrugged and Langham knew then that they'd got him. A public trial would establish that he'd been carrying out his mission and it would be a chance for him to show that he hadn't talked. If he was sent back without a trial the KGB would automatically assume that he'd cooperated and was being rewarded. Or turned yet again.

Bykov looked up at Langham. "Have your people talked with Moscow?"

"I think the boss has made contact at low level."

"How did they respond?"

Langham grinned. "I don't think they were very interested. I think they thought you'd been a bit careless. And there was some talk about money." Langham smiled. "You been salting a bit away, comrade?"

Bykov didn't answer but Langham could tell that he was worried. Better let him stew for a bit. He stood up and walked to the door.

"Wait."

"What is it, Bykov?"

"What happens if I cooperate?"

"You told us you were cooperating all the time."

"I mean further cooperation."

Langham walked back to the chair and sat down again and said quietly, "I could put a good word in for you."

"What is it you want to know?"

Langham shook his head. "You know what we want to know."

"The contacts, yes?"

"Yes."

"And if I tell you everything I know?"

"I think that would create a lot of sympathy for you, my friend. Quite a lot."

"You want to make notes?"

"Yeah, OK."

Chapter Twenty-one

Renshaw sat back in his chair, as always, relaxed and looking slightly bored as Hoggart told him about Lensky. When he finished Renshaw looked at him.

"Why isn't Fletcher giving me this information?"

"We've been working on it together. He'd had to go and fetch his wife from Bath or somewhere because her car broke down."

"You seem very worked up about this chap? Why?"

"Well first of all because we can prove he's told us a pack of lies. And he's here for some special reason."

"What reason?"

"I don't know for sure. But I think it's something to do with my chap Yakunin."

"Yakunin?" Renshaw frowned. "What on earth can it have to do with him?"

"I don't know, but Yakunin was really scared when he saw Lensky's photograph."

"Scared of what?"

"I don't know."

"Have you found who removed Lensky's file from Central Archives?"

"No. The girl looked at our IDs and said we didn't have high enough clearance."

"Who's we?"

"Fletcher and me."

"You say you've talked with Lensky. Who gave you clearance for that?"

"Nobody."

"What was your impression of Lensky?"

"Oh he was smooth as oil. Putting me at my ease. Playing host. Lots of charm. You'd have thought I was the defector and he was SIS."

Renshaw laughed. "All those class prejudices of yours must have been working over-time."

Hoggart smiled. "Maybe, but that's a fair description of his attitude."

"Anything else?"

Hoggart glanced briefly at his list on the card and then back at Renshaw. "No. That's all, sir."

"OK. Leave it with me. I'll think about what we do next."

• • •

It was when he was shaving the next morning that something clicked in Hoggart's mind. With lather still on half his face he put a wet hand in the pocket of the jacket hanging on the back of the chair by his bed.

He took out the card with his notes on and read it carefully. He'd put a mark against each point about Lensky as he reported it to Renshaw. There was one point with no mark. Slowly he sat down on his bed, closing his eyes as he tried to recall every word of his talk with Renshaw. And at the end he was sure that he'd forgotten to raise it.

For a long time he sat there staring vacantly towards the window, the razor still in his left hand resting on his thigh. More often than not intelligence work was a slow grinding away at apparent facts, sifting and sorting the pieces of the jigsaw puzzle, until there was a pattern that could end up as a picture. All too often you ended up with four corners, a frame and no middle. And sometimes you realised long afterwards that in fact the corners *were* the middle. It happened, as Hoggart well knew, when you went into some operation with clear-cut ideas on what you expected to find. The pieces you put together made a picture but you didn't see it because you already had a picture in your mind of something entirely different. When that picture wasn't there you didn't even see the picture you had put together. It was the difference between looking and seeing.

Suddenly everything fitted. There was only one snag. He didn't believe it. It was impossible. But there was a way of proving it. Maybe not proof that a lawyer would accept but proof enough to satisfy SIS.

Hoggart sighed heavily as he stood up, walked over to the wash-basin and finished shaving. He parked his car by the Imperial War Museum and walked back to Century House. He looked through the several piles of magazines on the table in the coffee annexe of the cafeteria and found the magazine that he was looking for. He had noticed it some weeks earlier. Picking up another magazine, a copy of *Country Life*, he made no attempt to hide them as he left.

• • •

It was mid-afternoon when he arrived at the Lamberhurst safe-house.

He gave Yakunin the two magazines and asked him to look at every photograph carefully. Five minutes later Yakunin pointed a shaking finger at the picture of the man and the pretty girl in the three-month-old copy of the *Tatler*.

• • •

Hoggart walked back to his own room at the other end of the house. For a few moments he stared out of the window. The leaves on the trees were already changing colour and there was an elm that was covered with noisy starlings which had flown in to escape the harsher winter of Europe. Finally he turned and sat down at the small table, reaching for the pile of scrap-paper and a pencil.

For nearly two hours he wrote out his case. Point by point. And he realised that over half the points he was making were not provable facts but the product of years of experience and training. When he had finished he read it through twice and found no reason to alter it. It wasn't a case he was making. More an excuse, a justification to himself for what he intended doing.

Hoggart looked at his watch. It was nearly 10 P.M. and it had long been dark outside. An hour later he was through Brighton and on the A27, the main coast road. He knew at the back of his mind that this wasn't the way it should be handled. And he knew that if it hadn't been for that one slip he wouldn't be making the journey. Renshaw had asked about the removal of Lensky's file. And he hadn't mentioned the problem of the file in his report.

CHAPTER TWENTY-TWO

Hoggart left his car in the boat-yard and walked round to Renshaw's mooring. It was after midnight and too late in the season and not a weekend so there was no sign of any owners as he picked his way carefully through coils of ropes and masts laid out on trestles ready for varnishing. It was a typical autumn night. Fresh and cold, stars glittering in a black sky and a breeze from the creek that set halyards rattling and canvas dodgers flapping.

He had to use his torch to find the finger pontoon where Renshaw's boat lay alongside, stern-on to the jetty. Unhooking the chain between the stanchions he stepped on board, his rubber soles squeaking on the dew-covered deck. Unzipping the cover over the wheelhouse, he shone his torch on the door down to the saloon and slid in the thin plastic to ease open the simple lock.

With the lights on in the saloon he looked around and was aware again of the luxury of the boat. A for'ard cabin with double bunks, a well-laid-out galley and another bunk on the starboard side and a luxury stateroom astern with a double bed and its separate shower and toilet. There was far more storage space then he remembered, but what he was looking for was not going to be in an obvious place. He found it wrapped in yellow oilskin, under one of the engine bearers. The ICOM-R70 short-wave receiver, the Minox camera, three cartridges of unexposed film, and a standard KGB microdot reader.

He was checking the for'ard rope-locker when he heard the car, and saw its lights as it swung from the road to the jetty. The engine was switched off, the lights extinguished, and a car door banged. He must have seen the lights on board but he seemed in no hurry.

The boat dipped and lifted as he came on board, his arms full of a cardboard box that seemed to contain groceries, as he came down the companion-way.

He didn't seem surprised when he saw Hoggart and put the cardboard box on the saloon table before turning to look at him.

Renshaw smiled. "Well, Eddie. No need to say make yourself at home."

"We'd better talk, Tony."

"By all means." Renshaw sat down opposite Hoggart on the cushioned bunk. "What brings you here a-visiting so late at night?"

"You know why I'm here, Tony. We don't need to play games."

Renshaw smiled. "Tell me all."

"Why? That's what I want to know."

"It's a long story, Eddie. It wouldn't interest you. Frightfully boring too. And why doesn't really matter, does it?"

"It does to me."

"But not to our masters. They are only interested in how and what. And they'd never understand the why."

"Maybe I would."

"Let's have a nice cup of tea first. Yes?"

"If you want."

"How many people know?"

"Just me."

"Are you armed?"

"No."

Renshaw smiled and went into the galley. He came back a few minutes later with mugs of tea, the tea-bags still in them, and milk and sugar on a tray.

Renshaw smiled. "Shall I be mother? Let's see. Milk and one sugar, if I remember rightly."

"You've got a good memory, Tony."

Renshaw shrugged. "You have to have a good memory, you know, in my line."

"You mean treason?"

Renshaw smiled. "I wondered how long before that word would rear its ugly head. A funny word. Do you know its origin?"

"No."

"Few people do. It's from the Latin *traditio* and that means a handing over." Renshaw smiled. "Sounds nicer in Latin, doesn't it?"

"Depends on the 'why.'"

"Really? That matters to you, does it?"

"It could do."

"In fact you'd need to know about the 'what' before you understood the 'why.' Nothing passed on to them would have affected our national security."

"It if didn't the KGB wouldn't have been interested."

"I'm afraid you're quite wrong there. Although the KGB were the channel it was people much higher up who benefitted. So did we of course."

"How could we benefit from giving away our secrets?"

"Well, as always in these things, it was on two levels. Lensky was my 'mole' in Moscow and I was his 'mole' in SIS. The only difference between us was that his people knew about both of us. Not that they knew what we were really up to. SIS knew only about Lensky. On one level we exchanged hard information, but who really mattered was the second level. And that was more often advice rather than hard facts or information."

"Like what?"

Renshaw closed his eyes for a moment then looked at Hoggart.

"On the facts level I would warn him that we might easily put one of their chaps in the bag if he didn't lay off contacts with certain politicians. It saved them losing an agent and us having to waste time doing surveillance of a new chap. And stopped the wretched politicians from playing silly games just for a free trip to Prague or Budapest.

"And on the second level I gave advice. What were the inner Cabinet's real views on removal of nuclear weapons. What was Mrs. Thatcher's real assessment of Gorbachev. And I'd get back a picture of the struggles inside the KGB or even the struggles inside the Kremlin itself."

"And the information you passed on was always factual and authentic?"

"On the second level it was never either of those things. It was the genuine views of a well-informed person who was not anti-Soviet or in Lensky's case not anti-British. Well informed because he was part of the inner circle."

"Did you pass on Lensky's information?"

"The hard stuff—the first level, was passed on to the DG verbatim. The second level came in my advice as if from me." Renshaw smiled. "I think the DG thought I used a crystal ball."

"You never had doubts that they might be using you?"

"Doubts, yes. But Lensky's comments were genuine, I'm sure. He wasn't always right. Neither was I. But our errors were made in good faith." Renshaw paused. "Lensky and I had a lot in common. Where politicians are concerned—he didn't trust theirs and I don't trust ours. I never have."

"Why not?"

"I was brought up among them. There were always half a dozen around at home every weekend. I heard them talking with one another, off the record. My father is a rich man and influential so they cultivated him. He didn't like them but he tolerated them. But I hated and despised them. It angered me that these men could influence and control all our lives. Send us into wars, decide how desperately poor you had to be before the State would help you. Change the law to suit their own interests. And I mean both of them—Labour and Tories. There's nothing to choose between them."

"But you trust the men in the Politburo."

Renshaw laughed. "No way. They're even worse than our lot."

"So why help them?"

"I don't. What I pass on to Lensky has often prevented them from some aggression that would inevitably lead to confrontation. When they're planning some move they always have to work out what they think the West's reaction will be. If our reaction looks as if it's going to cause them trouble they very often think again. It doesn't always work. It didn't work with Afghanistan but the mess they got into only showed them what it cost if they ignored the signals that Lensky gave them. Signals from me."

"So why not do it officially? Why the one-man band?"

Renshaw laughed. "Can you imagine what our lot would have said if I'd put the idea up to them? They'd have put me in the Tower or the place up in Scotland—the so-called psychiatric hospital."

And Hoggart knew that Renshaw was right. They would have genuinely thought he was crazy. Apart from being dangerous. His feet wouldn't have touched, despite his old man.

"How did you get to know Lensky?"

"Our planes were held up for six hours by fog at Tokyo airport. We got talking about politics and current affairs and I think after about an hour we both realised that we were in the same business. Anybody else would have backed off but we were both amused. And as we went on talking it was obvious that we both had much the same views and outlook on the world and our own governments.

"I think it was more or less as an intellectual exercise that we discussed how to use our positions to bring some sanity into East-West relations. Despite some doubts we decided to try it for a few months. Each of us claiming to have recruited the other." Renshaw smiled and shrugged. "It seemed to work—and we were in business."

"Why was Lensky sacrificed by Moscow?"

"He wasn't intended as a sacrifice. He was meant to counteract Yakunin and protect me."

"You know, I've just realised something."

"What's that?"

"You and Lensky are exactly like one another."

Renshaw smiled. "I wish I was half as handsome as he is."

"I don't mean looks, I mean personalities."

Renshaw laughed. "Tell me more."

"The charm, the self-confidence, Eton and Balliol, Moscow University, upper-class sophistication. All of it providing a perfect disguise."

"Disguising what?"

"Sloane Rangers outside but dedicated intellectual anarchists underneath."

Renshaw laughed. "Not bad, my boy. Not bad."

Hoggart said quietly, "Where do we go from here?"

"I thought I might make a little trip across the channel. That was my plan." Renshaw smiled. His charming smile. "With your very kind permission of course."

"What made you decide to leave tonight?"

Renshaw laughed softly. "The same thing that brought you down here too. Instinct. The little bells ringing and the little red lights flashing."

"Nothing more than that?"

Renshaw smiled. "Just a little. Do you ever listen to Moscow Radio's overseas request programme in English?"

"No."

"They play music requests. You write in to the English Service. From the UK or Ireland, the West Indies, the United States. West and East Africa." Renshaw shrugged. "Wherever English is spoken. And they play your piece for you." He sighed. "Sometimes it's not quite that innocent." Renshaw looked at Hoggart and smiled wryly. "Sometimes the request is fictitious, and the music is a signal. Only used in emergency, of course, when time is of the essence. There's a tune I'm very fond of. A kind of signature tune. It's an old, old piece called 'Deep Purple.' They played that on the programme tonight." Renshaw smiled again and said softly, "That's why I'm here."

"And what do I tell the people back at Century House?"

"They don't know you're here. Just be surprised when you are told. Just one more intellectual does a bolt. But an Oxford man this time, not Cambridge." He laughed. "That'll be some compensation for them. They won't want it to get in the press. They've got enough scandals to cope with already without adding to them unnecessarily."

"And Lensky and Yakunin?"

"You can tell Yakunin that I'll square things in Moscow for him as long as he doesn't work for SIS."

"And Lensky?"

"Ah yes, poor Lensky. He'll have to carry on for a bit while I work something out."

"I can't let David Fletcher go on with Lensky and just waste his time."

"Why not? Fletcher won't mind. He's not like you, my friend.

He's never been really involved in his work. He's opted for a personal life. And who can blame him?"

"And when things have cooled down I get a telephone call from some KGB goon with a message from you threatening to expose me if I don't do what Moscow wants."

"You read me better than that, dear boy. Don't you?"

"Will you answer me a personal question totally honestly?"

"I've answered all your questions honestly."

"When you were kind about my wife was it a piece of long-term insurance to get me on your side?"

"You mean insurance for what I'm asking you to do now?"

"Yes."

"Common sense should give you the answer. I didn't expect you to be here on the boat. I'd assumed that I should quietly fold up my tent like the Arabs and silently steal away. How could I have known that you would be so significant?" He paused and then said quietly, "I helped you about your wife because you were one of my men who needed help. A man who'd tried to find a small dream and found a nightmare instead. No other reason."

"Can I ask you what happened?"

"There were some problems about burial. There are still idiot parsons who won't bury suicides. But I found a place in the end. A pleasant place."

"Where?"

"You really want to know?"

"Yes."

"She had a proper funeral service and she's buried in my family's plot in a village church near my old home at Henley-on-Thames."

"Who was there?"

"Just me."

There was a long silence and then Hoggart said, "When do you want to leave here?"

"The tide's up now."

Hoggart stood up. "Thanks for what you did for me and Jacqui." He paused. "I hope you're happy in your new life."

Renshaw grinned. "What? With all those bloody grim-faced Russians? No way." Still smiling he said, "But we all make our little beds, don't we? And we all have to lie on them sooner or later. I'll send you a postcard when I'm settled in." He nodded and held out his hand. "Take care, Eddie."

Hoggart took the offered hand and said quietly, "You too." Then he turned and left, stumbling up the companion-way steps, across the deck and onto the pontoon that led to the jetty.

As he stood in the shadows of the trees by the small lake, he heard the boat's engines come alive and five minutes later she edged out from the mooring and turned towards the lock-gates. He could see Renshaw holding the warps, talking to the lock-keeper outside his control cabin. He heard Renshaw laugh and then with a wave of his hand to the lock-keeper he moved to the wheel and the boat nosed out towards the creek.

Hoggart waited until the boat's lights disappeared then walked slowly back to the boatyard and his car.

MORE MYSTERIOUS PLEASURES

HAROLD ADAMS
The Carl Wilcox mystery series
MURDER   #501 $3.95
PAINT THE TOWN RED   #601 $3.95
THE MISSING MOON   #602 $3.95
THE NAKED LIAR   #420 $3.95
THE FOURTH WIDOW   #502 $3.50
THE BARBED WIRE NOOSE   #603 $3.95
THE MAN WHO MET THE TRAIN   #801 $3.95

TED ALLBEURY
THE SEEDS OF TREASON   #604 $3.95
THE JUDAS FACTOR   #802 $4.50
THE STALKING ANGEL   #803 $3.95

ERIC AMBLER
HERE LIES: AN AUTOBIOGRAPHY   #701 $8.95

ROBERT BARNARD
A TALENT TO DECEIVE: AN APPRECIATION
   OF AGATHA CHRISTIE   #702 $8.95

EARL DERR BIGGERS
The Charlie Chan mystery series
THE HOUSE WITHOUT A KEY   #421 $3.95
THE CHINESE PARROT   #503 $3.95
BEHIND THAT CURTAIN   #504 $3.95
THE BLACK CAMEL   #505 $3.95
CHARLIE CHAN CARRIES ON   #506 $3.95
KEEPER OF THE KEYS   #605 $3.95

JAMES M. CAIN
THE ENCHANTED ISLE   #415 $3.95
CLOUD NINE   #507 $3.95

BILL PRONZINI
GUN IN CHEEK — #714 $8.95
SON OF GUN IN CHEEK — #715 $9.95

BILL PRONZINI AND JOHN LUTZ
THE EYE — #408 $3.95

ROBERT J. RANDISI, ED.
THE EYES HAVE IT: THE FIRST PRIVATE EYE
   WRITERS OF AMERICA ANTHOLOGY — #716 $8.95
MEAN STREETS: THE SECOND PRIVATE EYE
   WRITERS OF AMERICA ANTHOLOGY — #717 $8.95
AN EYE FOR JUSTICE: THE THIRD PRIVATE EYE
   WRITERS OF AMERICA ANTHOLOGY — #729 $9.95

PATRICK RUELL
RED CHRISTMAS — #531 $3.50
DEATH TAKES THE LOW ROAD — #532 $3.50
DEATH OF A DORMOUSE — #636 $3.95

HANK SEARLS
THE ADVENTURES OF MIKE BLAIR — #718 $8.95

DELL SHANNON
The Lt. Luis Mendoza mystery series
CASE PENDING — #211 $3.95
THE ACE OF SPADES — #212 $3.95
EXTRA KILL — #213 $3.95
KNAVE OF HEARTS — #214 $3.95
DEATH OF A BUSYBODY — #315 $3.95
DOUBLE BLUFF — #316 $3.95
MARK OF MURDER — #417 $3.95
ROOT OF ALL EVIL — #418 $3.95

RALPH B. SIPPER, ED.
ROSS MACDONALD'S INWARD JOURNEY — #719 $8.95

JULIE SMITH
The Paul McDonald mystery series
TRUE-LIFE ADVENTURE — #407 $3.95
HUCKLEBERRY FIEND — #637 $3.95
The Rebecca Schwartz mystery series
TOURIST TRAP — #533 $3.95

ROSS H. SPENCER
THE MISSING BISHOP — #416 $3.50
MONASTERY NIGHTMARE — #534 $3.50

VINCENT STARRETT
THE PRIVATE LIFE OF SHERLOCK HOLMES — #720 $8.95

AVAILABLE AT YOUR BOOKSTORE OR DIRECT FROM THE PUBLISHER

Mysterious Press Mail Order
129 West 56th Street
New York, NY 10019

Please send me the MYSTERIOUS PRESS titles I have circled below:

103 105 106 107 112 113 209 210 211 212 213 214 301 302
303 304 308 309 315 316 401 402 403 404 405 406 407 408
409 410 411 412 413 414 415 416 417 418 419 420 421 501
502 503 504 505 506 507 508 509 510 511 512 513 514 515
516 517 518 519 520 521 522 523 524 525 526 527 528 529
530 531 532 533 534 535 536 537 538 539 540 541 542 543
544 545 601 602 603 604 605 606 607 608 609 610 611 612
613 614 615 616 617 618 619 620 621 622 623 624 625 626
627 628 629 630 631 632 633 634 635 636 637 638 639 640
641 642 643 644 645 646 701 702 703 704 705 706 707 708
709 710 711 712 713 714 715 716 717 718 719 720 721 722
723 724 725 726 727 728 729 801 802 803 804 805 806 807
808 809 810 811 812 813 814 815 816 817 818 819 820 821
822 823 824 825 826 827 828 829 830 831 832 833 834 835
836 837 838 839 840 841 842 843

I am enclosing $_____ (please add $3.00 postage and handling
for the first book, and 50¢ for each additional book). Send check or
money order only—no cash or C.O.D.'s please. Allow at least 4 weeks
for delivery.

NAME _____

ADDRESS _____

CITY _____ STATE _____ ZIP CODE _____
New York State residents please add appropriate sales tax.